PRAISE FOR ROBERT BOYCZUK

"(P)age-turning thrills aplenty . . . Boyczuk borrows from sources as diverse as Tolkien, *Star Wars*, and Alan Moore, and integrates the miscellany admirably into a fast-paced plot. The dystopian human dynamics . . . are the stuff of an epic nihilistic hangover."

—*Publishers Weekly*

". . . the writing is vivid, the characters . . . interact in a believable and thrilling way, and there is enough tension to make us suddenly start turning the pages hurriedly. . . . [Boyczuk is] a writer to watch."

—**Paul Kincaid,** *The New York Review of Science Fiction*

"Boyczuk builds up his hauntings and often gruesome metaphors and imagery from the base of his stories' human relationships, which imbues his fiction with an uncanniness that mimics the feeling of being trapped in a maze-like dream. Readers need not worry, however. The horror here is very real—Boyczuk just wants you to have a little fun finding it."

—*Rue Morgue Magazine*

"Robert Boyczuk is a supremely talented writer."

—**Cory Doctorow, author of** *Little Brother* **and** *Pirate Cinema*

FIRST EDITION

The Book of Thomas, Volume One: Heaven © 2012 by Robert Boyczuk
Cover artwork © 2012 by Erik Mohr
Cover design, interior design, and Map of the Spheres © 2012 by Samantha Beiko
Additional interior layout © 2012 by Danny Evarts
All Rights Reserved.

Distributed in Canada by
HarperCollins Canada Ltd.
1995 Markham Road
Scarborough, ON M1B 5M8
Toll Free: 1-800-387-0117
e-mail: hcorder@harpercollins.com

Distributed in the U.S. by
Diamond Book Distributors
1966 Greenspring Drive
Timonium, MD 21093
Phone: 1-410-560-7100 x826
e-mail: books@diamondbookdistributors.com

Library and Archives Canada Cataloguing in Publication

Boyczuk, Robert W. (Robert Wayne), 1956-
    Heaven / Robert Boyczuk.

(The book of Thomas ; vol. 1)
Issued also in electronic format.

ISBN 978-1-927469-27-9

    I. Title. II. Series.: Boyczuk, Robert W. (Robert Wayne), 1956-
Book of Thomas ; vol. 1.

PS8603.O979H43 2012   C813'.6   C2012-904989-1

CHIZINE PUBLICATIONS
Toronto, Canada
www.chizinepub.com
info@chizinepub.com

Edited by Brett Alexander Savory
Proofread by Stephen Michell

Canada Council   Conseil des arts
for the Arts   du Canada

We acknowledge the support of the Canada Council for the Arts which last year invested $20.1 million in writing and publishing throughout Canada.

ONTARIO ARTS COUNCIL
CONSEIL DES ARTS DE L'ONTARIO

Published with the generous assistance of the Ontario Arts Council.

Printed in Canada

ROBERT BOYCZUK

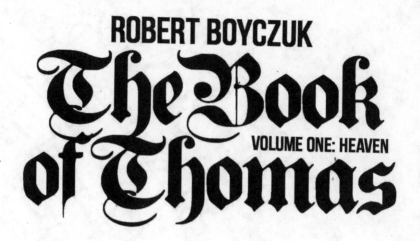

The Book of Thomas

VOLUME ONE: HEAVEN

ChiZine Publications

Heaven.

· the waters above. ·

· Lower Heaven. ·

the Sphere of Water

the Sphere of

the Sphere of

the Sphere of

the Sphere of

the Sph

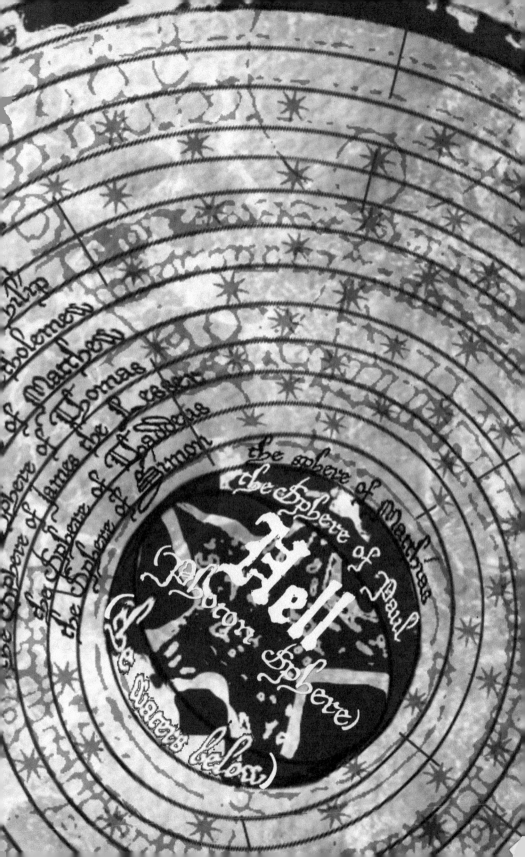

The mind is its own place and in itself, can make a Heaven of Hell, a Hell of Heaven.

—*John Milton*

Apology to Readers of This Work

Memory, even memory such as I have, is frangible. It is true I cannot forget the things I set out to remember, such as the minute details of a map I have studied for only a few minutes. Or those memories carved in my mind's eye because of their novelty or violence, moments thrust upon me freighted with awe, horror, or shame. These things I shall remember always, as clearly and precisely as in the moment they happened. Often, people have called this ability a gift from God, and they have mistakenly believed that, like God, this ability is absolute, perfect: that I can recall in totality everything I've ever seen or heard or smelled or touched. Nothing could be further from the truth. In many ways, my memory is unremarkable, no better than yours.

Although the events recorded in this volume are, for the most part, accurate in the smallest detail, there are certain incidents and conversations which are not reported verbatim. At the time they took place, they seemed inconsequential, and so made no special imprint on my memory. Upon reflection, however, I realized they were essential to my story. And so it is these scenes I've had to reconstruct imperfectly. As much as possible, I've tried to verify the details by interviewing others who bore witness, and I believe I have succeeded in capturing the spirit, if not all the specifics, of these moments. If these passages bear any inaccuracies, it is my fault alone.

I would also ask the reader to forgive any awkwardness in the language or structure of this work. Writing, beyond scratching a few numbers in a ledger or making a brief notation on a chalkboard, is somewhat new to me, and I am afraid the only written stories I know are the ones that were available to me in the *Bible* and its sanctioned *Addenda* (the Church having banned all other books two years before my birth). Of course, I've *listened to* plenty of stories. Not the kind of stories one tells about oneself—for instance, how one bested so-and-so at chess, or struck a particularly favourable deal at the market—the mundane stories of everyday triumphs. No, I mean the sort told by itinerant dramatists and singers. Stories about other people, other places, other times. Of victories, yes, and, *defeats*. Of truths larger than ourselves. Stories that teach us something important, even if the people in the stories never learn the important thing. Their learning is not the point. It is never the point. Remember that, and judge me, and my story, accordingly.

So, where to begin?

Perhaps it's best to start with the most important thing:

Orphanotrophium

My father is dead, I thought, shivering in the thin nightshirt I still wore, the one I'd been in when they'd seized me. *And I am to blame.*

Yesterday, I'd turned ten. At least I thought it was yesterday. But it was hard to tell how much time had passed in the dank, windowless cells beneath the monastery. Four days? Five?

I will never see him again—not in this life.

Or in the one after, if the Bishop was to be believed. Heretics, the Bishop had told me, were condemned to eternal damnation. But if I were to confirm my father's sins, my father could no longer deny them. He would be allowed to confess and repent—and to live. So I had nodded numb affirmation to all the Bishop's strange questions. Muttered the answers I thought the Bishop wanted to hear even when the questions baffled me. But I was, and still am, a bad liar. The Bishop didn't believe me, so my father had died unrepentant, while I bore witness. After, the Bishop had made me confess my lies. The ones the Bishop had forced me to make. My penance was light—two days of prayer and fasting chained in darkness. Improbably, the Bishop believed my soul could still be saved. But I knew better.

I killed my father.

After my penance, a silent Friar had unlocked my shackles and, with a crooked walking stick, prodded me up and through a small kitchen into open air. When I had been brought to the monastery it had been the dead of night. And now, as we emerged, it was night again. Or perhaps it had remained night the whole time. For all I knew, this might be a Sphere of perpetual night where the suns never kindled. I'd heard of such things. Perhaps that's why the Black Friars had built their monastery down here, because the darkness suited their work.

We followed a footpath through rocky fields and denuded trees, the Friar whacking me smartly across the back of my legs whenever I slowed. I lost a slipper—but it didn't matter, really, because my slippers were falling apart. A short while later I kicked off the other one. Once, we paused and I was allowed to go to my knees to scoop water from a small spring that crossed our path. My stomach rumbled; it had been two days since I'd last gnawed on a mouldy hind of bread.

At some point the path had become a rutted waggon track, and we walked past cultivated fields, the shapes of farmhouses and barns in the distance. Which meant people. And where there were people and fields, there were regular cycles of day and night. The kind that would allow those people to work and their crops to grow. There would be a dawn.

This knowledge failed to hearten me.

The path widened, became hard-packed dirt. We crossed a stone bridge over a fetid river that seemed nothing more than an enormous open sewer, and immediately trod a broad street paved with crumbling bricks. On either side of the bridge I saw that earthworks had recently been erected and that a crude tower was being raised, as if to defend the crossing. But the tower was only half-finished and seemed unoccupied—at least no one came out to challenge us. Even so, I took it as a sign of a bad place expecting worse.

As we walked, bits of crumbled brick bit into my soles. Houses stood shoulder to shoulder now, their porticoes set back a dozen paces from the thoroughfare. Here and there light leaked out around the edges of a shuttered window. The street narrowed, and the Friar and I turned, and turned again. The houses became taller and shabbier, pressing in on the street. None had porticoes, only doors and barred windows overhanging the lanes. There was no river here to carry away excrement, and the foul smell of fresh night soil in the gutters made me gag. Narrower back streets branched off ours, from which emanated the sounds of furtive movements. If the Friar heard anything, he ignored it, herding me impatiently through the labyrinthine alleys and finally down this last claustrophobic lane, no wider than my outstretched arms.

Rough hands shoved me; I stumbled over broken bricks and into a wooden wall that loomed out of the darkness. A dead end. I stood completely still, felt the wood damp against my cheek and under my fingers. Not sure what to do. I stiffened at a touch on my arm, but it was only a frayed hempen rope, suspended from something in the darkness above. For a time I waited, for a wordless kick or a blow, for whatever might come. When nothing did,

I turned, but the nameless Black Friar who'd brought me here had already faded away into the barrio. Without ever saying a word.

I had no idea where I was, nor why I'd been brought here. Until this moment I'd been stumbling through the night, not thinking. Numb. My father was dead. What point was there to anything beyond that fact?

A shuffling sound from the impenetrable darkness.

It occurred to me, then, that perhaps the Friar hadn't abandoned me. Perhaps he'd gone around the corner to relieve himself. . . .

But then I heard a retch and the sound of gobbing. A small, gaunt shadow congealed at the foot of the alley, ambled forward. "Yer a pretty one, ain't you?" A drunken voice, the kind that promised pain. And instantly, sickeningly, I knew why the Friar had left me here: to die. Not by the Friar's own hand—that would have been a mortal sin—but at another's.

A man reeled forward, emerging from the shadows—an indigent in ragged clothes, his face pocked, his left eye socket empty and scabbed. I snatched up a chunk of brick. The indigent took stock of the brick with his good eye.

"Now, now, boy. No need fer that." He offered a gap-toothed smile. "As God is me witness, I intend you no harm. I was just thinking, you being so young an pretty, and me knowing them what like that, there was a brass deacon or two to be made between us. . . ." As he spoke, the man patted his own clothing, absentmindedly, feeling for something.

A knife!

I retreated a step, felt something between my back and the wooden wall. The rope. In one motion I whipped the brick at the indigent and spun around, grabbing the rope with both hands. I heard feet pound behind me as I hauled myself up with all my might—the rope gave way and I landed hard on my arse, a bell tolling once, loud enough to wake the dead.

Or at least to make the indigent pause, uncertain, a few paces away.

The man glanced up to the impenetrable dark where the bell had sounded, then down at me, close enough so that I could see the knife's nocked and pitted blade. The indigent narrowed his eyes, advanced a step. I scuttled backward until my shoulders pressed against the wall—then tumbled backward as the wall swung inwards. A lantern flared, held aloft by an immense figure who stood astride me. The indigent raised a hand to block the sudden illumination. Waving his knife blindly, he backed away. "I seen him first," he whined.

"*Deus lux mea!*" boomed a voice that shook the walls of the alley.

The indigent flinched, then turned and fled, scattering a string of blasphemous oaths over his shoulder.

Softer now: *"Dominus vobiscum."* A benediction: May the Lord be with you.

The enormous man who stood over me was garbed in a brown, homespun robe the size of a tent. A monk. Reaching down, he grabbed me by the collar and hauled me inside without the least hint of exertion. He slammed the gate shut (for now, in the light of his lantern, it was recognizably a wooden gate) and barred it with a thick beam. The gate spanned the gap between the stone footings of two sizable buildings. Outside, the hovels must have accumulated over the years, anchoring themselves to these solid structures for support, a throng of beggars hemming in a rich man. Above the gate, the space between the buildings was closed off by sections of wrought iron bars, rising beyond the bowl of illumination, far higher than the roofs of the dilapidated structures outside. Difficult, I remember thinking, but perhaps not impossible, for someone to scale.

The monk grabbed a long wooden pole and put the handle of the lantern into a notch in the pole's end. He swung the lantern high onto a hook above the gate, so its illumination flooded both sides. Then he turned to me. "That way," he growled, pointing with the pole to a darkened passage. He shoved me harder than the Black Friar had, and I staggered. "Father Paul will be waiting."

"You rang the bell."

"I didn't. I mean, I did, but it was an accident." I sat on a small stool in the middle of an austere room, the lone decoration a dust-grimed portrait of a long-dead Pope. I had to crane my neck to look up past the edge of the trestle table at the gaunt, old priest wearing a threadbare and stained cassock. The huge monk who had brought me here, the one who'd opened the gate, had spoken to the priest in tones too low for me to overhear. Then he had gone back outside.

"Call me Father. Or Father Paul. You weren't looking for succour?"

They don't know, I thought. *They didn't expect me.* "I was brought here." This much of the truth, at least, seemed unlikely to betray me.

"I see." Father Paul steepled his hands. "Are you afraid, my son?"

"No."

"You lie." The priest said. "Lying is a sin."

I stared at a sputtering candle embedded in a mountain of wax on the tabletop. The only other thing on the table was a vellum-bound *Bible*. At some time in the distant past, a finger of wax had crept down the candle holder, split at the corner of the *Bible*, and snaked its way along two sides of the bottom cover.

"Do you have a name?"

"Thomas," I said after a moment's hesitation. When he furrowed his brow, I added, "Father."

He leaned back in his chair. "You lie again."

I had told few lies relative to boys my own age. Most of those I did tell, I owned up to when the inevitable guilt wormed inside me. Confession was the only balm for my soul. I believed all the things the Church had taught me: in right and wrong, in good and evil. That God loved me and watched over me. But now, after witnessing the inexplicable torture and death of my father, and after my own mortifying sin of betrayal, a small lie didn't seem so important. I vowed not to hesitate next time. The trick, I realized, would be to anticipate the lies I'd need.

"So. Thomas the doubter."

"No, Father."

"No what?"

"I . . . I believe, Father." At least this wasn't a lie.

"You say you were brought here, Thomas the believer." Father Paul smiled wanly at his own joke, revealing yellowed teeth. "Might I ask by whom?"

"A . . . a man, Father."

"What sort of man?"

"A cruel man, Father." I immediately regretted what I'd said—what were the chances this priest would believe anything I might say about another cleric?

But Father Paul misunderstood. "The man Brother Finn chased away?"

I nodded, no hesitation this time.

The priest looked at me oddly, but didn't accuse me of lying this time. "Was he your father?"

"No!" The word burst violently from me before I could control myself. Looking down, I said, "My father is dead." I tried to hide my trembling from the priest.

"Your mother?"

"She died when I was born."

"I see." Father Paul said. "Do you know what this place is?"

I shook my head.

"*Orphanotrophium*. The orphanage at *San Savio*."

Perhaps the Friar hadn't left me here to die after all. At least not the quick kind of death I had envisioned.

"And you seem to be an orphan," he said, eyeing me as if he was trying to peer into my soul. "Or at least abandoned. A happy coincidence, eh?"

I remained silent.

Father Paul shrugged. "No matter, the sanctuary lamp shines for all boys." He rose and walked around to stand in front of me, placing a knobby hand, as pale as the *Bible*'s vellum covers, on my shoulder. He stared into my eyes, the tips of our noses almost touching. I could smell the wine on his breath. "Those boys who pull the bell rope are petitioning for admittance. Sometimes children are brought to *San Savio*, like you, without understanding. The bell is rung for them. We do not make these children stay if they do not wish. Even though you rang the bell, I do not believe you did so knowingly. So the choice is still yours."

"I can leave?"

"If you wish," he said. He stared intently at me. "We are strict here. You won't go hungry, but neither will you grow fat. You will work hard and prosper or be indolent and wither. Do you understand this?"

I nodded.

"Once admitted, boys cannot leave until they are bound-out as an apprentice to a suitable family. In your case, this will be several years. Do you understand this?"

I nodded again.

"Well," he said, "what's it to be?"

I stared at my feet, contemplating my dismal prospects. I was lost and alone in the heart of this Godless city, two Spheres below where I had grown up. A five-day journey had brought me and my father to the Dominican monastery—and we'd been hooded, save during a few hours when we paused, after sun-off. And though I could remember every step I'd taken this night (as I related in my preface, God has gifted me the ability to recall anything I set my mind to recall), at best I could only guess at the route we'd travelled before the monastery, reconstructing it from scraps of sounds and smells, and from the subtle changes in air pressure felt in the eardrums and the churning of the stomach, marking the transition from Sphere to Sphere. Transitions usually only Clergy were permitted to make. Even if I managed to use these spartan clues to find my way home, to climb back to my own Sphere, no one would be there. The Church had taken us all from our beds, my father and his servants, even our cook and gardener and their families. Our modest estate would be empty. Or worse, already gifted by the Church and occupied by cold-eyed strangers. Nor would I find welcome from our friends and neighbours. It was a small rural community, and word would have spread fast. For the son of a heretic, there would be no welcome.

"I asked you a question, Thomas. . . ."

"Yes." I looked up at the priest. "I would stay, Father, if you would have me."

"We would." The priest smiled, giving my shoulder a squeeze before releasing it. He leaned back against the table, placing his palms on its edge. "Now I will give two pieces of advice. You can take them or not as you please, but know they are intended kindly." He paused, until I nodded.

"First, it's only in stories that children are reunited with their relatives. I don't know if you have an uncle or aunt you think favours you, but no one will claim you. In the thirty-one years I've been pastor here, no boy has ever been claimed. The sooner you realize that, the better."

I already knew this to be true, but to hear it said aloud by this priest made it real in a terrible and irrevocable way.

Father Paul reached out and pinched the collar of my nightshirt between his fingers, appraising it. "I can tell you've come from a family of some means. And I hear the education in your voice. Likely a Sphere or two above this poor one. The other boys will hate you. A lot are bigger than you—and are hard as stone. Have to be to get through what they have been through. Whatever has happened to you, whatever injustices you believe have been visited upon you, they've had it worse. Infinitely worse. You need to remember that when they beat you."

I was too exhausted, too empty, to be scared.

"My second piece of advice is this: you can do one of two things, Thomas. You can try to be harder and more ruthless than they are. And that may serve you well in the short term—until someone even more ruthless comes along. Or you can learn to forgive them. Which will serve you well on the day of reckoning when we ask God for His forgiveness." I must have looked at him quizzically, for he said, "Yes, even me, Thomas. I too must beg forgiveness." I heard the naked shame in his words. "We're all sinners, Thomas. Every one of us." Father Paul's shoulders sagged. "Forgiveness is our only hope."

Choir

I never quite understood the reason for my first fight. If you could call it a fight. Almost before I realized what was happening I was on the ground, gasping for breath, the sharp jab to my stomach delivered by the smallest boy in my form for a slight I was not aware I had given. As I lay incapacitated, the boy picked up a rock and scrutinized me as if he was weighing the merits of bashing in my skull. I looked up, daring him with my eyes. The boy dropped the brick. He spat on me and walked away.

I forgive you, I thought.

It was the morning of my first day.

The orphanage of *San Savio* at *Los Angeles Nuevo* had fewer than a hundred residents. The youngest boys looked to be about seven, the older ones perhaps twelve, on the cusp of puberty. I was placed in a form of twenty boys, all roughly the same height and, presumably, the same age, though most had run feral on the streets before coming to *San Savio* and likely hadn't an inkling themselves of how old they might be. We shared a cramped dormitory. School was six days a week, sixteen hours a day. At sun-on was Lauds, consisting of hymns, psalms, and a reading from the scripture. After a final short prayer and benediction, we were given five minutes to break our fast. Too little time to do anything other than cram in as much of the stale bread and cooling porridge as we could. The lessons that followed consisted of readings from the *Holy Book* or its *Addenda*, a lengthy discourse on those readings, then a regurgitation by the students. For lunch we were given a short time for small bowls of lukewarm soup and whatever bread might have been left over from breakfast, and an equally brief time to play in the courtyard, overseen by one of the clerics, a birch rod at the ready. After midday, three hours of Latin and two hours of chores. The only subject that was not taught by rote came late in the afternoon when we did sums on small, shared chalkboards for an hour. A meagre dinner at half-light, then Vespers before sun-out.

Sundays were devoted entirely to worship.

My name is Thomas.

By the end of the first week I'd come to think of myself as Thomas. It was Thomas who was beaten and bruised almost daily. It was Thomas who tried to make himself small, to pass unnoticed. Even in my dreams I was named Thomas. David was dead, as were all the people I'd known and loved. Sometimes at night I prayed for that boy. I'd whisper, *May God have mercy on your soul.*

I suffered the rod no more or less than other boys. I volunteered nothing but answered everything I was asked. Despite my indiffer-ence, I excelled. The simple reason was I forgot nothing I set out to remember. Father Paul, who taught us Latin, called my eidetic memory a gift from God. To me it was a burden. Or, more precisely, a condition. *Eidesis*, I'd named it: an inability to forget. Each moment of my father's inquisition, and my own complicity, was carved into my soul. While other boys would forget (or at least soften) their sins with the brush of time, I would carry my guilt to my deathbed, undiminished.

At the end of my first month, Father Paul advanced me to the form with the largest boys. Those I'd left behind, though disparaging their schooling with every breath, nevertheless beat me for my impertinence. I woke each morning to the throb of new welts and bruises. The boys in my new form mostly ignored me. I was too small for them to be bothered and, as long as I didn't excel at anything, I posed no threat. So I kept to myself and made sure as many of my answers were wrong as were right.

A few, though, looked at me with something other than hatred or envy. Something that made me squirm in my seat, that made me grateful they'd left me in the dorm with boys my own size, ones without the sprout of whiskers on their chins. Still, only a few days passed before three older boys contrived to catch me alone in the laundry room. I was pinned to the floor by two, while the third pulled my trousers down around my ankles, then lay on top of me.

It hurt, but no worse than anything else I had suffered.

Still, I felt a burning shame. And a craving for vengeance against those three boys. However, what bothered me most was that it bothered me at all. Somewhere, somehow, I was dismayed to discover that there was a kernel in me that had not yet surrendered to the sin of despair.

During my early stay, a dream plagued me. In it, I was back at the Dominican monastery, chained in my cell, asleep on soiled straw. Yet I could see and hear, as if awake. A warm glow danced across the stone walls of the passageway, growing in intensity, and an inhumanly tall figure flowed around the corner, a corona of pure light silhouetting it. The figure bowed under the archway to my cell, wings I hadn't been able to see until now, brushing ceiling and floor. An Angel. So indescribably beautiful, I ached. The Angel looked upon me—the sleeping me—with tenderness, its gaze as pure as that of a mother looking upon a newborn. A look of love. In that moment I knew I must love the Angel in return.

But then the Angel was gone, and with it, all certainty, its light dwindling as my sleeping form thrashed on the stone floor of my cell, drowning in the darkness of my troubled dreams.

The fights with other boys continued unabated. I had quickly learned that boys who don't fight back are doomed to be bullied forever. So I made a point of observing the tussles in which I wasn't a participant. I was particularly interested in those in which a smaller boy bested a bigger one. After a few fights, it seemed to me that size, though perhaps the most important thing, didn't guarantee victory. Speed and agility, and an understanding of leverage—how to use a larger boy's weight against him—could quickly turn the tables. I watched, and I learned. I practised my newfound knowledge whenever I could. Within a few weeks, only the biggest boys dared bully me. And with them I learned that sometimes one can win by losing. Winning against the worst bullies only seemed to enrage them, but losing to them (after I delivered several blows that would leave prominent and painful bruises), lessened their ardour for return matches. They'd won, after all, so what did they have to gain by provoking further confrontations?

In the classroom, I learned little I did not already know. But outside the classroom, in the dorms and the dining hall, in the courtyard and laundry room, in the larders in the cellar, my education continued.

I learned that it was best to eat everything under the watchful eye of the Brothers, rather than pocket a crust and have to fight another boy for it later.

I learned the Brothers could be as cruel as the boys—and invoked God the most when inflicting their cruelest punishments.

I learned that although it was always bad to be summoned by Brother Finn (who was fond of drinking undiluted wine, which fuelled his fondness for boys), it was especially bad when Brother Finn was drunk. Bad in a way that made even the toughest boys cry. So bad, sometimes, that Brother Finn wept, too.

And I learned that when I was first summoned to Brother Finn's office, on a day when he was particularly drunk, I had no tears left in me.

But perhaps the most important thing I learned was that Father Paul took immoderate pride in his choir. Which meant that choirboys were inviolable—not subject to schoolyard justice or the whims of the bullies. Off limits, even to Brother Finn's attentions.

At the start of my sixth month at *San Savio*, Father Paul announced choral tryouts. Tryouts were necessitated whenever a boy in the choir was bound-out as an apprentice, or when the onset of puberty ravaged an angelic voice. One by one the boys were summoned to Father Paul's office to sing the praises of God. After I sang, Father Paul declared that I had been doubly blessed: he told me that not only did I have a memory to be envied by the most renowned scholar, but that I'd been blessed with a voice that would make Angels weep.

I doubted this. I thought my audition poor and my chances a long shot. Singing had been forbidden in my father's house. And in the few places where I was free to sing—out of earshot in the fields surrounding our house, and on the road as I walked to school—my own voice sounded no better or worse to me than any other child's. But perhaps I inherited some modicum of talent from my mother. I knew she had truly been blessed. My father would speak of her voice with reverence. Describe it in such intimate detail that I could hear it. A voice that brought light into every corner of the house and every corner of my father's heart. He said her reputation was such that people, important people—Bishops and the like—would make excuses to visit, to stay to dinner, in hopes of coaxing a song from her. Our tightfisted gardener grumbled that my father squandered much of the harvest silver for overpriced copies of songbooks and the fanciful novels she loved to read. When, in the years leading up to my birth, the Church had finally banned all books save the *Good Book* and its *Addenda*, he told me my father didn't bring her precious books to the burning, but had built a cabinet with a false back in which to hide them.

On the day my mother died, on the day of my birth, my father collected every songbook and novel hidden in the house, and burned them all himself in the back garden.

Books, the Bishop had said, sadly shaking his head, *were the least of his sins. But a clear sign of a struggling soul, the beginning of his slide into iniquity. It must pain you that he blames you for your mother's death, but if you help me now, if you help me redeem his soul, he must forgive you. . . .*

I knew the Bishop said such things hoping to unnerve me, to elicit damning evidence from me. Nevertheless, I examined my memories in detail, but could find nothing to suggest that my father blamed me for my mother's death, or to make me question his love. (All the time, at the back of my mind, wondering how the Bishop had come to know the facts of the burning, imagining a day when I, older and stronger and more persuasive, might ask our gardener this same question.)

It would have been so easy for my father to blame me. But he hadn't. Had he?

These thoughts made my stomach churn with uncertainty. Although I could remember every small detail of my father's gestures, every expression of his affection, the seed the Bishop planted that day sprouted, sending forth tendrils of doubt that, despite my perfect recall, I would never know the secrets of my father's heart.

We choirboys had our own special form and a more spacious dorm room, as well as our own area of the dining hall where we enjoyed more varied food and larger portions, though it was still never quite enough. We were given clean albs and surplices to wear when we sang on Sunday—for the boys at sun-on, then later in the cavernous Church for parishioners at the two morning celebrations. Before Mass, when the great doors to the Church were swung wide and the parishioners filed in, I could see the broad steps and pillars outside and the subdued Sunday bustle in the square beyond. It was my only glimpse of the outside world.

Although I had believed I would never delight in anything again, I discovered an unexpected enjoyment in singing. I picked up everything quickly, never needing to be taught anything more than once. And when I sang, I mercifully forgot myself, lost completely in the sweep and exaltation of music, my soul soaring on its battered wings.

The fights stopped, as I knew they would. But not the naked envy, which I could see flashing in the eyes of the boys I'd left behind.

Still, I knew something like peace.

Eleven months to the day after my arrival, and three weeks before Christmas, Father Paul announced a special choral presentation to be held that Saturday after Vespers. There were to be no rites, no Liturgy of Eucharist, no Communion. Just song.

To my surprise, the other boys in the choir greeted the news with a simmering panic. They knew something I didn't. For the first time since I'd been at the orphanage I wished I had a friend, a confidant, I might ask. But I'd made a point of isolating myself from the other boys, of eschewing the few tentative offers of friendship. There was no one to ask. Especially now, after Father Paul had selected me to deliver a solo at the performance. I was a pariah.

"Yer sure to be bound-out," one boy hissed as he brushed past, "*castrato*."

I didn't know what a *castrato* might be, but from his intonation I knew it couldn't be anything good. I shrugged it off, mostly because there was nothing else to do.

The afternoon preceding the concert the boys in the choir were excused from study. We were directed to scrub ourselves pink in the laundry room, then to take turns picking the lice from each other's heads. Brother Augustino did his best to cut and comb our unruly hair with his ancient, palsied hands. When we were as shiny as we were going to get, special ecclesiastical robes, smaller versions of Father Paul's cassock (but without the collar), were brought out. They smelled of cedar—I hadn't smelled anything like it since . . . since running free on my father's estate. I willed back the tears.

With Father Paul sitting in the first pew, we sang the *Kyrie Eleison* and *Gloria*; the *Credo* and *Nicene Creed*; the *Sanctus* and *Benedictus*; and then *Agnus Dei*.

All for a scattering of oddly dressed men and women in the pews. They were a different sort of people. Different than the regular parishioners. Their clothes were finer, their shoulders squarer, their hygiene better.

Their fear of God less tangible. They sported brightly coloured garb, in crimson and gold and jade, lacking the sombreness appropriate to worship. Two of the women wore bodices that exposed their pale breasts. *Impious* was the word I might have used. None were parishioners. *San Savio* was in the heart of an impoverished district and these people were anything but poor. Perhaps they worshipped in more appropriate clothes elsewhere, in parishes more suitable to their station.

They sat there, looking not so much as listening, running their eyes over the boys in the choir with hard, calculating gazes, appraising us the way they might judge the quality of a heifer.

At the very end, I stepped forward for my solo, *Ave Maria*. When I finished, there was complete silence.

A dissipated man in a brocaded greatcoat stood up and pulled out a leather purse. "I've more than a few silver bishops aching to be liberated." He shook the purse and the coins jingled. The man's eyes were on me.

Father Paul paled, and propelled himself to his feet. "Not here," he rasped loudly, waving his hands and scuttling over to the man, darting glances at the vaulted ceiling as if God might be watching. He put a hand on the man's shoulder and levered him to a side door that led to the rectory. "All of you, please, this way."

I departed *San Savio* that day, bound-out. Not to the man who'd shown his purse. Instead, it was an obese man who'd sat quietly in the back during the performance, the least decadent of those assembled, wearing a plain brown cloak and mud-stained leather boots.

"Be thankful, boy," the fat man said as Brother Finn closed and barred the gate behind me. He held a rope in his sausage-like fingers that was looped around the neck of an overburdened jenny-mule. "If Georgie had another few bishops to his name, he'd have had you three times in three different back streets on the way to his brothel, then once more in his own chambers for good measure, before sending you to the front room for the pleasure of the *hoi polloi*." He eyed me. "If he dressed you up just right, say in that choirboy's outfit you were wearing, why I'd reckon he'd have made a pretty penny, too." He laughed a raucous, obscene laugh, and his jenny brayed in kind, which made him laugh even harder. He sobered and spat on the ground, wiping his mouth with the back of his sleeve. "But I have plans of a different sort for you. Pray you're worth the price I paid." Then he turned and clicked his tongue at the mule in a way that bespoke of a well-worn habit. Man and mule turned as one and ambled toward the mouth of the alley, their buttocks swaying in unison.

"Follow me, boy," said the fat man over his shoulder, "if you ever wish to see Heaven."

The Society of Jesus

Rather than risk the deepening gloom of the streets of *Los Angeles Nuevo*, we stayed that night at a ramshackle brothel not far from the orphanage at *San Savio*. After loosing a brass deacon from his purse and passing it over to the establishment's wary-eyed mistress, my new master instructed me to stable the mule around back. We didn't keep large animals on my father's estate, so I wasn't quite sure what to do—but I'd heard stories and thus knew enough to give the animal's rear legs a wide berth. She was docile, though, and I managed to unburden her without incident. After much fumbling with the buckles and straps in the fading light, I also freed her from her bridle and harness. As I did this, I noticed her long ears swivelled around sedately, inquisitively, and her tail hung loose, not twitching—both of which I later came to recognize as signs of contentment. After I finished, I stroked her snout, which she seemed to like.

Free of her encumbrance, I saw the mule bore another burden, one of which I could never relieve her: her coat had a whitish line running from her mane along her spine to her haunches and intersected a similar line across her withers, as if a crucifix had been painted on her back.

"Her name is *Cross*, though she's anything but." The fat man stood at the entrance to the stall, a steaming wooden bowl in his hand. "You need to brush her, too. Give her a lick of salt and some grain. But not too much. Overfeeding will make her sick. Mules were bred for the desert, and like desert food, so never anything rich." He handed me the bowl, from which rose a smell that made my stomach rumble—and I realized that in preparation for the concert, I'd somehow missed supper, and was now ravenously hungry. "And make sure there is enough clean water in the trough for her to drink." He scratched the mule on her snout affectionately, then pulled a carrot from his pocket and allowed her to nibble on it. "Give her a carrot every day if you wish her to be your friend." The fat man glanced around the rickety stable, at the saddlebags and packs I'd stacked in a corner. "There's not a great deal of value in those bags, but it would irk me to loose them nonetheless." He kicked one. "There's a blanket in this one if you get cold."

With that he turned and ambled away.

I threw myself down next to the saddlebags and greedily scooped the stew from the bowl with a cupped hand, in my rush spilling as much as I ate on my ragged shirt. It was a wonderful concoction. Unlike the fare at *San Savio*, it had onions and carrots and peas that weren't shrivelled and chewy, and boasted potatoes and chunks of chicken thick enough to chew. The sauce was beyond my wildest expectations, so good that I didn't even care that I scalded my hand and my tongue and the roof of my mouth in my rush to eat.

When it was all gone, I licked the bowl—and sat back to think.

It had been my intention, at the first opportunity, to part company with my new master. Such a moment was upon me. I had feared I would be shackled, or at least closely watched. Not left on my own where escaping was as simple as walking out the gate, nor with the ample provisions the saddlebags might provide. In my callowness, escape seemed not only possible, but likely. My reasoning was thus: the city was of such formidable size that it would have been near impossible to find me. And I believed that my time at *San Savio* had hardened me sufficiently so that I was every bit as tough as the other boys in the orphanage. And, if they could make their way on the streets of *Los Angeles Nuevo*, why couldn't I?

Only I found myself reluctant to leave.

As I sat there, I felt the twinge of incipient guilt. As if in fleeing I'd be stealing the price he'd paid for me. For the same reason, I knew I couldn't bring myself to take anything from his baggage. To this day, I have never cheated or stolen from another person intentionally, even those who have stolen and cheated me. If I was going to escape, I wanted it to be clean, without debt.

There was a second reason, as well: his simple gesture of affection toward his mule. It had made me realize that in my time at *San Savio*, I'd seen no such gesture pass between the boys and their teachers. There was something in me that hungered for that kind of effortless affection, the kind my father had once shown me. As foolish as it sounds, I was jealous of the mule, and in that moment he rubbed its snout, I would have given anything for him to tousle my hair with the same casual affection.

Thus, I made my excuses to stay: *Don't be impulsive. Take advantage of a safe haven for the night. A good sleep. And perhaps on the morrow* . . .

I checked the gate at the end of the alley leading to the stable, making sure it was shut and barred, and gave the rest of the place the once over, until I was reasonably sure that no one would trouble me that night. Then I sat with my back propped against the saddlebags, clutching a cracked and greying axe handle I'd found, ready to defend my master's meagre possessions, as he had bid me.

From the brothel the sounds of revelry washed around me, rising in volume through the heart of the night. Twice I thought I recognized the boisterous guffaw of my master, and once a series of explosive grunts I imagined to be his. But it was only a guess, for business was good, and it wasn't until the small hours of the morning that the sounds of rowdy ecstasy had diminished enough for me to drift off to sleep.

I was awoken by a kick from my master. He held a small lantern that struggled to push back the pitch black. Behind him, the brothel's windows were shuttered and dark. I had no recollection of curling up next to the mule on the hay, but my back was pressed against her warm spine.

"I want to be out of the city by sun-on," my master said, nudging the mule's haunch with his foot, rousing it. The animal snorted in complaint, but tucked its legs under its belly and levered itself awkwardly erect. It sauntered over to the trough and dipped its head. "See if you can manage the bridle. Not too rough around her ears, though. Mules are particularly sensitive there, and if she gets annoyed she'll thrash her head and likely knock you silly." A sheen of sweat covered my master's brow, his eyes were bloodshot, and the smell of stale wine oozed from his pores. Hanging his lantern from a peg, he walked to the trough and bent over next to the mule, splashing water on his face. Then stood straight, stretched, and farted loudly. "Do what you can and I'll be back to check your work in a few minutes." Leaving the lantern, he ambled back into the house, rubbing his temples.

When he returned a ten minutes later, two bulging wine skins slung over his shoulder, he seemed surprised that I'd not only managed the bridle, but the pack saddle, too, and had almost finished loading the mule. When I'd unsaddled Cross the previous night, I'd memorized the positioning of the straps and ropes, and where and how they were knotted, as well as how the packs had been suspended from the harnessing. Cross had been cooperative, and I had replicated the whole arrangement with little difficulty. My master waved me away from the mule and eyed my work critically, tugging here and there on a strap, then nodded, looking pleased. "Seems you have more than just a pretty voice, eh?" He laughed, and slapped me on the back. "Now finish the job," he said, unshouldering the wine skins and dropping them in my hands. "But pack these last, eh? Want to keep them handy. . . ."

After I did this, my master, holding aloft his small lantern, led Cross down the alley and out onto the street in front of the brothel, the lonely clattering of hooves on the cobbles the only sound in the silent city to mark our passing.

During the two hours it had taken us to wend our way through the city, we had seen only a handful of drowsy people, none giving us more than an indifferent glance. Now on the outskirts, we started to pass wains loaded with produce and livestock coming in to the city, whose drivers favoured us with the curt, wordless nods of the brotherhood of early risers. With the first intimations of sun-on, we reached the river demarcating *Los Angeles Nuevo*. It was as wide as the river I had crossed upon first entering the city, although this one was nowhere near as filthy. On the far side was a small city of tents and other hastily erected shelters, the threads of dozens of cooking fires streaking the morning sky. On both sides of the bridge were manned guard towers and earthworks. However, the guards were focused entirely on those petitioning to enter the city, and they gave us not so much as a glance.

As we trekked into the countryside, the suns began to brighten. Lengthy shadows grew on our left, and so I knew we must be travelling north. It had been night when I'd first entered the city, almost a year ago, but I was pretty sure that the line of suns had been perpendicular to our route. Which meant that we had been moving in one of two directions: north or south. After the first sun-on at the orphanage, I retraced the twists and turns of that journey in my mind, and was able to determine that we had been travelling by-and-large north, which meant the Dominican monastery lay south of the city. It was a relief to know that we were now moving in the opposite direction.

We stopped to break our fast an hour outside the city, near an attenuated, cloudy brook whose waters were nonetheless sweeter than anything I'd tasted in the last year. After sating myself, I doused my head and shook it, water spraying everywhere. Despite the few hours of sleep I'd managed, I felt more awake than I had in some time. My master didn't look nearly as energized; his face was a pallid oval, and his hands shook as he unwrapped a cloth containing farmer's cheese, a small loaf of bread, and a stick of cured salami. Using his knife, he cut portions, but ate only a little, leaving most for me. Then he poured himself a half-cup of wine, diluting it with an equal amount of water from the brook. Muttering, "*Sanguinis Domini,*" he downed it in one gulp.

Blood of our Lord.

I suppose my shock at his blasphemy must have been apparent because he squinted at me and mumbled, "Hazard of the profession." Some colour had returned to his cheeks. He poured himself a second tot of wine, but didn't dilute this one. "You can't drink God's Blood as part of your job everyday, and not develop a fondness for the taste, eh?" He tossed back the wine and started to laugh, which abruptly degenerated into a racking cough. He spat out a sickly gob of phlegm, then wiped the remaining strands from his lips with the back of his coarse sleeve.

He began packing up the gear. "Before my fall from grace, I was Father Ignatius of the Society of Jesus."

A Jesuit. I had been bound-out to an ex-Jesuit. In the enlightened Spheres everyone knew them as "God's marines." They ran the colleges and seminaries with intellectual and physical rigour, and more famously served as missionaries, their duty to proselytize and defend the faith, to convince and ultimately to convert. It wasn't uncommon for a Sunday sermon to be larded with an example of their courage and sacrifice. Many stories ended with their deaths. In my mind's eye they were more than mere priests: they were selfless adventurers, heroically carrying the light into the unenlightened and Godless lands of the lower Spheres.

Ignatius secured the food pack on the mule and turned to me. "I am an excommunicant, *ferendae sententiae*, sentenced by the ecclesiastical court." He picked up Cross's lead. "I no longer serve the Church as a cleric. But the Church, in its mercy, has seen fit to allow me to continue to serve in another capacity." He pointed a pudgy finger at me. "By securing talented boys for their choirs." He rubbed thumb and forefinger together in the universal gesture of anticipated coin. "For a lucrative finder's fee, of course." He laughed his raucous laugh, setting off a minor earthquake in his belly. "You see, I have an ear for these things. Before the Church and I parted ways, I was choir-master at the *Capella Sixtina*."

I found it hard to imagine this man, in his stained and frayed cloak, in such a sacrosanct setting, standing on the very same altar as the Pontiff did when celebrating Mass—and where the Conclave of Cardinals met after the Pope's death to elect his successor.

"You sing like you don't know it, but you've got the goods, boy. You're almost ready for the Sistine Choir. It's not all there yet, but with some coaching, a great deal of practise, and a little more confidence, who knows? You might even make it to Heaven."

It had never occurred to me that there might be actual choirs, or any other human affectation, in Lower Heaven. I had always envisioned It as an ethereal place where Angels drifted serenely to and fro, fulfilling the unfathomable tasks God had set them. After I chewed on it a bit, though, it made sense that someone must take care of the mundane jobs that kept the Sphere functioning. But a choir?

"Don't look so gobsmacked, boy." Ignatius turned and flicked the lead, man and mule ambling onto the road. "Heaven ain't all it's cracked up to be."

For the next month we travelled from Parish to Parish and recital to recital, staying at brothels and, occasionally, at less dubious inns when no convenient brothel presented itself. Ignatius was greeted with familiarity at every establishment. I much preferred the inns because, other than their more acceptable moral character, they were invariably cleaner and quieter, and I was allowed to share the room when there was bedding enough for two. During this time, Ignatius didn't see fit to purchase another boy. Indeed, at times he seemed agitated, and he left halfway through two of the recitals, muttering to himself.

The journey itself was largely unremarkable, save for the unusually large number of travellers moving in the opposite direction, always towards *Los Angeles Nuevo*. Men, women, families. Even ragged children by themselves. All on foot, a few drawing wains packed with their meagre belongings. They were thin and stoop-shouldered, looking more than anything like beaten curs. Most didn't raise their eyes as we passed, but those that did stared coldly at Ignatius's girth and Cross's stuffed bags.

"This is an impoverished and troubled Sphere," Ignatius told me. "Two straight years of drought. Five of the last ten. These migrants are largely those who worked the fields, but there is no work for them now that much of the crop withers before it can be harvested. So they head for larger cities, thinking their lot will be better there, but most will never get past the poxy camps. Many will die there."

I could see this was a poor Sphere, certainly much poorer than the one where I'd been born. We'd had a few lean harvests in the last few years, but our fields and forests were hardy and green, and there was enough work that there were few migrants and certainly no camps—at least none I knew of. At *San Savio* I had mistakenly associated the miserly portions of food with the orphanage, not realizing the problem was endemic to this Sphere. Now that I was out of *San Savio*, the signs of hunger, and its attendant unrest, were unmistakable. In the city, beggars choked the streets; outside, the ragged masses huddled in seething camps, held at bay only by heavily armed *Guardia*. And beyond, where we now travelled, the most telling sign, the sere fields and wilting crops.

Aside from the migrant workers, the only other travellers we encountered were patrols of young men, most mounted, a few on foot. Sometimes they were uniformed *Guardia* from the nearest city, under the disciplined command of a *Hauptmann* wearing the blue uniform and black beret of the *Gardes Suisses*. Other times they looked more like a rag-tag band of brigands, armed only with farming implements. Ignatius told me—and my own subsequent experience has borne this out— that wherever there are young men without work, trouble follows. So I suppose arming these young men and sending them out on patrol was better than leaving them idle, and risk having them foment violence in their own villages.

For the most part, the patrols left us alone, probably because we looked respectable enough. But when they did stop us, Ignatius quickly produced a beautifully inked vellum from the Vatican, guaranteeing us safe passage. A few eyed it dubiously—but never the *Suisse*, who, eyes widening, seemed to recognize it immediately. In the end, though, all let us pass.

"Don't you fear being robbed?" I asked Ignatius one day after we passed a patrol herding three gaunt prisoners, their wrists roped behind them.

"Worse," he said, clucking his tongue reprovingly at Cross, who'd veered to the side of the road to nibble on a small patch of green grass. "But don't fret, we're relatively safe. For now. Most still fear God more than they fear hunger. And when God will no longer suffice, there is always the Church and its *Suisse*." He pointed at a makeshift cross that had been erected at the crossroads through which we were about to pass. It was like a dozen other crosses I'd seen on our journey. Then I noticed something about this cross, something that had been hidden by the angle at which we approached: bodies hung from both ends of the horizontal beam. It wasn't a Holy Cross. It was a gibbet.

"The fear won't last forever, though," Ignatius said. "No matter how pious you hope to be, or how much you might fear the noose, in the end, hunger always gets the better of you."

Flies buzzed both corpses, and a crow worked away at the eye of the nearest one. Behind the gibbet, the field had been trampled, and there were two rows of unmarked mounds. Those in the last row had freshly turned earth. We passed in silence, and I mouthed a prayer for their wretched souls.

"Why come here?" I asked, perhaps a kilometre farther on. "Why risk it?"

"Because the Church, in its wisdom, deems only orphans fit for its most exalted choir."

"But—" I stopped, mid-sentence, suddenly understanding. The wealthier Spheres, closest to Lower Heaven, would present fewer opportunities and more problems. Parents would be either intractable or make ridiculous demands. But an orphan . . . what orphan wouldn't prefer a life at the Vatican to the misery of *Orphanotrophium*? And where better to find a surfeit of orphanages than in a troubled Sphere?

"A buyer's market," I said.

"Down here, Thomas, the Church is very poor. It does what it must."

I was suddenly angry, when I really had no cause to be. But I was too young to know that. "God will not abide moneychangers in his temple," I said. "'My house shall be called the house of prayer; but ye have made it a den of thieves.'"

"'Judge not that ye be not judged.'" Ignatius quoted back at me.

"Selling the boys. It's . . . it's a sin."

He laughed. "Is it, now? Did you ever think one man's sin might be another man's blessing?" He put a hand on my shoulder. "Where do you think the boys go after *San Savio*, Thomas? Most end up on the street. They become beggars, thieves, and prostitutes. More than half don't likely reach the age of twenty-five. Those who find work in a brothel, well, they are the lucky ones."

"No good can come of sin," I said obstinately.

"Tell that to the boys at *San Savio*. The coin I paid for you will feed them all for half a year." He stopped, and stopped me, too, with a look. "You might choose to starve yourself for your piety. But would you starve them, as well?"

The notion of the relativity of sin gave me pause.

"I didn't make the world," Ignatius said wearily. "And I didn't make the hearts of men. If you must blame someone for this mess, blame the one who did."

It may seem unnaturally naive, but I couldn't fathom what he was saying, and I am sure it showed on my face.

So he said it unequivocally for me: "God, Thomas. If anyone's to blame for this mess, it's God Almighty."

In the next week, the sad procession of migrants became a trickle, then gave out abruptly. The patrols, too, became much less frequent. We learned from the Parish Priest conducting the next recital that the Pope, hearing of the dire situation, had issued an edict forbidding men to move from place to place within the Sphere, except for Clergy and those who served them. In the same edict, he also allowed those in the camps to remain, and bid the Parishes of the cities to do what they could to help those unfortunate souls. It was a test, he said, of all men's faith.

So the journey became almost peaceful—we passed few travellers, and those were largely Clergymen or Deacons, hastening on Church business. The only sign of trouble was the dark smoke of sizable fires that sometimes smudged the horizon, and the haze of rain that showered down on them. Perhaps those restless young men, who no longer had to protect their towns and families from pillagers and outlaws, had begun turning their anger on their neighbours, the only people left to blame. In any case, the fires were always distant, and whether it was merely field burning to clear the land for the next planting, or something more calamitous, was impossible to say.

As we tramped the road, Ignatius tutored me. It quickly became apparent he surpassed Father Paul, in every respect, as a teacher. Whereas Father Paul stuck rigidly to a series of lessons he had developed over the years that focused exclusively on choral music, Ignatius understood the capacity of the human voice apart from any particular style of song. His expertise was more intimate and fundamental, one that preceded style and technique—the sort of knowledge that, once acquired, enabled one to master any form of vocal music.

For my part, I was an eager student. In the mornings he taught me a series of exercises to wake up body, nose, and voice: breathing and humming exercises, pitch patterns and arpeggios. When we paused to break our fast he held his hand on my rib cage and throat as I sang, directing me to observe the proper movement of my *musculus intercostalis* and *diaphragma*. In the afternoons he had me sing to the fields the Mass I'd been taught. Then he sang me other Masses in falsetto and had me repeat them. When he discovered my ability to parrot the Masses after hearing them only once, he immediately questioned me to learn the extent of my gift, then changed the manner in which he taught me to better suit my abilities. He also began addressing me more as an adult might address another adult. I felt flattered, and I suppose he meant me to feel this way. Even so, at first I thought him needlessly exacting, picking at tiny differences in tone and timbre that were impossible to distinguish. But then, after a day or two passed, I realized I could hear the variations he was hearing, and wondered how it was I had never heard these glaring differences before. After this pattern repeated twice more, it occurred to me that he wasn't so much teaching me to hear things I hadn't before as he was teaching me to listen to *myself* in a way I hadn't before. When I asked him about this, he replied, "Thomas, one of the most useful qualities a man can cultivate is the ability to hear himself as others hear him." The sense of this, as it applied to improving my voice, was obvious. But it was clear he meant it also as a more general apothegm.

One evening, when we shared a room, and wine had made him forget himself more than usual, he paced the room in an uncharacteristically dark mood because of the lack of suitable prospects at the Church we had visited that afternoon. Five weeks of travel and I was his only find— apparently an inauspicious start to the season. I didn't know what to make of his candour, so I let him ramble, listening to his complaints, grunting the minimal affirmatives he seemed to require. All of a sudden he stopped and spun on his toes, teetering, but not losing his balance. He let himself down onto the creaking frame filled with straw that constituted his bed.

"Boy, I'm going to teach you the most important thing about singing" he said, slurring his words slightly as he leaned towards me where I sat on my own meagre pile of straw. "How to sing with conviction, even when you have no experience upon which to draw." With this, he burst into a song with a deep, basso voice I'd not heard him use before:

> She lay all naked on her bed and I myself lay by;
> No veil but curtains about her spread, no covering but I.
> Her head upon her shoulder seeks to hang in careless wise,
> And full of blushes were her cheeks, and of wishes were her eyes.
>
> Her blood still fresh into her face, as on a message came,
> To say that in another place it meant another game.
> Her cherry lip moist, plump and fair, millions of kisses crown,
> Which ripe and uncropt dangled there and weighed the branches down.
>
> Her breasts, that well'd so plump and high, bread pleasant pain in me.
> For all the world I do defy the like felicity;
> Her thighs and belly, soft and fair, to me were only shown:
> To see such meat, and not to eat, would anger any stone.
>
> Her knees lay upward gently bent, and all lay hollow under,
> As if on easy terms, they meant to fall unforc'd asunder;
> Just so the Cyprian Queen did lie, expecting in her bower,
> When too long stay had kept the boy beyond his promis'd hour.
>
> "Dull clown" quoth she, "Why dost delay such proffer'd bliss to take?
> Canst thou find out no other way similitudes to make?"
> Mad with delight I, thundering, threw my arms about her,
> But pox upon't 'twas but a dream, and so I lay without her.

"Now you try it," he said, clapping me on the back.

I did. He listened with his head cocked, then smiled when I finished. "You sang it well, as if you truly knew what you were singing."

"I know things," I said, as any boy my age would, feeling the colour rise in my face.

"There's knowing and there's knowing," he said, grinning salaciously at me. "And if you knew too much, you'd be useless to me." He must have misread my confusion for discomfort, because his smile fell away and he looked at me with concern. "Now there, boy, no need for that face. It's easy to overvalue the things we've never had. What you do have is talent, and it's a great honour to sing in the Choir of *Capella Sistina*. And an easy life to boot. Your balls are a small price to pay."

How foolish it must sound that I hadn't an inkling, until this moment, that I was to be castrated. Of course Ignatius wouldn't have invested so much money and time in me if he were to lose everything when puberty wreaked havoc with my voice. The taunt at *San Savio*'s, the one I hadn't understood, now came back to me so clearly it rang in my ears. I whispered, "*Castrato*."

Ignatius placed a meaty hand on my shoulder; his eyes brimmed over with sadness and what might have been pity. He nodded. Then he dropped his hand back to the bed, bringing the depleted wineskin to his lips for a pull, then stoppered it. "You're a good lad," he said, laying back on the bed and flinging the wineskin into my lap. His eyes fluttered shut. "Never forget that."

The idea of castration seemed to bother Ignatius more than it bothered me. The next day, and in the days that followed, he averted his gaze and quickly changed the subject whenever our words threatened to take us back in that direction. For a man given over almost completely to his baser desires, I suppose the idea of castration was the worst fate imaginable.

But for me it was different.

My only experiences of sexual desire had been those compelled upon me by Brother Finn and the fumbling boys at the orphanage. I'd also heard the unruly sounds of sexual congress that issued from the brothels we had visited, which reminded me of nothing so much as the frantic sounds of rutting dogs. The Church, while it said little about sexual desire, had told us unequivocally that desire was a sin. That only within the sanctity of marriage, with the explicit purpose of procreating, was this kind of desire acceptable. In all other cases these urges must be thwarted through heroic efforts of will, a task at which most were wanting, and which invariably led to all kinds of evils—some of which I had suffered first hand. To my thinking, then, castration in exchange for a life of ease, as well as freedom from unruly desires, didn't seem like such a bad deal. No worse, say, than having an aching tooth pulled before it became septic. I foolishly imagined it would impart the same kind of relief. . . .

So I reconciled myself to my fate, determined to be the best *castrato* whose voice ever echoed the magnificent frescoed ceilings of the Sistine Chapel.

The New Boys

Ignatius's luck abruptly changed—at the next concert at the orphanage of *Saint Alban*, he purchased two more boys for his peripatetic choir. They couldn't have been more unalike: Ali was thin, dark-complexioned and furtive; Lark was round, pale, and gregarious. Both boys seemed, at least initially, as shocked as I had been to be walking in tow behind Ignatius's broad bottom. But children are infinitely more adaptable than adults, and what seemed incongruous on the first day took on the veneer of routine by the end of the second. As at *San Savio*, I kept my distance from the boys, even though they seemed, for the most part, less inimical. Even so, I found myself unaccountably happy to once again be in the proximity of boys my own age. I was less happy, however, that Ignatius now had to divide his attention three ways.

Both boys had fine voices—perhaps not as good as mine, but then I'd already had the benefit of six weeks of Ignatius's tutelage. Of the two, Lark had the better natural voice but lacked discipline, while Ali had wonderful control, but only in the octaves he'd mastered. At first Ignatius split his time in half, tutoring the new boys together in the mornings, then tutoring me in the afternoons. However, because of the diametrical nature of their talent, and because it quickly became apparent Lark would need more direct instruction, Ignatius rejigged his approach, teaching Lark in the mornings, and spending a shorter amount of time with Ali in the afternoon. My lessons stalled completely, although Ignatius still exhorted me to practise and, from time to time, drew me into the other boys' sessions to demonstrate a point when his own falsetto was inadequate to the task. Lark always listened carefully to me, and did his best to mimic me; Ali, on the other hand, made no secret of his resentment, and glared at me as I sang, then attempted to outdo me—which, more often than not, bit him on his own arse, as Ignatius was fond of saying.

When Ignatius tutored Ali, the two walked abreast on the road, Ignatius pulling Cross in his wake. I would tramp a half a dozen paces behind the mule, and Lark would amble beside me, talking incessantly about anything and everything, but mostly about the parsimonious portions of food and the malicious bullies at *Saint Alban*. I bore it patiently, not wanting to offend. When it was Lark's turn for a lesson, the boys switched places, but Ali said not a word to me and quickly dropped another half dozen paces behind. From time to time I felt his dark scrutiny prickle the hairs of my neck, and I would snap my head around to try to catch him at it, but his eyes were always averted, on the yellowing wheat stalks, tracing a bird in the sky, or absorbed by the small dust cloud kicked up by his feet.

It soon became apparent Lark and Ali would not get along. Though they had come from the same orphanage, they had had nothing to do with each other (Ali having arrived only the month previous); now the overtures of friendship Lark essayed, Ali rebuffed with disdain. Indeed, Ali showed the fat boy nothing but contempt—having only a modest appetite, Ali had taken to dumping whatever leftovers he had into the stable muck, while Lark looked on forlornly.

It fell to me to teach the other boys how to care for Cross. Lark showed little interest and was a poor student; Ali took to it readily enough, though. After showing him the routines twice (Ali never asking a single question), he jumped in the next day and performed them without hesitation. He asked for no help, and seemed to want none, so I was glad to give these duties over to him completely. I found I missed brushing Cross and stroking her warm muzzle; I even missed the rough feel of her tongue when she licked salt from my palm. But the work occupied Ali, and his moody silences seemed not to bother Cross at all.

Towards the end of our first week together, as we were passing through withering corn fields, Ali disappeared.

Ignatius was up front with Lark, while Ali had been lagging farther and farther behind each time I looked back. Then he was gone. I'd been humming an exercise to myself, but had stopped abruptly—Ignatius glanced back and halted. He frowned for a few seconds, then turning his back, he picked up right where he'd left off in his lesson as if nothing were amiss.

I hesitated for a moment, but there seemed nothing to do. So I followed man and boy and mule.

Less than a minute later, when I glanced back, Ali was there again, as if he'd never left.

Initially, I suspected that Ali had run off, then thought better of it. Ali didn't seem stupid, and there would have been far better places and opportunities to make good his escape than a desiccated corn field in the middle of nowhere. My second notion was that he'd darted into the stalks to relieve himself. I, too, would have used the cornfield if I'd felt the pressure of an imminent bowel movement. But if it had been that, it had been remarkably quick. For a piss, he would have used the side of the road like we all did. It made no sense, and bothered me, though I couldn't have articulated why I should care a whit about anything Ali did.

It also bothered me that Ignatius seemed unperturbed. Perhaps he knew something I didn't.

When Ali went forward for his lesson that afternoon, I took the opportunity to quietly grill Lark. He told me that Ali had arrived at the orphanage only a week before Ignatius purchased him. "He weren't from around our village," Lark said. "I heard his Da came looking for work in the fields, only there weren't none. What with the rains the last few years, there's been a whole lot less to harvest." He scuffed his foot along the ground, kicking up dust to illustrate his point. "When Ali's Da didn't want to leave, those others that came before him, looking for work, too, well, they did for him, on account of they was afraid of losing what little work they had." He sniffed. Lark had little else of importance to add, other than he'd heard Ali's father had brought him into taverns and inns to sing for their supper. "I think it were a man who'd heard him sing what brought him to *Saint Alban*," Lark told me, shaking his head.

I thought back to my first months at *San Savio*, the raw wound of my own father's death, my unrelenting memory keeping it as sharp as the moment I'd witnessed it. And better understood Ali's sullen demeanour. Nevertheless, I watched him more closely the next two days, as we camped just off the road under crude canvas tents during the night showers ("Noways like the real rain we used to get," Lark said, nodding sagely, a brown stalk of grass hanging from the corner of his mouth), and then stayed in a brothel's stable the following night. On both days

I observed Ali surreptitiously darting into cover as he had done before, then reappearing moments later. The only other thing that caught my attention was that Ali seemed to have developed an affection for Cross and now walked with her as much as he lagged behind.

The next morning, as Lark was stumbling over the first new Mass Ignatius was attempting to teach him, and Ali drifted listlessly behind me, I mulled over everything I could recall of Ali's time with us. You might think it easy for a person gifted with perfect recollection to see patterns in his memories, but it's not. Often it's the opposite. To apprehend a pattern, one must sift through recollections, selecting only those that are relevant and arranging them into a meaningful pattern—not unlike building a puzzle. But when one has an almost limitless store of memories, the puzzle goes from a few pieces to thousands of pieces, and the possible combinations of those pieces, as well as all their possible arrangements, is vast beyond measure. The task becomes, well, daunting. Indeed, I was so lost in mulling over the possibilities that I jumped when a hand closed on my shoulder and spun me around.

"Yesterday," Ali said, his face a hands-width away, his grip tightening, "you made me look a fool."

I shrugged off his grip. "No," I said. "You did that yourself."

He surprised me, then, nodding curtly, but without rancour. "Sing it," he said.

So I did. I sang the arpeggio he'd stumbled over the day before. And he repeated it, only this time without trying to out-sing me. His effort was much improved, and it was my turn to nod.

"Again," he said.

We went back and forth in this manner for the balance of that morning. At the end of our session, Ali didn't glower at me, as he had almost incessantly since he'd joined us, which I took for a rough expression of gratitude.

The next two mornings, I continued tutoring Ali. Ignatius glanced back from time to time, but without comment. The afternoon of the third day, Ignatius told us he'd require extra time with Lark, and so we found ourselves together the entire day. I think both of us worked harder that day than we had on any other. I was exhausted by the time we reached our brothel for the evening. After we finished eating, Ali put his half-finished bowl on the ground beside his makeshift straw bed, then turned his back. I was so tired that the significance of his action didn't register.

But Lark, coming back from taking a piss, didn't miss a beat. As soon as he saw the half-full bowl, his face lit up like it was Christmas morning.

In the next few days, two important things happened.

The first was that Ignatius had the three of us sing together. We had not done so before. It was after another fruitless audition, this time in the massive stone Church of *Saint Isidore* at *Los Cruces*. With the travel ban, Ignatius had been the only buyer in attendance; Lark, Ali, and I sat quietly in a pew behind him. He had us wait until the Parish priest ushered out his boys, then Ignatius bade us take their place in the choir stall and sing a Mass he'd taught us. He cocked his head and listened closely.

At first we were tentative, cowed, perhaps, by the gloomy resonance of the Church. But after a few false starts, we sang together for the first time. I was so surprised at what emerged, at how it was far better than anything I could have imagined, that I almost faltered. With an effort of will, I blocked my mundane concerns, and settled into the task, losing myself utterly in the joyous song. We sang praise to God's glory, our voices twining, transcending our meagre individual talents, rising above this poor benighted Sphere, groping upwards towards Heaven. I felt rapturous. Awed to be part of such a glorious endeavour. Even now, as I sit here writing this, after having traversed more Spheres of the Apostles than any living man and witnessing their countless marvels, after having served as the very agent of the Angels of Lower Heaven, I still mark that moment as the one in which I came closest to God.

The Mass ended and our voices fell away.

Ignatius nodded, then hustled us out the door and back to our brothel.

That night, laying in the stable, I finally understood the extent of Ignatius's gift: not only was he an exceptional teacher, he also had a divinely inspired ear, one that could discern, in unschooled voices of disparate children, the possibility of the sublime.

The second important thing happened the next morning as we were preparing to depart *Los Cruces*. "Yesterday," Ignatius said, "I was very pleased with your performance. If I searched to the ends of this Sphere I don't believe I could find boys with more suitable talent." He smiled at each of us. "So, this morning, we strike out for Rome."

I felt a flush of pride.

Lark fairly beamed, while a short-lived smile—but a smile nevertheless—flickered across Ali's thin lips. I supposed neither had ever seen an Assumption, let alone been out of their own wretched Sphere. For them, it would be a grand adventure.

What immodest pride I felt soured almost immediately, for I knew Ignatius lied. I could see it in his face, in the set of his shoulders, in the manner in which he wouldn't hold any of our gazes for more than a second. I had always been good at that sort of thing—figuring if people were lying or not. The more time I spent with someone, the better able I was to read them. At first I'd thought I'd been blessed with a marvellous intuition, until I realized it was just another aspect of my other gift: I had been subconsciously drawing on my store of memories to correlate the small ticks of the liar—their facial expressions, their gestures, the ways in which they held themselves—with their lies. As long as I spent enough time with someone to catalogue a few lies, it became easy. The only people this didn't seem to work with were those addicted to the truth and, of course, Angels. I put them in separate categories, for it turns out that Angels are not wholly truthful.

In Ignatius's case, there was also other evidence that confirmed the lie.

His praise notwithstanding, I knew there had to be boys in this Sphere with voices equal or better. And, from what he'd told me, it was his habit to wander six months to a year in an impoverished Sphere, collecting upwards of ten boys. Yet he'd been in this Sphere for only a few months and had only three boys. So why so soon? As we'd passed more and more gibbets at the roadside, as we'd watched ominous black smoke slouch across the horizon, I'd also watched Ignatius grow increasingly anxious. It was fear that was making him impatient to depart—fear that the troubles of the Sphere might overtake him.

If I needed any further evidence, it came the next morning in the form of a tall, sinewy man named Kite, who joined us as we were loading Cross in the stable-yard. He appeared as a ghost might, materializing without so much as a breath of sound, observing us from a few paces away. Ignatius stepped over and greeted him jovially. He explained to us that he'd met Kite the previous evening over a cup of ale. When they'd discovered they were journeying the same road, they'd decided to throw in with each other. It was clearly another lie.

Kite was like no other traveller I'd seen. He carried a small pack slung across his shoulder and resting on his hip. Although his clothes were threadbare and faded, they were still recognizable as the blue and yellow striped doublet and breeches of the renown *Cent Suisse*, the Papal Guard; on his head he wore the traditional morion, it's red plume gone save for a few tattered and grimed ostrich feathers. Over his shoulder he bore their weapon of choice, the halberd—but with its ceremonial ring cut away, so that it didn't make a loud clinking sound with each step he took. Unlike his uniform, his weapon was in good repair, oiled and looking sharp enough to cleave a hair. His arms were roped with long strands of muscle—the sort you would need to swing a halberd effectively. (If you've never seen a halberd in use, I can attest it is a long and potentially awkward weapon—really three weapons, to be precise: an axe, a spike and a hook—and it takes a man with the right kind of strength and agility to wield it proficiently, and not kill himself in the process.) Kite's uniform fit too well for him to have taken it off another man, which meant he was either a deserter or had been turned out of the *Cent Suisse* in disgrace. The fact that he still possessed his halberd (of which he would have been stripped in a court-martial) led me to believe it was the former. In either case, he was here now, a long, hard fall from Rome. And like Ignatius, he'd found a place where he might still profitably ply his trade.

"In these troubled times," Ignatius said, clapping Kite ostentatiously on the shoulder, "it is heartening to meet trustworthy fellow travellers."

Kite's eyes flickered at the hand on his shoulder so quickly it would have been easy to believe I imagined it. But Ignatius pulled his hand away as if it had been scalded. Then he laughed, a nervous fluttering thing.

Kite said nothing; he just continued to look at us as a vulture might eye carrion.

Ignatius had been, in my limited experience, a good judge of character; he had always handled the people we'd encountered adroitly, including the *Guardia*. I suppose you would have to have good instincts if you spent all your time travelling dangerous Spheres, as Ignatius did. In this case, however, I questioned his wisdom.

I wondered how trustworthy Kite really was, and if that trust had been purchased with Ignatius's coin. If so, I wondered whether the amount Ignatius had agreed to pay him up front was both large and small enough to keep him from relieving us of everything else we had of value before we reached our destination, including our lives. Mostly, though, it worried me that Ignatius had been worried enough to engage him in the first place. What did he fear on the road so much that he felt it necessary to put his trust in a man like Kite?

I didn't have to wait long for my answer.

The Captain

We were set upon in the middle of the night. It was dark, as dark as it gets, and my mind was still cloudy from sleep. All around me confusion reigned. There were shouts and thudding footsteps. My feet were pointed towards the embers of our fire, as was my habit, and as I levered myself up onto my elbows I made out two men grappling, one of whom had Ignatius's telltale girth. Then my view was eclipsed as someone tripped over my feet and fell full on top of me, knocking me back and crushing the air from my lungs. It felt like a sack of grain had been tossed on me. Before I could catch my breath, the person was up and gone, fleeing into the forest on whose periphery we'd made our camp. Two dark figures, clutching what looked like cudgels, bolted past me in pursuit. They didn't seem to see me—in the dark, lying flat on my back as I was, I probably made an inconsequential lump.

Without willing it, I found myself on hands and knees, scrambling for the tree line, too. I threw myself headlong into the undergrowth; branches whipped me. I dove into a clutch of blackberry bushes, and bit my tongue to keep from screaming as thorns raked my face. On my belly now, I wormed deeper into the bushes, until I was certain I couldn't be seen, then lay as still as I could.

The sounds of the scuffle had ceased. I heard muted voices, and a man's groans, pitched too high to be Ignatius's basso. I listened hard and, with a slight sense of relief, thought I could pick out the distinctive sound of Ignatius's wheezing, but it was impossible to say for certain. At the campsite, one of the brigands now spoke distinctly enough for me to hear: "What should we do with the big one, Cap'n? Finish him?"

"We will show him the same courtesy he'd have shown us." A cold, quiet voice. The sort that believed unequivocally in its own authority. "Let him have the balance of the night to think on his sins. If he's alive in the morning, we'll decide then."

From deeper within the forest, where the two men with cudgels had been thrashing about, I heard a squeal, and a shouted, "Got 'im!", followed immediately by a man's screech.

"Well?" The cool voice again, projected over me.

"The son of a whore bit me hand, Cap'n."

I heard what could only have been a vigorous slap, and a high-pitched cry of pain. Laughter from the brigands by the fire.

"Shut it," the Captain said, and the mirth fell off abruptly. "Paolo, fetch the lantern. Dermot, bring him here."

"But he bit me hand, Cap'n—"

"I asked you to bring him here."

"He's the fat one, Cap'n. It ain't him . . ."

There was a moment's silence, and if the Captain's voice was cold before, it was ice now. "*Bring him here.*" The last three words were delivered *staccato*, like three hammer blows that would seal the coffin of the man who didn't heed them.

I heard the two men crunch their way quickly out of the forest, twigs snapping beneath their boots, passing so close I could have reached out and touched them. Between them they dragged a whimpering Lark. I heard him grunt as they dumped him unceremoniously on the ground. A lantern sputtered to life, and blades of light cut through the bushes. I turned my head and stuck my hands under my belly, trying to hide any flesh that might give me away.

"Lash him to the other one," the Captain barked.

"It don't matter, Cap'n, if he gets to the Assumption, *The Meek*'ll do for him anyhow."

"Dermot, you're a loud-mouthed fool." There was the sound of a blow, then a grunt, and what was probably a body crumpling to the ground.

"Well, *boy*," the Captain's voice was suddenly so loud it seemed to shake the bushes in which I was hiding, "now that Dermot's let you know that we know you're out there, I won't insult your intelligence by pretending that we don't know. You're lying quiet, hoping we won't find you. Maybe thinking you'll wait until we get bored and leave, then somehow manage to get to the Assumption on your own. But I'll tell you why it's a vain hope if ever there was one. First, we aren't going anywhere. Peter and Damian here are fine trackers. We will find you, and if not this night, when sun-on comes. Second, Dermot, despite his general stupidity, has it right: should you manage to elude us, should you somehow manage to find your way to the Assumption, *The Meek* will eat you alive. Literally. They number fifty thousand now, I've heard, and are so desperate for sustenance they have taken to cannibalism. Third, in the unlikely event that you do persuade *The Meek* to let you pass, without your escort and the fine vellum I hold in my hand, the monks at the Assumption will never believe you." I heard him take a few steps closer; the slashes of light moved in such a way that I knew he was lifting the lantern high and scanning the depths of the shadows. "I have a proposal for you. If you come out of hiding right now, and save us the time and trouble of the hunt, I will treat you fairly and with honour, and your friends, too. I will even do what I can for your master, though he's taken the kind of wound from which few recover. I tell you this not to scare you, but so you know I am being truthful with you. You should also know there is no help coming from other quarters. Your other man seems to have forgotten his halberd in his haste to run off." I heard the *chunk* of a weapon being driven into the ground. "So what's it to be, boy? Will you accept my terms?"

When I didn't answer, he said, "I'll give you five minutes to think on it. But be warned—if I have to send my men into the woods to smoke you out, then our bargain is forfeit, and I'll give both those boys to Dermot to do with as he pleases."

Until now I had been buffeted by circumstance and events not of my own making, dragged along by the whim of others. For the first time in my life I would have to make a decision that would be utterly and irrevocably my own. One whose consequences would dog me until the day I died. My stomach knotted. *What should I do?* The question whirled in my mind, over and over. *What should I do?* My legs began shaking.

I knew I must calm myself.

So I quietly performed a breathing exercise Ignatius had taught me. It did the trick. I stopped shaking and my mind cleared. The first thing I realized was that my chances of escape were not quite so bleak as the Captain would have me believe. Clearly, none of them had seen me dive into these blackberry bushes, or they'd have already pulled me out. The canopy was so thick here that within a few metres of the tree line a perpetual gloom enveloped everything, and in the dark it would be extraordinarily difficult to see the signs necessary to track me. I also knew that as soon as they started stumbling around looking for me they would make enough racket to cover any sounds I might make. If I made a dash for it now, while there were several hours of darkness left, I was fairly confident I could elude capture. Once away, the forest was immense, and the undergrowth thick, providing endless opportunity for concealment. No doubt the Captain knew all of this, too—and that's why he'd proposed his bargain.

What then? What would I do after, without food or money or Ignatius's letter from the Vatican? Even if I could evade the patrols, I'd find no succour in communities struggling to feed their own children. Nor did I entertain the faintest of hopes of reaching the Assumption on my own. And there was still Lark, Ali, and Ignatius. Without my surrender, all three would likely die. With my surrender, all three might live—but only if the Captain was as good as his word.

I hesitated not because the decision was difficult, but because I first had to convince myself there was no other way. I played out the alternatives in my mind, hoping against hope to see something. But I came up blank: there was simply no way to escape the relentless guilt that would follow me if I abandoned my companions. So, when I judged five minutes had elapsed, and no other solution had presented itself, I pushed myself onto my elbows, and said in a clear voice, "I acc—"

A rough hand clamped over my mouth.

Before I knew what was happening, I was pulled from my hiding place; my breath was crushed from my lungs as I was tucked under a stone-hard arm like I was a bundle of sticks. My captor loped away from the lantern light, deeper into the forest, weaving around the trees, carrying me as if I weighed nothing more than an idle thought. Behind were confused shouts, followed by the sounds of several men crashing through the underbrush. Above it all I recognized the Captain's voice, shouting for order, trying to stop his men as they fanned out in the woods, calling for them to be quiet, all to no avail. We drove straight into the forest while the sounds of their frantic search covered our retreat, and within a minute the noise of their thrashing faded entirely. All I heard was the deep, rhythmic breathing of the man who carried me, and the steady thump of his boots on the humus of the forest floor.

His hand was like a vise over my mouth, and his arm crushed my chest, making it difficult to breathe. Tears blurred my eyes. After a time—probably only a few minutes, although it felt like more—just when I thought I might faint, I heard the sound of running water, and abruptly we broke out of the trees and crashed through a shallow river, its ripples scattering the reflected light of the dimmed suns overhead. Cold drops spattered my face, shocking me back to consciousness. As soon as we were on the other side, and behind the cover of a thicket, my conveyor deposited me roughly on the ground and collapsed in front of me, gasping to catch his breath.

Kite.

I pulled myself up unsteadily, still dizzy. "I've got to go back," I managed to croak.

He looked at me as if I was crazed.

"If I don't, they will kill the others."

Kite reached over and, with barely an effort, pulled me down so hard my backside slammed the ground painfully. I glared at him, and he returned my gaze with indifference. "No."

"Why? Why won't you let me go?"

"You wouldn't understand, boy."

"Maybe I understand more than you think."

He arched his eyebrows slightly.

"You knew Ignatius," I said. "From before, when you were both at the Vatican. You were in the *Cent Suisse*. There are only one hundred Papal Guards, and there's only one choir-master at *Capella Sixtina*. You had to know each other."

There might have been a twitch at the corner of his mouth.

"Your meeting with Ignatius wasn't coincidental."

He spat. In the one day we'd been together, I hadn't heard Kite string together more than two words; mostly he made himself understood with dark, pointed silences. So it surprised me when he wiped the back of his mouth on his sleeve and said, "You're smarter than any pretty boy has a right to be." He narrowed his eyes. "What else do you *understand*?"

There was no reason for holding back. "That Ignatius was excommunicated around the same time you were expelled from the *Cent Suisse*." I paused. "Or maybe at *exactly* the same time."

This time there was a definite twitch.

"I saw the way you looked at him when he put his hand on your shoulder," I said. "I saw the way he reacted."

"You know nothing."

I leaned forward and, though I was scared to, forced myself to put a hand on his shoulder, the same shoulder Ignatius had clasped. It was like grasping a rock. "I know you love Ignatius. Or once did." Kite went rigid. "You needn't surrender. I heard them talking. I don't know why, but they seem only interested in me."

He batted my hand away. "They will kill the others, regardless." He said it with the certainty of a man who'd dealt with their kind before.

"Are you so angry at Ignatius for betraying you that you'd let him die?"

"Betraying me?" He barked out a harsh laugh. "You got that backwards."

I knew Ignatius had been excommunicated because of his expansive appetites. Despite his professed disbelief, he had once been pious. So I had assumed that his guilt over his transgressions with Kite had gotten the better of him, and led to a confession that ended in their joint downfall.

"You betrayed Ignatius," I said aloud, rearranging things in my mind. "So you owe him." The *Cent Suisse* were nothing if not honourable. He had come back for me because it had been part of a debt he believed he owed Ignatius. "You promised something, to atone for what you did. You promised Ignatius you'd protect me."

"I don't care a whit about you, boy."

"Then you promised to get me to Rome."

He didn't deny it. Instead, he said, "I will not let you surrender yourself."

"If you won't let me go back, then rescue them."

He snorted. "Eight men—"

"Nine," I said, "counting the Captain."

"Nine, then, against one? And without my halberd?"

"You have a dirk in each boot."

He sneered. "You think too highly of me."

"I think well of a man who honours his debts, but not of one who does so at the cost of a friend's life."

He growled at me, and I flinched backwards. Yet he looked shamed, too. I knew then I had a chance. "They won't be expecting you to return. None of them came straight after us, which means that none of them saw you grab me. As far as they know, you'd already run off for good, or else the Captain wouldn't have said what he did about you. They think you a mercenary who values his own skin more than his word."

He rolled forward onto his haunches; anger creasing his features. "I'm no coward."

"I didn't say you were." I paused, waiting for him to speak. Waiting for him to tell me what he needed to tell me.

He did, after a moment's silence. "Ignatius was on watch. I stupidly gave him my halberd. I'd have fought without it, but there were too many of them, and it was easy to see they weren't new at this business. I'd have only gotten myself killed." He glared at me. "What use would I be then?"

"You did what you had to do."

His shoulders slouched the tiniest bit, and he stared off into the gloom.

"There were four skins of undiluted wine on Cross," I said. "There's a pretty good chance they will be emptied in the next hour." That caught his attention. "If you go back after that, it will still be dark. . . ."

"No."

"What choice have we? To flee? You can't force me to go with you. I suppose you could carry me under your arm. But how far could you get?" He glowered at me, but said nothing. "I don't know why, but they seem eager to find me. Eager enough to track me into the forest. Come sun-on, they will see the broken twigs and our footprints, the moss scraped from the rocks in the stream bed. Without food, with me squirming under your arm, you won't be able to outrun them. They will overtake us and kill you, and so your promise to Ignatius, whatever it might be, will go unfulfilled."

All expression drained from his face, masking whatever thoughts were passing through his mind. I suppose it was a deeply ingrained habit from years of service, where an inscrutable expression was an asset. He mumbled something I couldn't make out, then looked at me in a calculating way that chilled my blood. "Do you know what you're asking, boy?"

His tone unnerved me, made me hesitate, though I thought I had reasoned it out pretty well. "I'm . . . I'm asking you to save my friends. To save Ignatius."

"Then a clever boy like you must know I can't do it alone." Pulling the dirk from his left boot, he tossed it on the ground in front of me. "So the real question, boy, is how do you feel about doing some of your own dirty work?"

I stared at the knife, dubious about what use I might be in a fight. Still, I didn't doubt that Kite knew his trade. Otherwise he wouldn't have tossed the knife towards me.

I was scared. Of being killed, yes. But I think I was even more afraid of killing. Several thoughts plagued me. First, when it came to the moment, would I have the nerve to do it? Second, what about the men I wished dead—did they deserve to die? Lastly, I wondered if I might be condemning myself to eternal damnation. To kill another man was a mortal sin; the only exception, Exodus tells us, is that of self-defence: *If a thief be found breaking in, and be smitten that he die, there shall no blood be shed for him.* Creeping up on sleeping men hardly seemed to qualify, no matter their moral makeup.

But wasn't it as shameful a sin to allow my friends to be killed?

I knew the Church's teachings well enough to know that God doesn't split hairs, and that evil done for the sake of good is evil nonetheless. What I would be doing would be murder. And even if I didn't wield a knife, Kite's point still pertained: *your own dirty work*, he had called it. It was my idea. Some think God judges us on our actions, but this is not true. It is our intentions. In asking Kite to do murder, I was as culpable as he was in wielding the knife.

One way or the other, I was damned.

I picked up the knife.

A Skirmish at Night

Gripping the worn cloth handle of the dirk tightly, I followed Kite through the woods. He moved like a shadow, as silent and sure of himself as any man I have ever met. I watched where he planted his feet and tried as best I could to mimic him. Even so, every few paces I managed to snap a twig or rustle some fallen leaves. I was so engrossed in this process that I nearly ran into him when he stopped. He put his lips next to my ear and whispered, "*Stay,*" then vanished into the shadows. A few moments later he rematerialized and motioned me to come after. I judged we were pretty close to the campsite, and thought it curious that Kite, as silent as a ghost, seemed indifferent to the noise I was making. In a moment, though, I saw the blaze of a large fire through the tree trunks, and heard its intermittent pops and crackles, loud enough now to cover any sounds I might make.

Kite led us right back to the blackberry bushes in which I had hidden, and this close we were greeted with the loud snores and mumbles of men who'd had their fill of drink. They had posted a sentry facing the woods. He sat on the ground, legs pulled up, a short sword across his lap, his head resting on his knees. He appeared to be asleep. At the other end of the camp I could make out another figure sitting up; only this one looked wide-awake, for I could see the glint of the flames as they danced in his eyes. Behind the fire were the prone figures of the other brigands, fallen into their stupefied sleep; set apart slightly from them were shapes I took to be Ali, Lark, and Ignatius. I was surprised things seemed to have fallen out exactly as I had told Kite they would.

With hand gestures, Kite made it clear that I should stay here, while he was going to leave the cover of the forest out of sight of the camp and circle round to approach from the rear, where the grass was long enough to allow him to creep right up on the man who was awake. I was to wait until Kite struck, and when he did, I was to run at the sentry whose attention would have turned to Kite and whose back would now be presented to me.

As plans go, it didn't strike me as a terribly clever one. Later, however, I realized this was probably its greatest strength. Kite knew from experience that a plan is only good in the first few seconds of a fight, and the simpler the plan, the less likely it is to go awry.

Kite slipped away.

I inched as close as I dared, watching the sentry for the least sign of movement. Then I waited, holding the hilt of the dirk as tightly as I had ever held anything, focusing on the man whose life I was supposed to soon end.

He looked peaceful. I felt like I was going to vomit.

Our plan fell apart almost immediately.

There was a commotion, and the sentry rose, turning his back to me as Kite had said he would. I dashed from cover—and immediately tripped over a root and sprawled to the ground, grunting loudly. I looked up in time to see the startled sentry spin around and stare at me. A few of the other brigands had been roused, and Cross, who I'd forgotten about, was also on her feet, braying loudly, kicking her hind legs into the air. One of the brigands, a tall fellow, had the end of Cross's rope wrapped around his hand and was struggling to control her. In all of this, however, Kite was nowhere to be seen. The sentry who'd been sleeping stepped forward and grabbed me by the collar, hauling me to my knees, pulling my face to within inches of his. Maybe he was still half drunk or half-asleep, or maybe he expected that I was surrendering myself. In any case, he didn't expect the dirk in my hand. I planted it in his neck. He wrenched backwards, yanking the knife from my grip, making a strangled screeching sound. I watched him, horrified, as he reeled through the fire, hands clasped around his own throat; I shall never forget the sound of his blood, jetting from the base of the dirk, sizzling as it hit the flames. He collapsed, small licks of flames nibbling at the edges of his trousers and shirt.

I was still on my knees. Everyone was staring at me now. On the ground in front of me was the sentry's short sword. I swept it up and staggered to my feet. The one holding Cross's rope said, "*Get him!*" in the Captain's unmistakeable voice.

Three of them fumbled in their blankets for their weapons; the third came straight at me. I slashed prematurely, and this fellow was sober enough to leap out of way. He pulled a knife from his boot and circled me.

"Don't hurt him," the Captain barked. "He's worth nothing to us dead."

Despite what the Captain said, the sentry took a step towards me, murder in his eyes.

That's when I finally saw Kite.

He flitted out of cover and streaked past the Captain, slashing with his dirk so fast his arm was a blur. He was on the other three before the Captain's knees buckled and he fell to the ground, Cross's rope still wrapped around his hand, his throat gaping open. The others fared no better, even though one had managed to grab hold of Kite's halberd and spin around to face him. Kite darted in under his first awkward swing, his hand plunging the dirk into the man's breast. Releasing his knife, Kite sprang back, snatching the halberd from the dying man's hands. He swung it towards the brigand in front of me, and in that instant I wondered how he could hope to strike a target so far away; but he let the force of the swing pull the shaft through his palms so that, with his arms, its arc extended four metres. It struck off the right arm of the brigand and sliced into his ribs like a butcher's cleaver would slice into a side of beef. Kite planted his feet, twisted and jerked his halberd free, and the man's body crumpled towards him.

By now, the remaining men were awake and huddled together in a small defensive knot. They were a sorry looking lot, and I think two of them were still so drunk they hadn't any clear idea of what was transpiring. I had expected Kite to make short work of them, but instead he stepped back, planting the shaft of his halberd on the ground; blood slipped from its blade and ticked onto his boot.

"Your Captain's dead," he said matter-of-factly. "If you drop your weapons, you may leave."

I hadn't expected this from him.

The brigands eyed him nervously. None seemed willing to challenge him.

"I'm as good as my word," Kite said. "I will not harm any man that leaves now."

One of the brigands immediately dropped his sword and bolted. The other three shrank back, clutching their swords and knives.

"*Without* your weapons," Kite repeated, raising his halberd and taking a step towards them. This was enough; all three dropped whatever they were holding and fled into the field.

I dashed over to where Ali and Lark lay; both sported bruises, but otherwise seemed fine. With the short sword, I sawed through the rope binding them. I had imagined they would leap and embrace me with joy. Instead, Lark just rubbed at the ligature marks on his arms and stared at me sullenly, while Ali raced after Cross, who'd bolted, dragging the Captain's corpse back towards the road.

I turned my attention to poor Ignatius.

He wasn't bound; there was no need. He'd been sorely wounded, and was prone and shivering, his pale face covered with a sheen of sweat, as if in the grip of an ague. Through parched lips, which moved like those of a landed fish, he wheezed moistly.

"Out of the way, boy," Kite said, and I let myself be pulled aside.

Kite knelt, and lifted a dirty rag that had been pressed on Ignatius's stomach wound. Gently, he let the cloth back down. Cupping Ignatius's head, he levered it up slightly. That's when I noticed the unstoppered wineskin in his other hand. He upended the skin and dribbled its dregs between Ignatius's lips, and I saw the big man's throat muscles contract under his chins. Kite looked at me, and I knew immediately what he wanted—I pulled a brand from the fire, and in short order found two of the three other discarded skins. I handed them to Kite, who repeated the process, then lay Ignatius's head back down. Ignatius's breathing slowed and became regular. For a few minutes he seemed at peace, and it would have been easy to imagine he was just sleeping.

Then, with Kite kneeling next to him, and his choir surrounding him, Ignatius shuddered and drew his last earthly breath.

Our New Master

We buried them in shallow graves, scraping parched earth over top of them as best we could. I knew there was no chance of a Christian burial, but I had insisted that we do at least this, and to my surprise Kite had acquiesced. I made small crosses for each of the brigands out of twigs and bits of rope, and said a prayer over the remains of the one I'd killed. After that, we dug a deeper hole for Ignatius. It took all four of us to wrestle his body into the grave. When I tried to plant a cross at its head, Kite would not countenance it. He took the sticks and flung them deep into the forest. "He wouldn't have us petition God on his behalf," he said.

There's not much else to tell about that night. We broke camp as hastily as we could, Kite choosing a few of the brigands' better weapons and securing them to Cross, then we were back on the road before sun-on. Though no one said anything, I'm sure those men who had fled were on everyone's mind. We marched quickly and in silence, Kite leading Cross at a taxing pace, the three boys in the mule's wake. After a while, I noticed Lark and Ali had lagged behind. Initially, I thought they were having trouble keeping up, but when I glanced back they had fallen behind no farther, and I realized they had done so, consciously or not, to keep their distance from me. I suppose it should have bothered me more than it did, but I'd had little sleep that night and was too exhausted to worry about much of anything other than trying to maintain Kite's exacting pace. I was also working hard not to think about the blood on my hands—and Ignatius's death. I walked as in a fever-dream, my head bowed, grateful for the other boys' silence when I thought about it at all.

We marched through the day, resting every few hours. When we halted, the boys would collapse on the ground, while Cross would graze or lap from a stream. (About halfway through the day, it occurred to me these breaks were for Cross's benefit, not ours.) The whole time we rested, Kite scanned the road in both directions, never once sitting himself. Much to Lark's dismay, our respites were too short for us to prepare a proper meal, and it seemed we were back on the road after we'd managed only a few hurried bites and a small swallow of water.

As we approached sun-off, our feet began scuffing up ash. A thin grey-white layer covered everything. We passed a sharp line demarcating the periphery of a blaze and found ourselves surrounded by scorched fields. A few hundred metres farther along, we crested a small rise and saw what had been at the epicentre of the fire: a group of burnt-out stone buildings, a Church in their midst. Threads of smoke still rose here and there. One of the buildings had collapsed entirely, leaving just a foundation covered by a pile of rubble, and only the Church had the vestiges of a roof. Something about the scene struck me as familiar.

Kite sniffed the air and had a good look around before saying, "The Monastery burned three, maybe four days ago. No one's likely to come around tonight. We'll camp here."

As soon as Kite said the word *monastery*, I could see it: the square of huddled buildings that would have housed the monks and their offices, the flattened area behind that would have been the gardens they tended, and to the north the blackened, skeletal trees that had once been their orchard. It was the Black Friar's Monastery where I'd been held and forced to witness the torture and death of my father. When I'd been brought down to this benighted Sphere, I'd been hooded, but we had not travelled far from the Assumption before arriving at the monastery. I hadn't thought about it, but it shouldn't have been surprising that we might pass it in returning to the Assumption.

Staring at the ruination, I wanted to feel some satisfaction. But I didn't. What I felt instead was a great sadness that men could perpetrate such cruelties on one another. Not just the ones I'd witnessed, but this, too. Some might claim that this was God's punishment, but a loving God would not countenance such wanton killing, no matter how unrepentant the sinners. No, this was man's hand at work. I said a prayer for my father, and for the souls of those dead monks. But most of all for the men who had done this, for they were the ones who would have to live with their sin until judgement day.

As we approached the buildings, a light rain began. We passed several charred corpses; arrow shafts jutted from them. Most of the shafts were still unburnt and feathered, which meant those poor souls had been pierced after they'd been ablaze. In all likelihood the Monastery had been torched to rout those inside; as they fled the conflagration they'd been killed, one by one. We walked through the front gate and into the cloister, then made our way across to the Church. Just inside, we had to step over another shrivelled body in the narthex, its mouth frozen in the rictus of an agonized scream. In its blackened fingers it clutched a crucifix.

The rain was coming down harder as we crossed the nave. The bit of roof that was left hung above the altar, and it was there that Kite and the two other boys threw their blankets. I couldn't bring myself to do that. Instead, I wandered away and huddled in the northern transept, where the inward meeting of two walls afforded some shelter. I was numb, past exhaustion, in a kind of waking sleep. I stared off into the gloom, my mind turning over and over everything that had happened in the last day.

Later, I became aware that Kite was sitting next to me, watching me; in his hand he held a dirk. The one I'd plunged into the brigand's neck. He held it out to me and said, "You may have use of this again." When I didn't take it, he laid it down next to me, then caught my eye. "They deserved to die."

I looked away.

"I felt bad the first time I killed a man," Kite said. He touched me lightly on the shoulder, then withdrew his hand almost immediately. A clumsy attempt to comfort me. Only I didn't need comforting, at least on that score. I had intentionally killed a man who intended me no hurt, and in so doing had likely damned myself to the eternal torments of Hell. Yet I didn't feel the horror of it as I thought I would. If anything at all, I felt relief. And shame that I didn't feel worse.

"You can't let it get to you," he continued, "or the next time you have to act you will hesitate—and you will be killed."

I didn't try to correct his misapprehension; instead, I nodded. He made a move to leave, and I put a hand on his arm to stop him. "Why did you let the last four go?"

He chewed his lip for a moment, then returned a question: "Why fight when it's unnecessary?"

"Because of what they did to Ignatius."

"They did what they were forced to, by circumstance or otherwise."

"I didn't think you the merciful sort."

He shrugged. "There are always other reasons."

"Such as?"

"I've seen too many fights, boy, where one side was expected to win. Only no matter how good the odds, it doesn't always turn out that way. Things can go wrong in hundreds of ways you would never expect."

"Like tripping over a root."

"Like tripping over a root," he agreed. "The odds weren't with us last night. We got lucky. I didn't want to push our luck."

I doubted he really believed we'd gotten lucky. We both knew he could have taken the last few brigands without breaking a sweat.

"There was nothing to be gained," I said, "and everything to be lost."

"Those who fight with their heads, keep them. Those who fight with their hearts, lose them."

"If I tell you my thoughts about what happened today," I said, "will you tell me if I'm right?"

He nodded.

"You poked Cross to create a distraction while remaining concealed. You knew as soon as she started braying I'd run out and make a scene. If I killed the sentry, that would be one less you'd have to worry about. If I didn't, you knew they weren't going to kill me. Like the Captain said, I wasn't worth anything to them dead. In either case, they were only expecting me and so they'd all turn towards me, which would make it easier for you to kill the only man who had his wits about him, the Captain."

"Some of the others had their wits about them, too."

"Then you went for their leader, because you knew they were undisciplined and would panic without him."

He nodded again.

"Who were those men? Why did they want me?"

"I know as much as you, boy."

I didn't believe him. "May I ask one more question?"

"Suit yourself."

"Why do Ali and Lark hate me?"

"They don't. They are shamed that you killed a man they wanted to kill. And they are angry that they are beholding to you. No man wants to owe another."

I could see the truth of it. Even though I felt they owed me nothing, I would have to find a way to let them believe they had balanced the accounts if I wanted them to like me again.

With his last answer, Kite stood up and walked away.

I had one more question I had wanted to ask him, but I let him go because I had worked out the answer for myself. I knew what his promise to Ignatius had been. It was the reason he had let me return to the campsite, why he'd brought the dirk, and why he'd answered my questions just now. His promise had been more than returning me safely to Rome.

Kite was to be my new teacher.

The Postulants' Camp

Before us was a sea of ragged, makeshift tents the size of a substantial city. Fifty thousand souls, if the Captain's figure was to be credited, all desperate to leave this unhappy Sphere. The encampment bearded the hill upon which the lily-white Assumption sat, and fanned out onto the plain below, the disarray of the camp a sharp contrast to the pristine, geometrical precision of the hallowed structure. The stench of human excrement assailed us well before we reached the camp's extremity, and Kite tore pieces of cloth for us to press over our noses and mouths. We were on a meandering path that no one else travelled. In the distance, however, we could see a steady stream of refugees entering the camp on well-marked roads, all in defiance of the Pope's edict. Why, I wondered, would they risk such a journey to come to a place like this?

We entered the camp and discovered why no one else followed our route: we were in a *lazarette*. Sick people had been laid out in a rough grid, and harried physicians moved amongst them attempting to provide what succour they could, while hollow-eyed priests administered last rites. Most of the ill, I learned later, had cholera. Few attendants or patients looked at us, and those who did gazed at us with a combination of surprise and wariness, as if to say, *Why are you, the living, here amongst the dying?* We encountered a tall, gaunt drayman wearing only a loincloth, dragging a cart laden with bodies. He grunted at us to give way. The dray trundled past, its wheels creaking under its load, leaving behind the sickening stench of putrefaction that no thickness of cloth could ameliorate. After picking our way through dozens more rows of the ill, we came to a sort of buffer zone between the *lazarette* and the rest of the camp, demarcated by a fouled river whose banks were covered with all manner of filth and detritus.

It was here, where the runoff from the camp accumulated, the stench was greatest—so much so I gagged and almost fainted. Ahead of me, Lark went to his knees, heaving violently. Kite dragged him to his feet and pushed him forward, towards a rickety bridge that spanned the foul river.

I knew little about doctoring, but enough to know that the ill recover more readily in sanitary conditions. It seemed madness to place an infirmary next to a river of excrement—unless, of course, the sick were not expected to recover.

Crossing the river, we entered the camp proper. The stench abated somewhat, a stiff breeze blowing it back over our shoulders. Save for Lark, we all dropped our cloths. Kite picked his way between ragged tents, past their sullen occupants. I could feel eyes on us, see the sharp set of hunger in their gaze as they watched Cross, with her fat packs, clop past.

The Meek, they had named themselves. Yet I had no doubt they were bold enough to rob us of our goods—and perhaps our lives. *Blessed are the meek, for they shall inherit the earth*. Was the appellation one of resignation because they knew there was nothing left for them in this life and their only hope was for the next? Or was it a not-so-subtle threat to those who controlled the Assumption?

Both, I decided, the stares prickling my back like thorns. I had seen enough of the world now to understand that violence all too often stalks the loss of hope.

I was relieved when we finally hit a road of sorts—a wider, hard-packed path, really, but broad enough for four men to walk abreast. It seemed less likely we'd be troubled here. People wandered up and down this avenue, clutching pots and water-skins; some looked dazed, others utterly defeated. A few sat at the side of the road, gazing off into the middle distance. At regular intervals, *Gardes Suisse* were stationed beside wooden huts. Set up next to each were two tables and a stool. A scribe sat on the stool, busily inking large quarto sheets on one of the tables, while a line of men and women and children looked on anxiously. On the other table were ledgers, stacks of blank quarto paper and a burning candle. I thought this odd, the candle, because it was not quite yet dusk, but more so the reams of empty paper. There was a fine for those in possession of more than three sheets of paper, except for those with dispensation from the Church, so I'd never seen so much blank paper in one place. Not only that, but the sheets were of the size used in printing books—well, *The Bible* since no other books were printed now—four pages per side. I could only see them as unformed books.

Books were the least of his sins, the Bishop had said to me, *But a clear sign of a struggling soul, the beginning of his slide into iniquity.* They had led to my Father's downfall, because of his love for my mother; and the sins of my father had been visited upon me. I got a small chill, looking at all that paper. Not because of the misfortune they had brought to my family, but because of the promise of their empty pages: *tabula rasa.* And though I felt it likely to be a sin, I was seized momentarily by the strange idea that, had I the means, I could rewrite my story—in more favourable terms—on those sheets.

As we passed the next guard house, I saw a scribe finish his document, roll the page neatly, then seal it by dripping wax from the candle and impressing his signet ring. He passed it to a large man with massive forearms, who I took to be a smith. The man poured some coppers into the scrivener's outstretched palm—and then I understood what was transpiring. The scribes were professional petitioners.

"Agents of Rome," Kite hissed softly, as if he'd read my thoughts. "For those who can afford their services." He spat, his disdain undisguised.

Any person, I had learned at *San Savio*, had the right to petition the Church. At the time, I had liked the idea that the Church had such a mechanism, enabling its most humble parishioner to directly petition the Pope. Father Finn had said to us, "But before you boys all run off to write the Pope a letter, there is one more thing you should know. . . ." The catch was that the petitions had to be in a prescribed format. It had to be on quarto-sized sheets, addressed to the Most Holy Father (*Beatissme Pater*), followed by the name and diocese of the petitioner. It had to be written in the language of the Church, Latin. This was done, Father Finn said, to ensure fairness, expedite the requests, and reduce frivolous requests, such as ours would have been.

But here, in this camp, where many couldn't write (and of those who could, only a few understood Latin), and where tens of thousands screamed for the Pope's leave to escape this unholy Sphere, it suddenly seemed an absurd prerequisite, serving no purpose—except, perhaps, to line the pockets of Rome's agents.

I couldn't believe the Church was enforcing this ridiculous requirement.

Despite what I'd suffered, I still believed in the essential goodness of the Church, and that the Pope was God's chosen vessel, our Holy Father. Had the Pope been aware of the injustice of my father's inquisition—or of the myriad of injustices, small and large, at *San Savio*—he would not have permitted them. But he was not God, he was a man, and couldn't be everywhere at once. Besides which, he had bigger fish to fry, next to which my sufferings amounted to nothing.

But this?

I began to understand Kite's disdain.

We came to a crossroads. On the corner to our left, a large white tent, a cross at its apex, had been erected. At its entrance, several *Gardes* were measuring meagre portions of food and water into cups and bowls extended by wasted men, women, and children, while half a dozen other *Gardes* struggled to keep order of a hopelessly long line that snaked down the road perpendicular to ours. From within the line, sunken, hungry eyes turned towards us with undisguised envy and hatred. I am sure they would have swarmed us had Kite not swung his halberd from his shoulder to the ready. In the eyes of several men I witnessed the glint of desperation give way to the wariness of self-preservation. Taking advantage of this, Kite pushed unceremoniously through the mob, stopping before the two *Gardes* posted at the tent's entrance. Under their berets both were pimply faced, and looked to be only a handful of years older than me. I could feel people pressing in behind us, almost feel their breath on my neck. From the corner of my eye, I saw a hand dart out and touch one of Cross's packs.

"Let us inside," Kite said, "or you'll have a riot."

The *Gardes* took in Kite's halberd, and then looked nervously to the crowd. The older of the two pulled back the flap and said in a voice that broke, "*Go!*"

The pressure of the crowd seemed to waft us inside. I felt a palpable sense of relief as the heavy flap fell behind us.

Bales and crates and casks filled the space—and, of course, more *Gardes Suisse*. Farther back in the tent, a half dozen sat at a trestle table on which was the remains of their evening repast. They were somewhat older, but all were still well under twenty if I was any judge. They looked untried, more like a gang of sulky teenagers than the vaunted *Gardes*. It was worrisome, that things had deteriorated to the point where men this green were being deployed. The oldest one—a major, from the single star embroidered on his epaulettes—rose from the table and approached us where we stood with Cross. A bit older, perhaps in his early thirties, he was a tall, black man with a commanding air. I could see him taking in Kite's faded uniform.

"Are you mad?" he said, in a pleasant enough voice. "Walking through the camp with *that*." He waved his hand at Cross.

The men at the table watched in silence.

Kite reached into this satchel, pulled out Ignatius's vellum, and proffered it. The major unrolled it and frowned as he read, then handed it back to Kite. I had feared he'd simply strip us of our goods and turn us out, but by the way his expression had changed, I could tell the letter had its intended effect. He turned to the young men at the table and nodded in a way that said, *I will handle this.* They returned to their meal.

"Rome grants you passage," he said. "That's clear enough."

"And aid," Kite said.

"More precisely," the Major said, "it exhorts us to '*render what aid possible.*' These days, little is possible. What is it you want?"

"An escort to the Assumption."

The major laughed. "You *are* mad." When Kite's expression didn't waver, the Major said, "I can't spare a man. We'd be overrun." He glanced at the table of young men and sighed as if he found them wanting. "We might be anyway," he said so they couldn't hear. Then he looked at Cross. "Even if I did give you an escort, your mule would still be on a spit before you got ten paces. You, too, if the whispers are true."

"We won't take the mule," Kite said. "Nor most of what she bears."

Ali went rigid; it was no secret he'd developed an affection for Cross. Truth be told, I had similar feelings and was sickened at the prospect of losing Cross. But I knew Kite was right. We'd be lucky to make it through the crowd on our own, let alone dragging an irresistible prize like Cross with us.

"The boys will each take their possessions and one short sword," Kite said. "The rest is yours."

This seemed to spark the major's interest.

"Perhaps," he said, "I might spare one man." He stepped over to Cross and examined the contents of her packs. Ignatius had provisioned us well, and with a quality of food unlikely to be found in the camp. Certainly better than the remnants on the table. The major turned back to Kite. "However, I cannot allow the weapons." He pointed to a pile of rusty swords, picks, axes, and knives in a corner. "We are also charged with disarming those in the camp. Weapons are forbidden to Petitioners."

I had tucked the dirk Kite had given me inside my pants and shirt to hide it from Lark and Ali; its wooden handle pressed insistently against my ribs.

"We are not Petitioners," Kite said.

"Civilians, then."

"I am not a civilian," Kite said.

Despite its ragged appearance, the uniform of the *Cent Suisse* still seemed to command respect, and the major didn't challenge his assertion, even if he did look slightly dubious. "Be that as it may, I cannot allow your boys weapons. There are many patrols in this camp. Too many to avoid. And they will not find your letter as—" he glanced at the fat packs "—as palatable as I do. Martial law prevails in the camp, and it is a capital offence for all but the *Gardes* to bear arms."

"Then," Kite said, "we must be *Gardes*."

The major looked perplexed.

"We are in the service of the Church," Kite said. "As much as you and your men. We only lack the trappings."

"The trappings?"

"Uniforms," Kite said.

"You want your boys to pass as *Gardes*?" the major said, astonished.

"There are only a few years between my boys and your youngest. The uniforms will fit. In a few hours it will be dark and difficult to make out their ages."

"What you ask is impossible. My men will not part with their kit."

"They do not have to. Once at the Assumption, we will return their uniforms with your man."

"No," the major said, "too risky. If you are stopped . . . or my man doesn't make it back . . ." He shook his head.

"The letter exonerates you."

"Perhaps," the major said. "But I'd prefer not to find out how much weight your letter really carries at my court martial."

"If the letter alone will not suffice," Kite said, pulling a gold pope from his pocket, "will this help buy our commissions?"

The major's eyes widened; he nodded slowly. "It would." He paused. "For *my* part."

"A silver bishop for each man who lends a uniform, and one for our escort."

"In that case," the major said, taking the gold piece from the cup of Kite's palm and slipping it under his belt, "who am I to refuse those who serve the Church?"

Amongst the Meek

Ali and Lark were taller than me by a hand, and we quickly found uniforms for them which required only minor adjustments—in Ali's case, this meant he wore the borrowed uniform over his other clothes to make it look like he had more meat on his slender frame. However, none of the *Gardes* were near as small as me. I had to roll my shirt sleeves and pants legs up, and tuck them in so their ill fit wouldn't look too obvious; I slipped the end of my belt into the side of my pants and tried to conceal it with a fold of the overflowing shirt. Kite even stuffed rags in my over-sized boots to add another few precious centimetres to my height; still, my short sword looked like a long sword at my side, the tip of its scabbard almost scraping the ground. I was implausibly small, but at night, surrounded by the others, I might go unremarked. The boys whose uniforms we wore sat at the table, in varying degrees of nakedness. If they were dubious about the bargain, it didn't seem to have affected their appetites—they gorged themselves on food they'd liberated from Cross's packs, eating with gusto.

Ali removed Cross's packs and harness, then brushed her down one last time while we waited for sun-off (when the patrols, the major told us, were less frequent, and those that were out, were less likely to confront or be confronted). Each night, the major himself would send out two of his own patrols, and we were to depart with the first, a contingent of six men, around midnight. Kite bid us try to get what sleep we could in the interim.

I slept fitfully, Kite sitting next to me. It seemed only a few minutes, but must have been several hours, when something dragged me back to wakefulness. I opened my eyes a sliver to see the lamps had been lit; on the other side of the tent the major was sitting by himself, turning Kite's coin over and over in his hand. He seemed discomfited. Abruptly, he rose and walked over to Kite, who sat on a barrel a few feet away from me, sharpening his halberd.

"I am shamed," he said to Kite. "I like to think myself a man of faith and honour. But I have shown you neither. If your letter be real, as I believe it to be, an honourable man would not take your coin." He held out the gold pope.

Kite refused to take it back. "Keep it," he said. "Or use it to buy food for these people."

The major considered for a moment, then tucked it away. "Nor can I take your mule. I will hold her for you as long as I can. If we are ordered to go, I may have to press her into service. Or leave her behind."

"I do not know if or when I will return," Kite said. "But I thank you, Major."

"Abraham," the major said. "My name is Abraham Osei."

"Kite."

They shook hands.

After the major had walked away, Kite looked at me; he waited until I opened my eyes fully, then returned to sharpening his halberd. From the manner in which he had regarded me, though, I knew he meant it to be another lesson. On honour? Perhaps. Or maybe a much more practical one on the guilt that consumes honourable men. I never found out, because moments later our patrol began forming up, and I became occupied with rousing myself and pulling my gear together. As I was doing so, Ali folded his arms around Cross and hugged her one last time, his silent tears falling on her neck. I longed to do the same, but felt doing so would diminish Ali's gesture, so I contented myself with offering up a silent prayer as farewell. (Of course, animals have no souls, but I like to think they might have their own sort of heaven, one in which my prayer might have been heard.)

The major had picked his smallest remaining men, and had them cluster around us so that we stood a decent chance of blending in. We filed out of the tent into the darkness and marched down a narrow, hard-packed path, the lead man carrying a lantern. We moved, more or less, in the direction of the Assumption, which was no longer visible save as a large square absence on the hilltop. Like everything else, firewood was in short supply, so the few fires we'd seen earlier had burned out. In some places, I could make out hunched figures staring silently at dying embers. For such a large gathering, the silence was eerie, the only sounds throat-clearing coughs, the buzzing of snores, and murmured words too indistinct to make out, and too intermittent to determine whether they were part of a troubled sleep or a whispered conversation. Twice a dark shadow darted across the path ahead of us, and once, a lump of night soil fell in our midst, narrowly missing Kite. It's origin was impossible to determine, and it seemed our assailant was more intent on blending into the darkness than on launching a second volley. Still, it worried me; the ground was peppered with stones that would make much more effective projectiles.

Half an hour on, we came to a small stone bridge that spanned a dried stream bed; the patrol, having reached the limits of its territory, did an about-face, and marched off into the dark, parting company without a word. The man who was to act as our guide, the company's sergeant, led us across the bridge, the three boys following closely—Lark, then Ali, then me—our berets pulled low over our eyes. Kite brought up the rear. Although it seemed impossible, the petitioners' crude dwellings were even more crowded on this side. Now we travelled without the benefit of a lantern; however, the sergeant seemed sure of his way, and quickened the pace.

When a torch flared several hundred metres ahead, the sergeant broke left onto a path so narrow we were forced to go single file between makeshift hovels and ragged tents—even my narrow shoulders brushed against canvas as we squeezed through. Although our progress slowed, we encountered no one. Soon, the ragged tents gave way to a mixture of more robust structures, cobbled together out of wood and string and canvas, and we found ourselves slogging through muck. Small things, hidden in the mud and filth, cracked under the soles of my boots. And with the more treacherous footing, my too-large boots had also begun shifting on my feet, and I could feel blisters forming on my soles, fluid filling them. Each step became agonizing. I grit my teeth and ignored the pain.

We walked and walked.

Four times we crossed overflowing latrines on boards, one only a hand-span wide. The stench, always bad, was horrific in these places. I kept my eyes squarely on Ali's feet, following him step for step, my blisters throbbing each time I planted a foot. Foolishly, I decided that if I broke the blisters, the pain might diminish, so for a few steps I slammed my feet down; I was rewarded with a tickle of warm, sticky fluid between the toes on both feet. But instead of the relief I sought, the agony intensified, almost beyond endurance, so much so that I had a notion to pull my boots off. However, I retained enough of my wits to realize it would be madness to discard them and walk barefoot through the filth. So I kept them on, more fluid seeming to seep between my toes with every step, my entire world collapsing into two searing points of pain that were my feet.

That's probably why I missed the abrupt transition: the chaotic jumble of improvised shelters had fallen away and we were back on the semblance of a road at the foot of the hill. Above us, a kilometre distant, the Assumption brooded in the half-light of sun-on.

I hadn't cried since the night my father died, but I almost cried then.

I struggled to contain myself, to push my agony to the back of my mind and keep step, for the sergeant had redoubled our pace.

Perhaps it was the pain or lack of sleep or that I had, for the past hours, focused only on the march of feet in front of me, but somehow I had also missed the camp stirring to life. All about us, in ones and twos and threes, petitioners shuffled slowly towards the gates of the Assumption, clutching their rolled petitions. A few glanced at our company, and there might have been a raised eyebrow or two, but for the most part their suffering was such that I don't think it would brook distractions. The crowd thickened, and I heard a deep voice hollering "*Postulants to the right!*" over and over. Everyone surged right and slowed; we went left. The petitioners thinned out, and the few still in front of us came to an abrupt halt, looking uncertain. Blocking their way was a gated wall, and in front of that, a squad of *Gardes* with pikes, standing ready. Their sergeant, a rotund man with a red face, was bellowing directions. "Postulants to the right!"

A bewildered-looking fellow, torn petition in hand, stumbled up to them.

"*Back,*" growled the *Garde* directly in front of him, the tip of his pike inches from the man's chest.

Despite this, the fellow raised the hand clutching his petition. "I—"

Before he could get out a second word, the *Garde* batted him on the temple with the side of his spike; the man went down like a sack of bricks. The other postulants backed off.

"You drop 'em, you drag 'em," the sergeant said to the *Garde* who'd swung. He nodded to the side of the road. "Put 'im over there." The *Garde* hustled out of line, dragged the fellow he'd cold-cocked to the side of the road, and rolled him into the ditch.

"Well," the sergeant said turning his attention to us, "What's this?" His eyes must have been bad because he squinted at us. The other *Garde* gaped at us, at three boys in their ill-fitting uniforms, but said nothing.

"It's Maur," said the sergeant who'd been leading us.

"Maur! God's blood, is that you?"

"It is."

"You're not due for provisioning for another five days."

"Got four going up."

The sergeant raised his eyebrows.

Kite stepped past me and proffered his rolled vellum. He was close enough that his uniform seemed to register with the sergeant. He took Ignatius's letter in his right hand and weighed it for a moment, then turned it upright; a silver bishop spilled out of the tube and into his left. Pocketing the coin, he passed the vellum to a corporal who stood behind him. After scanning it closely, the corporal said, "Looks real enough."

"Major thought so, too," said Maur with no trace of irony.

During this exchange, I'd forgotten about the postulants behind me, but now I felt a hand on my shoulder. I turned.

A sizable crowd had accumulated. At its fore was a woman of middle-age, clutching her petition. *My mother.*

I'd never seen her, but a fine portrait hung above her dusty piano.

"Please," she said, shoving the roll against my chest; I instinctively grabbed it. For a moment her eyes pinned me; they were startling, the colour of pure jade, and I thought, *Those aren't my mother's eyes.* In the the painting they'd been blue.

Maur raised his hand as if he made to strike her; she turned and fled.

And in good time. For the *Garde* had advanced to disperse the crowd, holding their pikes horizontally at chest height, forming a bristling picket. They swung wide, to swallow our party, and closed around us. Most of the petitioners managed to dance out of the way. But those at the back of the crowd, who probably couldn't see what was happening, were pushing forward, hoping, perhaps, this might be a way to skirt the long line. Something light glanced off of my head, and fell to the ground. Then again and again: a rain of petitions. I could see arms over top of heads, flicking the rolls towards us, desperate for someone, anyone, to heed them. Where the crowd was the thickest, the mass of people surging forward overwhelmed those trying to retreat. I watched in horror as several people were pushed back towards us and impaled; directly in front of me the tip of a pike slowly pierced the back of a scrawny young man trying to squirm out of the way. He howled and thrashed, the barbs on the pike head keeping it firmly embedded, while the *Garde* held on to the other end of the pike for dear life, looking for all the world as if he was landing an enormous fish. Blood pooled under the young man's jerkin and ran down his back and legs. He collapsed to his knees, then fell to his side. The *Garde* dropped his pike and stepped back, letting another pikeman take his place.

Over the general tumult, I heard a piercing cry: "*They're killin' us!*"

The crowd was thrown into a swivet; bodies heaved this way and that, and wordless screams rent the air.

"Take them to the Assumption," the sergeant shouted over the melee. I looked down, thinking he meant the petitions at our feet. But strong hands grasped me, dragging me away. Dragging all of us away.

I craned my neck for one last look, searching the crowd for the woman with the green eyes; but all was a thrashing, panicked confusion. The only thing clear was that the *Gardes* had resumed their advance, the soles of their black, scuffed boots crushing the carpet of discarded petitions into the mud.

Assumption

Viewed from half a league distance, the Assumption appeared pristine. At the front gate, however, the alabaster stone blocks of its foundation were clearly stained and pitted with age, and there were deep grooves between the blocks where the mortar had spalled. I barely had time to take this in as we were hustled beneath a raised iron portcullis, the pointed teeth on its bottom flecked with rust. We found ourselves in a narrow passageway in which three men could walk abreast. A dozen metres and the passage was barred by a second portcullis. On either side, smooth stone walls rose ten metres, and overhead was not the vaulted ceiling I had expected, but a flat wooden one, which had six closed hatches along its length. Spaced regularly along the walls were narrow vertical openings, no more than the width of my palm, behind which I sensed, more than saw, the movement of men. As we approached the far gate, I heard the rattle of abruptly untensioned chains and the rasp of sliding metal issuing from behind us; I turned in time to see the first portcullis clang down. Almost immediately the gate in front of us began to rise to the groaning of hidden winches. There were few fortifications in my Sphere, that of the Apostle Andrew; and the ones I had seen thus far in this Sphere had been hastily erected in the recent past. So it took me a moment to apprehend the reason behind this design: if the opening and closing of the two gates was managed right, attackers would be trapped; and the arrow-slits at the side and murderous holes above would allow the defenders to slaughter them.

We passed under the second gate, and immediately our escort fell back; the corporal, no doubt anxious to attend their comrades, barked out a command, and the winches went to work again, reversing the process.

In a low-ceilinged room illuminated by lanterns, we stood before a squad of *Gardes*. While the troops outside had looked bedraggled, half-beaten, and uncertain of their roles, one glance told me these men were hardened veterans. Their faces held none of the wariness or malice or anticipation I'd become accustomed to seeing in the *Gardes* and local patrols; rather, they appraised us with cool detachment, standing in disciplined formation, ready to execute with precision any command given.

"Stand at ease," said a short priest, emerging from behind their rank, his voice commanding despite his stature. He wore the black cassock and collar favoured by Jesuits. The *Gardes* relaxed marginally, widening their stances.

I threw myself on the ground and tore off my boots. Pulling out the cloths that had been stuffed in them, I made strips to wipe away the viscous, pink fluid first, then to bind the open blisters on my feet. As I did so, Kite proffered his vellum again, and the priest accepted it; there was no coin inside this time. He read it and furrowed his brow. "Ignatius?" the priest asked, looking up.

Kite shook his head.

I rose and took a few tentative steps. The pain, as bad as it was, seemed manageable.

"I warned him," the priest said, returning the scroll. "I shall pray for his soul." He bowed his head and clasped his hands, as if he was going to pray then and there. But if he did, it was a very short supplication. "Come," he said, and moved off into the gloom behind the *Gardes*.

We followed him—me limping behind—into a room illuminated by candles in sconces. In its centre was what looked like a large trap door set into the floor; behind it was an inverted T of metal arms. The horizontal arm at the top was adorned with cylinders. The priest had us stand on the trap door. It shifted slightly downward as we did so, and I couldn't help shooting a nervous glance at Kite. He looked unperturbed. So I tried to dismiss my fear. The priest began moving the cylinders that were not fixed to the arms, and I realized what he was doing: we stood upon a large scale, which he was using to weigh us. When he balanced the arm, he moved over to a small writing desk and scrawled some figures in a ledger.

"Come," he said again, and we followed him into a short corridor. At its end, the priest touched a single finger to what I thought was the wall of a dead end and stepped back; a door swung inward, revealing night.

Only it wasn't night. It was the heart of the Assumption.

There was nothing save a round, wrought-iron cage set in the centre of a fuligin plane. Inside the cage, the face of another Jesuit floated, the outline of his cassock nearly impossible to distinguish from the background. The inner walls of the atrium were composed of the same material as the floor and, without windows or doors save the one through which we entered, they formed the interior of a featureless ebon cube, open at its top. As far as I could tell, there were no joints anywhere, which meant that each of the five planes had to have been moved in place as a piece, but by what extraordinary means I couldn't conceive. The material itself was like nothing I had ever seen, improbably smooth. Although it was now full sun-on, the material didn't reflect the light, but rather seemed to absorb and refract it down to impenetrable depths, leaving me with the disorienting feeling I was staring into a bottomless abyss.

A long, worn carpet led from the door to the cage, and the priest stood aside and bade us follow it with a curt wave of his hand.

Ali took the lead and I followed—and immediately understood the reason for the runner. Without it, I would have been overwhelmed by the vertiginous sensation of walking over a void. I swayed, but managed to maintain my balance, fixing my eyes rigidly on the cage. Ahead of me Ali stumbled and would have fallen had I not caught him by the shoulders and steadied him. He glanced back at me, eyes wide, disoriented and near panic.

"Fix your eyes on the cage. Don't look down or sideways or beyond."

Ali regained a semblance of self-control and nodded; thus we moved forward, my hands on his shoulders, until we passed the Jesuit who stood just inside the cage. Ali immediately seized the bars to steady himself. I thought he'd be grateful but the look he gave me was withering, and I realized in helping him I had inadvertently stoked his resentment.

Lark hadn't fared as well as Ali, for Kite entered the cage carrying him under one arm, much as he had carried me the night we'd run from the Captain. The poor boy had his hands pressed tightly over his eyes; he shook uncontrollably and his face had taken on an ashen pallor. Kite did not look at all unsettled, but then he'd given me the impression he'd travelled in several Spheres of the Apostles. At the minimum, he'd been through three Assumptions: the *Cent Suisse* were in Rome, three Spheres above this one, one above the Sphere in which I'd been born. Kite had to pry Lark's hands free as he set him down next to Ali, then he, too, grasped a bar. I don't know why, but this made me feel better.

The Jesuit latched the gate behind them. The small priest who had followed us now walked backwards on the carpet, rolling it up as he went. When he reached the door, he touched it in the same spot a second time, and stepped inside. The door swung shut soundlessly and disappeared into the featureless wall as if it had never been there.

I had thought I would feel better at making it to cage, but this wasn't the case. Being in the centre seemed to make everything worse. I could feel my equilibrium slipping away; I began swaying.

"It's always hard on you the first time," the Jesuit said. "Best if you do as your friends are doing and close your eyes."

I'd paid him no heed until now, but his voice brought me up short. Even though I had only heard him speak Latin through the gunny sack over my head, I recognized his raspy voice.

"This isn't my first time."

He looked at me with what might have been curiosity, but said nothing. Then, in silence, he positioned us within the cage and bid us not move. Stepping to the centre, he stood astride what I had taken to be a wooden Crucifix embedded in the floor. But the lengths of the arms were equal, and when I looked closer, I realized it was two carpenter's levels fixed perpendicularly, small glass cylinders with spirit bubbles on each end. Directly above them a silver bell had been suspended from the roof of the cage. The Jesuit pulled the rope attached to the clapper so a loud, clear note rang out. Then he bowed his head and began to pray in Latin, the same prayer I remembered him uttering at the start of my descent. A moment later, I heard the note returned, but muffled, as if from some distance; I couldn't be sure, but it seemed to emanate from beneath us. There was another distant sound, only this was like stone being dragged over stone. It vibrated through my soles, and into the broken blisters on my feet, and I ground my teeth and swallowed back the pain.

Then my stomach lurched as we began to rise.

The Jesuit's prayer broke off, and he peered intently at the levels, his hand on the rope. As we ascended, he rang the bell—each time he'd pull the rope from one to four times in quick succession, reminding me of the Sanctus bell rung during Mass.

On my descent, I'd had no way to gauge our speed, unable to see the distances; but now, unhooded, I determined we were rising a metre every few seconds. Within a minute we had crested the walls of the Assumption. The edges of the platform that bore us were now distinct, and were far enough away from us that they hid the postulants' camp below. However, I could see the great curving reaches of the Sphere in every direction. Here and there rose black plumes of smoke, like those we had passed on our journey, and around them the grey smear of rain God had sent to douse the fires. A moment later, the structures of a distant city hove into view; inside its wall were many benign threads of smoke rising from chimneys. But at its heart a massive column of smoke bellied upwards. At its base I could see the tiny, yellow flicker of flames. The size of the fire must have been enormous to be evident at this distance. Yet there was no rain to quell it. I watched in horror, wondering why this, of all the fires, God had left unquenched.

"His will is beyond our ken."

I turned to find the Jesuit regarding me, keeping half an eye on the levels, and one hand on the bell rope.

A few days ago I would not have essayed a response. "I . . . I came from such a city."

He shook his head sadly. "For a want of ten righteous men. . . ."

God had agreed to spare Sodom and Gomorrah if Abraham could find fifty righteous citizens. When this proved impossible, God, in His mercy, lowered the number to forty-five, then forty, thirty, twenty, and finally to ten. To no avail.

The burning city soon passed from view as the edges of the platform obscured the ground in every direction. Only the gentle curve of the sky remained.

Intermittently, the Jesuit rang the bell. With nothing else to see, I watched him.

"You are sending instructions on how to keep us level," I said.

He smiled, and it occurred to me he had a kindly face. "Yes."

"The number of bells indicate adjustments to make."

He nodded.

"It must be difficult, to keep it in balance."

I didn't expect him to answer, but he did. "Right now, the plate at our feet weighs less than you might think, and that makes it difficult to balance." He tapped a red line on one of the levels with the toe of his sandal. "If the edge of the bubble passes this line, it will flip, and the Assumption will be lost." There were only a few millimetres clearance on either side of each bubble. "The plate upon which we stand, and those directly below, work in opposition to one another." He was warming to the explanation; I imagine very few Clergy ever asked about his work. Except, perhaps, for fellow Jesuits. Their order seemed to have a natural curiosity; they were renown for studying the natural world avidly—sometimes to the dismay of the Church. "There are damping plates, too, that ameliorate the vertical acceleration caused by gravity." My puzzlement must have been evident, for he asked, "What do you know about gravity?"

"Only what I've been taught: that gravity weighs us down while we live, pulling us towards the inferno. And when we die—well, if our soul is heavy with sin, it plummets to Hell. But if it is light enough, it escapes the pull and ascends to Heaven."

Kite, who held his peace until now, snorted derisively.

The Jesuit took it in stride. "Indeed," he said, smiling tolerantly. "That teaching is more in the nature of, ah, metaphor. Gravity is not punitive— it is a natural force, and behaves as all such forces do, in a predictable fashion, just as God has willed. Certainly gravity draws us down towards Hell, but that does not make gravity malign. Weight is merely the force exerted on the body by gravitation. And Hell is an unimaginably dense mass. So massive, that if you were to move close enough to it, you would never be able to escape." The priest threw Kite a look. "This gives rise to some of the more fanciful explanations."

"You said *right now* the plate at our feet weighs less than we might think. Do you mean it weighs more at other times?"

"Weight varies depending on the magnitude of the local gravitational acceleration. At the centre of our platform you weigh roughly the same as you did below. But if you were to step beyond the edges of this cage, your weight would be, well, negative. You would be pulled up. Above and below us are plates that damp or enhance the effect of the gravitational acceleration of the Sphere. By moving them just so, you ameliorate the effect of gravitational acceleration from below, and increase it from above. Since the pull down on the area of the cage is less than the pull up on the rest of the plate, we rise."

I thought about this for a moment. "Why not make the middle as light as the rest? Then there would be nothing holding the platform down."

"True. But if you were to step outside this cage you would, at the very least, lose consciousness. The transition is too pronounced. Your body has grown in the context of a certain gravitational acceleration, and so its systems depend on this to move your fluids. Changing the gravity too quickly would disrupt the flow of these fluids and cause you to lose consciousness—or worse."

"You said we weigh *roughly the same*. Not *exactly* the same."

He nodded.

"It's hard to tell, but I think I feel lighter."

"Yes."

"And I felt heavier as we went down Spheres." Until now, I had attributed the heaviness I'd felt to my state of mind rather than a natural force.

"As you get closer to Hell, your weight increases. In the lowest Spheres, the crush of weight is such that men cannot survive there for long."

"So that means gravitational acceleration increases as we descend Spheres."

"Or becomes weaker as you rise, yes."

Kite, who I'd thought had lost interest in the conversation, said, "And so Angels fly."

I expected the Jesuit to get angry, but he didn't. "Angels can fly because God gave them wings."

Kite turned to me. "It's why they can't leave Lower Heaven, boy. Those flimsy wings of theirs would be worse than useless below Heaven. A few Spheres down and they'd be pulling themselves on the ground like crippled beggars."

I wasn't surprised so much by Kite's blasphemy, as I was by his boldness. The Jesuit looked as if he'd been slapped.

"Is it true Angels can fly anywhere in Lower Heaven?" I asked him quickly, hoping my inquisitiveness would soften Kite's goading. "And they can't in lower Spheres?"

"That's likely," he said, collecting himself. "But we don't know for certain, because they never leave Lower Heaven."

"Then the stuff of which the Spheres are made, the earth itself, must also work like these plates."

"Precisely!" the Jesuit said with enthusiasm, obviously glad to focus on my interest, and skirt Kite's provocation. "The effect is greatly reduced, but their masses are vastly larger than the plate upon which we stand." It was clear he was excited that the natural world exhibited an explicable order, and that he had an audience with which to share his beliefs. "It's the application of the same principles that allows the Assumption to move, and that keeps our Spheres equidistant from one another, so that earth doesn't crash into sky." It had never occurred to me such a disaster was possible; I shuddered at the thought. "God made the Spheres to lessen the pull of Hell," he continued. "Thirteen Spheres of the Apostles, all contained within another, each diminishing the pull of Hell, until it is barely noticeable in the highest Sphere of Lower Heaven. So God keeps the Spheres of the world in harmony. In balance. Like the balance of this plate."

Kite said, "So you are God of this plate?"

"No, no, no. That's not what I meant!" The Jesuit's face turned red. "We . . . we, are humbled by his works. Our understanding is small. Less than a single leaf in a vast forest. Just enough so that we might use God's gifts as he intended. His ways, as mysterious as they are, have meaning and order. But to grasp them, even a small part of them, one must apply *reason* to the natural order."

"Or perhaps," Kite said, releasing the bar and taking a step towards the Jesuit, his halberd loose in his hand, "the Church bends reason to fit circumstance."

The bubbles in the levels edged slightly towards the red lines. The Jesuit blanched. "Please," he said, "you must stand still." As he spoke, he rang the bell sharply three times, paused, then rang it twice more. The bubbles moved marginally towards the centre. "No more talk! I must attend to my work."

"Father," I said. "One more question and I promise we won't disturb you again."

"We?" the Jesuit asked, shooting a look at Kite.

I looked at Kite, too, and to my relief he essayed a curt nod.

"Ask, then," said the Jesuit. "But no more moving!"

"Why can't the Meek be assumed?"

He said nothing for a moment, eyeing his levels intently. "Their numbers are too great," he said, turning his back to us. "They would disturb the balance."

Kite caught my eye, but said nothing, as he'd promised.

In silence, we rose.

I looked to see how soon we would reach the zenith. But the colour above was uniform in all directions, making it impossible to gauge distance. I could see no opening and was seized by the irrational fear that we'd be crushed against the sky—until my ears popped and I felt a slight lurch in my stomach. And by that I knew that we had passed from one Sphere into another. Looking around, I realized we were in a cube identical to the one below, save that its interior was the colour of the sky, thus making the opening virtually invisible from below. The Jesuit rang his bell and a door, matching the one below, appeared in the wall. A rolled carpet was heaved onto the plate.

Five minutes later, the portcullis of the upper Assumption clattered down behind us. We stood in a glade. A well-maintained brick road cut through flower-speckled grass to a wooden bridge and thence over a brook. Birdsong rose from the surrounding wood. An altogether idyllic scene—in contrast to what lay only a few hundred metres below. A huge sense of relief, and an equally profound guilt, stirred uneasily within me.

"Where now?" Ali asked.

"To the next Assumption," Kite said. He pointed. "Two months march." When I'd been taken, we descended two Spheres in five days before reaching the Black Friars' monastery. I was certain this was the second Assumption we'd used, but a two month's journey meant that the next Assumption, the one back into the Sphere where I was born, was a different one—and that much more distant from my boyhood home. Though I knew there could be nothing there for me, it still made me sad all the same that we wouldn't be passing near on our journey to the Vatican.

Lark, who Kite had had to carry out of the Assumption, wobbled unsteadily behind us, took two steps away into the deep grass, went to his knees, and vomited. I waited until he wiped the back of his dirty sleeve across his mouth, and offered him my water bottle. He turned away with a small shake of his head, spurning my offering. In our passage through the Meek, Ali and Lark's resentment had been forgotten, but now that we were no longer facing imminent danger together it seemed to have resurfaced.

"The Jesuit lied." Kite's voice startled me. "There is no reason the Meek cannot be Assumed—if the Church wished it." I'd thought so, too, but when I said nothing, Kite continued. "Balancing the Spheres would be more about the distribution of mass and not the relative amounts in each Sphere."

"Maybe he believes it."

"So much the worse if he does," Kite said. "If he believes it, then he is deceiving himself and betraying the faculty of *reason* the Jesuits claim to hold in such high esteem. And if he doesn't believe, he is betraying his humanity in letting the Meek suffer."

"Perhaps he fears betraying God," I said.

"The Church," Kite said with utter conviction, "is not God."

This made me angry. "He's a priest. He cares for us. For our souls." I felt my face flushing. "You had no call to taunt him."

Kite shrugged. "I did it only to show you how men deceive themselves. And to show you the desperation with which they wish to stay deceived. You can insult a man's mother, and yet make amends. But show him how he has deceived himself, and he will drag you to Hell sooner than forgive you."

It was another lesson, one I found difficult to accept. "So you provoke him for being a man?"

"For being a coward or a dupe, or both." Kite locked eyes with me. "I can see you are angry, boy. And for what? Because I tried to show you how you deceive yourself?"

This brought me up short.

Kite barked out a laugh. "See what I mean?" He swung his halberd over his shoulder and started down the road, leaving me behind to smart.

Ali smirked at me, then followed Kite; Lark thrashed out of the high grass to catch up.

I didn't want to believe that men were men, whether they wore a collar or not. I wanted to think better of those chosen to be God's ministers.

Except I knew Kite's lesson to be true. I'd seen it at my father's inquisition, at *San Savio*, and amongst the Meek. It is not those who are unashamedly evil that we need fear the most, for their intentions are plain; rather, our fear should be reserved for those equivocators who would allow evil to flourish, and name it good so they might sleep better at night.

My Secret

The next morning, after we had broken our fast, Kite collected three stout sticks from the wood that skirted our road, and handed one to each of us. He paired me off against Ali and, with a gesture, bade us fight.

Since the night of the ambush both Ali and Lark had treated me with indifference and silence—Kite had attributed it to their shame the night we rescued them. So, to try to balance the accounts, I resolved to let Ali best me.

I need have made no such resolution.

Although slight, Ali was taller, had a longer reach, and was remarkably quick. And I was slowed by my blistered feet. Ali peppered my shoulders and arms with half a dozen blows before I could execute a clumsy thrust—from which he easily danced away. My resolution completely forgotten, I lunged at him with force, only this time as he skipped out of the way he swung his stick so it smacked my cheek. This infuriated me so much that I yelled and charged at him, swinging with all my strength—and ended up in the dirt as he deftly ducked my clumsy slash while kicking my feet out from under me. I sat up, my palms scraped from the fall, knowing a bruise or two would soon colour my skin. My mock sword lay uselessly on the ground several metres away. Ali stood above me, the tip of his stick hovering an inch from my nose. His eyes shone above a crooked smile.

Kite stepped up and wrapped his long fingers over Ali's, lowering his stick and tapping it against my chest, directly over my heart. "Here," he said, releasing Ali's hand. "Not the head."

Ali nodded.

Then he lowered his stick and extended his other hand. I reached up to grip it and he helped me to my feet.

"Now see if you can do any better, boy," Kite said, pointing at Lark.

He did, indeed, fare better, landing a blow or two, and once, when they grappled, Lark used his weight to stagger Ali. But Ali danced around him much as he had danced around me, and I could see he was taking it easy on Lark. My cheeks burned at my false pride in thinking I might do the same to Ali.

"Switch," Kite said, and Ali started to walk away. Kite raised his hand. "No. You fight until you lose."

So Ali and I went at it again, only this time my resolution was to take what I observed in Lark's fight and my own, and use it to my advantage. Once, I managed to crack my stick across his ribs with great force; but he was as tough as he was fast, for he didn't even wince. He thrashed me soundly a second time. If I could take any satisfaction from this bout it was that, at least between me and Ali, the books were more in balance.

When Kite called a halt to the practise (Ali having won every bout), I was surprised to see by the shadows that we'd been fighting for what must have been two hours. Ali was lathered in sweat, as was I. And poor Lark was on the ground grunting for breath.

We broke camp shortly after.

On the morning's march, Kite spoke at length about what he observed us doing, and what we could have done to best Ali. Some of his observations were the same as my own, but most were things I hadn't considered. In the afternoon, Kite lapsed into his characteristic silence, and I took the opportunity to reflect on how I might best apply his advice. That evening, I had a chance when Kite had us do it all over again. Ali, who'd no doubt been considering the same words, bested us again.

And so Kite supplanted Ignatius as our teacher. In the days that followed, we kept to the same pattern: an hour of sparring each morning, followed by Kite's discourse on the art of combat as we marched; a silent afternoon in which to consider his words; and then an evening bout before we supped. We quickly developed blisters on our hands; but these burst and, by and by, were replaced with calluses. Kite didn't restrict us to swordplay. He also taught us the use of the dagger and long knife. In all this, our true weapons, the short swords we had brought with us from the Postulants' camp, stayed sheathed, and we used what sticks we could find. Ali continued to excel, and I could see improvements in Lark. But I felt like I was making little progress. If I was improving at all, it was in such tiny increments as to be unnoticeable;

I became despondent as I watched a multicoloured garden of bruises flourish on my skin.

"You don't practise."

This was on the seventh day out from the Assumption. Ali sat on his haunches on the other side of the fire's dying embers; Lark, exhausted, snored heartily into his bedroll; and Kite lay perfectly still in his, whether awake or asleep or in some state between was impossible to judge.

"I do," I said, puzzled.

"For the choir, I mean."

"Oh," I said. "Well, neither do you and Lark." Since Ignatius's death, none of us had sung.

"I just thought . . . I mean, Kite said it would take us three months to get to the Vatican. We've only got a month left. Maybe less. We should practise."

Ignatius had never told us what happened to the boys who weren't taken into the Sistine Choir, but it was easy to imagine. So I understood Ali's concern. Still, I shrugged, pretending indifference. After all, how could I tell him I already knew I would never sing in the choir?

"Are you afraid we will outshine you?"

It would have been easy to make him believe that simply by not denying it. "No," I said, unwilling to lie to a friend—for I *had* come to think of Ali as a friend.

"Then why will you not help us?" I knew this must be hard for him, asking a favour.

"I will help you," I said, considering. Ali and I had repaired our relationship, but Lark still harboured some resentment. Perhaps this would help. "I will coach you both as best I can, and try to teach you what Ignatius taught me. On two conditions."

He looked at me, wariness settling on his face. "What?"

"That you do not ask me to sing."

He looked surprised. "Why not?"

"That is the second condition: that you do not ask me why I choose not to sing."

He hesitated, but having no other choice, nodded agreement. We shook on it.

And so the next afternoon, as we marched towards the next Assumption, Ali and Lark sang and I directed them. I feared Kite might object, but if he thought anything about the juxtaposition of the martial and choral training, he never said a word.

The problem was, I couldn't think of a good excuse for not singing. So in the moment I'd struck the deal with Ali, I thought myself clever for attaching the condition that I'd have to make no excuses. But as the days passed, I realized that all I'd done was to push the question to the side, not banish it. I could see Ali wondered, as did Lark. But both kept to our agreement. And who knew what Kite was thinking? I began to regret not taking the time to fabricate a lie that would appease everyone, rather than publicly harbouring a secret.

Knowing there was no place for me at the *Capella Sixtina*, I had formulated a plan to slip away from Kite and strike out on my own at the first reasonable opportunity. Yet now I found myself reluctant to leave—I recognized the practical value of Kite's training, as difficult and frustrating as it was for me, and was reluctant to forgo it. And this Sphere seemed largely agrarian, the few towns through which we passed more villages than anything, where everyone knew everyone else. There were no other travellers, and few inns (which Kite would have refused to use, in any case). A boy on his own here would stand out. I also had no knowledge of this Sphere, for what geography lessons we'd had were only on our own Sphere. Why learn about other Spheres when you are never expected to leave your own? No, if I was to have any hope of surviving, I decided, I would wait until after our next Assumption. At least then I'd be back in my own Sphere. Though I'd travelled little as a boy, I'd seen maps of the Sphere and knew the names of all the major lakes and rivers and cities (and many of the minor ones). Better yet, I'd heard gossip, and knew something of places by their reputations. Enough, at least, to form an opinion on where my chances might be best.

I couldn't sing, or they would immediately know my secret and, at best, I would be left at the first orphanage we came upon. You see, I was precocious for a boy of my age, and with the onset of puberty my larynx had begun to lengthen and my voice change.

Kite's Secret

As the days passed, and no one challenged me, my fear of discovery abated. I knew there would come a time when I'd be confronted, but I tried, as much as possible, to put this dread from my mind. I pitched my voice lower and lower, reduced it almost to a whisper, and spoke as little as possible. I made no excuses; rather, I let them concoct their own. It would be a month (by Kite's estimation) before we reached the next Assumption, and if I could make it that far then I was fairly confident I could successfully strike out on my own.

We fell into a rhythm, much as we had with Ignatius.

Despite my apprehension, I recall those days with great fondness. The Sphere through which we journeyed was a marked contrast to the one below. It was verdant and serene, undisturbed by strife. When we saw other people, it was almost always at a distance in the fields, ploughing or harvesting. Most essayed a friendly wave. After half a dozen such encounters, our suspicions dissipated and Lark and I waved back. Time moved apace, probably because I found myself occupied constantly with Kite's lessons morning and afternoon, and my tutoring in between—and pleasantly exhausted at day's end. During this period I enjoyed restful sleeps troubled by few dreams. Most of all, though, I enjoyed tutoring Ali and Lark. Pedagogy, I discovered, was fraught with challenges and frustrations, but also with great joy. When the boys sang beyond my expectations, I felt a surge of pride. Not a sinful, self-aggrandizing pride, but the humbler satisfaction of playing a small, but essential, role in the accomplishment of others. Life was calm and ordered and meaningful in ways it hadn't been since I'd been taken by the Church.

Five days before we were to arrive at the Assumption my uneasiness returned; if I was to part company shortly, I'd have to prepare. I resolved to surreptitiously gather a small supply of food, enough for two or three days travel. But I didn't. I deferred that first day, then the next, reluctant, I suppose, to spoil the respite. When I slipped a small piece of hardened cheese into my pocket on the third day, I felt sickened, as if I had somehow betrayed my friends. It made no sense, for there was no danger of starving now: we carried an ample supply of dried and cured food, and fresher provender was not in short supply as we passed through villages. Nevertheless, I couldn't assuage my guilt. As we walked that day, I rolled that lump of cheese between my fingers until I'd ground it into a pocketful of tiny morsels—most of which fell through a small hole and trickled down my leg and onto the hard-packed earth of the road.

"You won't make it."

We were pitching camp in a small clearing at the side of the road. I was on my knees, arranging sticks into a cone over the tinder and kindling for our fire. Lark and Ali had wandered off to gather bulkier fuel that would last well into the evening. A short distance away, opposite me, Kite sat cross-legged. Until he had spoken, the only sound he'd made had been a slow, rhythmic *snick, snick, snick* as he ran his sharpening stone across the blade of his halberd.

"I don't know what—"

"You do." He fixed me with a stare, the stone poised over his blade.

There was no point denying my intention; Kite seemed to know what I was thinking before I'd thought it myself. "I can't go to Rome."

"You can and you will."

I felt an urge to tell him why I couldn't go, but saw no gain for me—at least not yet. I wanted to get through the Assumption first. Once back in my own Sphere, I'd still attempt my escape. If I failed, then I'd tell him my secret and he'd leave me in an orphanage. It wasn't what I'd hoped for, but better than being abandoned here. So I said, "Okay."

"You will have to lie much better than that in Rome."

I felt my face flush. "What do you want from me?"

"Do not attempt to flee."

"Why shouldn't I?"

He swung the end of his halberd out, knocking over my carefully constructed cone.

Anger got the better of me, and my voice rose sharply. "I tell you I will never sing with the Sistine Choir!" In the vehemence of my response, my voice cracked.

"No need to look horrified," Kite said, barking out a sharp laugh that was like a slap in the face. "I already knew your little secret."

I was nonplussed. "I . . . I don't understand. If you know, why have you not left me behind?"

"Rome," Kite said flatly, "is more than a choir." He turned his attention back to his blade, and resumed rasping the stone against its edge. His movements were precise and careful. Affectionate.

"Why?" I asked again. But I knew he'd already said as much as he was going to say, leaving me to reason it through on my own.

I gathered the disarrayed sticks, chewing my lip, thoughts tumbling over and over in my head.

Rome is more than a choir.

I began reassembling my cone, examining the sticks one by one, then placing them in exactly the same positions they were before, as if building a puzzle.

Kite knew my secret, but didn't care. Which meant he wasn't taking me to join the choir at the *Capella Sixtina*. Yet, he was still determined to take me to Rome. For what purpose? I confess my first thought was of the other boys who'd been bound out at the same time as I, and I remembered the man Ignatius had called Georgie, who'd wanted to buy me for his brothel. Could Ignatius's commission have been to find boys suitable to be catamites? I could hardly credit that. I was certain there was an ample supply of willing boys (or, at least, guardians who were willing) closer at hand. Such boys could be procured with far less trouble. No, there was something else . . . something about *me*. I'd suspected this before, when we'd been waylaid by the brigands. But false humility had made me reject this as too absurd. How could I possibly be that important? Yet the Captain had known who we were, and seemed willing to do whatever it might take to capture me alive, including murder. And, for his part, Kite had demanded I flee with him, abandoning Lark, Ali and Ignatius—once his lover—to their probable deaths. And he would have, had I not demurred. My stomach knotted, for it sickened me to think that there was something about me important enough to have cost Ignatius his life.

Rome is more than a choir.

With a shock I realized what it was that Kite had wanted me to work out: Lark and Ali meant nothing to him. If I fled, they would never see the Vatican. I had insisted on rescuing them; and now Kite counted on me not to betray their hopes. And he was right, for as soon as I realized this I knew I couldn't flee. If I did nothing else, I'd see them through to Rome.

Why? I wondered. *What was so important?* I'd thought Kite was bound to see us there because he was honouring a debt to Ignatius. Now I knew different.

I stared at my fragile pile of sticks, then at Kite who endlessly sharpened a blade that needed no sharpening. I knew it likely that I might never apprehend his reasons. Kite was the sort of man who kept his secrets—unto his grave.

First Love

After waking from a restive sleep before sun-on, I stole away from camp.

I'm not entirely sure why I did so. At the time, I remember rationalizing it as an urge to revisit the habits of my childhood, to rekindle the peacefulness of wandering field and forest by myself. But now, looking back, I suspect that was more an excuse. I'm sure I did it more to provoke Kite. It galled me that he was confident I wouldn't run away, and I suppose I wanted to shake his confidence. But if he heard me rise, he gave no sign. His eyes did not flicker, nor did the regularity of his breathing change. He appeared as fast asleep as Ali and Lark.

Only I knew he wasn't asleep. Or, at least, not asleep in the way of ordinary men. I was certain he was aware of my movements on some level; I had no doubt it was as much an autonomic reflex as his heartbeat.

I backed towards the margin of the forest where the undergrowth was thick; still he appeared unperturbed. Turning with disdain, I pushed my way through some brambles and plunged into inky shadows beneath the trees, stumbling onto a deer run. After my eyes adjusted to the dimness, I followed the narrow path for a few minutes, pushing aside slender young branches as I made my way. I came to a fork and paused; in the stillness I heard morning's first birdsong and the rush of a river. I took the left branch, which ran in the direction of the river.

The sound grew. Through the leaves I saw flashes of whitewater.

All at once I was out of the forest, standing on a flat rock, overlooking the foot of deafening rapids. Cool spray licked my face and drenched my clothes. To my left, a few metres away, the river abruptly broadened and its course levelled, and the threshing water swirled tranquilly into a series of inviting pools.

I pulled off my shirt, intent on a long overdue ablution, and took a step towards the edge of the rock to climb down to the nearest pool—then froze. A naked figure rose from where it had been sitting in the pool, its back to me.

I threw myself on the ground and scuttled back into the bushes, shirt clutched in my hand.

I was so shocked, at first I thought to run back to camp to tell Kite—then immediately dismissed the idea. That's what Kite would expect me to do. So after my heart slowed and my breathing became more regular, I edged back towards the pool on my belly, wriggling into a clutch of myrtle bushes, where I might observe the bather unseen.

It was a young woman.

Although I'd never seen a naked woman before (except for the few crude renderings of my classmates at *San Savio*)—and, angled away from me as she was, her slender waist, the curve of her hips and buttocks, and the small prominence of her breasts were unmistakeable. Her skin was dusky and unblemished, her limbs lithe and sinewy, her hair jet black and cropped short in a boyish cut. Around her waist was a finely wrought gold chain that hung from the curve of her hips and glittered in the morning sun. She stood thigh-deep in the pool, leisurely scooping water over herself, slowly running her hands over the sculpted muscles in her arms and legs, luxuriating in the sensation. Until now I'd only ever seen the exaggerated sensuality of Ignatius's prostitutes, and found it of little interest, thinking it contrived and laboured, anything but arousing. However, watching this woman, believing herself unobserved and thinking only of her own pleasure, I felt an intense arousal unlike I'd ever felt before. The heat rose in my face, and burned in my groin, too, where unbidden an erection pressed urgently into damp earth. When she ran a hand up her leg and slipped it between her thighs, my heart leapt into my throat. For a moment or two her hand lingered there, then she let it fall into the water; but it rose again to her flower and she brushed her fingertips lightly back and forth, barely touching herself. Slowly, then, her touch turned to strokes, her hand slipping in and out with growing urgency. I don't know how long passed this way; it could have been a minute, it could have been ten. I was stricken, unable to think, unable to breathe, unable to move. When she clenched her buttocks and arched her back, crying out in pleasure, my world seemed to cant sideways.

I spilled my seed then.

Not as a boy does in his dreams, but awake, as an adult, for the first time in my life. I shuddered in diminishing waves that matched her own, gasping for breath, then squeezing my eyes shut fearing I would lose consciousness.

When I opened them, she was there, in the pool, doubled over, her shoulders heaving, her hand still clamped between her thighs. She caught her breath, then stood, withdrawing her hand, unashamedly examining her glistening fingers in the incipient morning light.

My thighs were sticky; I was horrified at the madness that had possessed me. The Church, if it wavered in other areas, held firm on this: seed was for the propagation of man only. To waste it was a grave moral disorder. I knew I'd committed a sin, a mortal sin, yet she was beautiful beyond words, a perfection of form and physique. I could not take my eyes off her.

What is it about images like this that catch in our imaginations forever?

In the intervening years I have been with women I thought I might love, some of whom other men would declare far more beautiful than the young woman I now observed. Never for me. In that moment by the river, this woman's raw beauty, her unabashed sensuality, was burnt indelibly on my mind; I would not recognize it until much later (and to the detriment of those who had the misfortune to love me more than I could ever love them) but I can now see the pattern of how I have vainly tried to relive the intensity of those feelings—and failed. You may ascribe it to the infatuation of a boy, but if it is, it is one that had stayed with me throughout my life, and pains me still. For the only love that stays with us, the only love that remains sharp and untarnished into our declining years unto death, is the one we can never have. You see, what I did a few moments later forever destroyed that possibility.

The young woman began singing; as difficult as it was to hear her over the roar of the rapids, I could make out snatches of the Mass we'd been practising the last week, the phrasing and intonation unmistakeable.

She turned, and I saw that it was Ali.

I suppose any sensible person would have quietly slipped away in that moment. But I didn't. I was too astonished—and confused—to move.

Ali waded out of the water, her body glistening in the light of sun-on, drops of silver dripping from the dark tangle of hair on her pubis. I thought then that she looked up at me; but I think she must have been searching for a handhold, for she disappeared beneath the lip of the rock, then gracefully swung herself up onto the flat stone in front of me. She folded herself onto the ground, sitting cross-legged only a few hand-spans away. I was astonished she hadn't seen me.

Leisurely, she wrung water from her hair; I watched as tiny rivulets slid down her shoulders and ran onto her small breasts. One drop hung pendent from her long, dark nipple; she casually flicked it off. Then she lay down to sun herself, her head toward the river.

Transfixed, I marvelled at her, watching her chest rise and fall, her eyes shut as if asleep. How could I have been so fooled?

I thought I might inch back experimentally, to see if sounds of the river would be sufficient to cover my movement. But just as I was about to do so, she cupped her hand over her pubis and began to pleasure herself again.

I am ashamed to admit it, but I became hard instantly.

She rolled over onto her stomach, her hands beneath her now, her hips rising and falling, rising and falling. Her legs were apart, her toes curled hard against the stone; from my vantage I saw first one finger sliding into the pink folds of her labia, then two, while with her other hand she caressed her clitoris in a slow, circular motion.

A madness possessed me; without volition I was on my feet and atop Ali. I heard her gasp as I grabbed her wrists and pinioned her arms. Then I took her from behind, as the boys had done to me at *San Savio*.

There are times too traumatic for ordinary memory to process; when this happens, it is not uncommon for people to say their memory went blank. Sometimes, it turns out these memories are not wholly gone, but are suppressed, pushed so far away from consciousness that they manifest only as shapeless ghosts that haunt dreams.

My memory, however, reacts differently. I have never wholly blanked out. Instead, my mind tears apart memory, shreds it, as if it is trying to make it a jumble of disconnected and incomprehensible moments that elude meaning. If it didn't, I am sure guilt would consume me and become unbearable. This was one of those times. As clearly as every detail of Ali bathing in the river had been burned into my mind, I have little recollection of my greatest shame.

I raped her. That I know.

The rest is fragments. A flash of her struggling beneath me pointlessly, my madness giving me pitiless strength. The cold metal links of her gold chain pressed between belly and back. Of me lying next to her, spent, as she wept into her hands. The blows she rained down on my head and shoulders with her fists and then a branch (when had she picked up that branch?), while I sat hunched over on bare buttocks, breeches at my ankles, head on my knees. There are disconnected moments of her expressions, too, of astonishment, of shock and anger. Of the revulsion etched in every line of her face as she screamed at me. But the sharpest spike of memory is that of her standing over me, sometime later, dressed again as a boy, her cheeks flushed, her eyes flashing hatred. "Pull up your pants," I remember her saying, and that drew me back, as if out of a dream; memory snapped back into place.

I did as she asked and stood, but my self-loathing wouldn't allow me to meet her gaze.

She punched me in the face, and I staggered backwards; a second blow felled me.

I lay on my back, and she stared down at me, murder in her eyes. I'd have welcomed death, too, only she didn't strike again. "You won't tell." Not a question, a demand, Ali squatting next to me, the tip of her dirk pressed against my throat.

I shook my head, at first thinking she meant what had happened, then realizing she meant about her being a girl. *A woman.*

"I know why you won't sing." This was her threat: she would expose me if I exposed her. But I would have sooner cut out my own tongue than said anything.

The walk from the river back to the camp is clear in my memory; conjuring it in my mind's eye, I see how it would have been beautiful had my disgrace not coated everything with a grey pallor. I resolved then and there, in the way boys are wont to do, to make things right, no matter what it might take. Yet by the time we reached camp I realized how naive I was being. I was no longer part of the world of boys, a world in which everything can be fixed—or forgiven. I had done murder and done rape, and had no hope of absolution, in Heaven, or here on earth.

Ali would hate me always.

Entering the world of adulthood, I knew despair.

Second Assumption

I own what I did.

Some men might blame a sin such as mine on possession. I will not. Yes, I believe in Satan. But I do not believe he, or any of his demons, were in me that day. At least no more than they are in any of us on any day. Still, I cannot explain my act other than to say I was possessed. I did not understand the darkness that moved me, yet I knew it to be part of me. I also knew that no matter what I might do, no mater how hard I prayed, the darkness would always be there, coiled inside me, waiting. That I could harbour such a thing frightened me.

I must have looked a mess when we returned to camp. One of my eyes had swollen shut, and I bled from several unstaunched cuts on my head. My nose throbbed relentlessly, and a strand of bloody snot ran down my lip whenever I snuffled.

Kite merely glanced at us, as if we'd just returned from a morning stroll, then turned his attention back to dividing the hard rounds of bread that had become our morning staple. Lark gaped, but had the good sense to snap his mouth shut and busy himself with other things.

I did not break my fast, nor join that morning's sparring, and Kite let me be.

The day's march passed in a haze. I conducted no singing. When we halted for lunch, I gave my portion to Lark.

I tried to find guidance in the Good Book that afternoon, but failed.

It's no secret that a literal reading of *The Bible* quickly reveals its contradictory and often vexing nature. Indeed, I have often heard the uneducated bend a passage to serve their own selfish ends. This, however, is born of an ignorance (a willful one in the unscrupulous) of our doctrine. It is not for us, the laity, to interpret God's word. It is the purview of the Church. The Catholic faith holds that the Word of God is manifest in the Holy Scriptures; but it also holds that interpreting the Word has been entrusted to the episcopate—so named the *Magisterium*—whose teachings on faith and morality are infallible, as promised by Christ. Thus, the Bishops interpret God's word for us.

Flee from sexual immorality. Every other sin a person commits is outside the body, but the sexually immoral person sins against his own body.

I did not need the Magisterium to interpret this passage. God spoke plainly. I had sinned against myself as much as I had sinned against Ali. Turning memories like pages, I searched passages from both Testaments, and found few that spoke to what I had done. The only one that seemed apropos was from Deuteronomy, and it was one my teachers had never brought to our attention: *If a man meets a virgin who is not betrothed, and seizes her and lies with her, and they are found, then the man who lay with her shall give to the father of the young woman fifty shekels of silver, and she shall be his wife, because he has violated her.* At first I thought the passage admonished me to take Ali as my wife. This I would have done in a heartbeat. But Ali had no father, and I had no shekels. And the passage also contained the proviso, *"and they are found."* What I supposed was meant by this was that once it was common knowledge a woman had been defiled, her prospects of securing a husband diminished, and so the rapist was duty-bound to take her as wife. Only, we had not been found. The more I thought about it, the more I believed that this exception had been put there for the woman's sake. As odious as was my first trespass, trying to force her to marry me—when she might find a better, more-deserving husband—would be tantamount to committing a second unforgivable violation.

No more verses spoke directly of my sin, although there was no lack of passages about the sin of lust. James was perhaps the most apt. *But each person is tempted when he is lured and enticed by his own desire. Then desire when it has conceived gives birth to sin, and sin when it is fully grown brings forth death.*

I understood this, and felt it to be true in my heart.

However, many of the verses that dealt with sins of the flesh only confused me, like Matthew's admonition: *But I say to you that everyone who looks at a woman with lustful intent has already committed adultery with her in his heart.* We'd been reminded of this passage several times at *San Savio,* and it was easy to see what Matthew meant by this and why the Priests, in a school brimming with pubescent boys, returned to it time and time again. But having now reached physical maturity, I could not comprehend how a man could act contrary to his nature—a nature God had given him. If sin be a thought, then I could not see how any man could avoid Hell.

In all this, I wondered about Kite, too, for the Bible seemed clear on his sin: *If a man lies with a male as with a woman, both of them have committed an abomination; they shall surely be put to death; their blood is upon them.*

How could the Magisterium interpret this otherwise? Yet Kite and Ignatius had not been put to death. They'd only been excommunicated. And as light as my punishment of fifty shekels had seemed, by the same measure theirs seemed overly harsh—and both were, by my reckoning, good men otherwise. I counted myself lucky to have known them.

Warnings and reproofs spun round and round in my head until I was dizzy and sickened, and still I had no better understanding of what I should do, nor if there was any possibility of redemption—in God's eyes or in Ali's.

When I recovered my senses, my back was pressed uncomfortably against a large rock; Kite loomed over me. Behind him, Lark stirred our small, dented pot, while Ali cut potatoes in her palm. The smell of stew swirled around me.

My confusion must have been apparent, because Kite said, "You fainted when I set your nose."

Kite had waited until the swelling subsided a bit. The last thing I remembered was his cold palms pressing against the sides of my deformed nose, and an intense flash of pain, like someone had smashed me between the eyes with a hammer.

Kite cupped my chin to examine his handiwork. "It'll never be fully straight again, but near enough." He let my head drop. "Shame," he said. "Such a pretty face. . . ."

Lark scooped some broth into a cup and brought it over to me. My stomach rumbled and my mouth watered. I glanced over at Ali, but she kept her eyes resolutely fixed on her potatoes. I waved away the stew.

Lark's round face creased with concern. "You haven't eaten all day. You've got to eat, Thomas."

"Leave him be," Kite said. "He'll eat when he's hungry enough." Then he walked away.

Lark leaned and whispered to me, "Ali caught you. You'd have hit your head on that rock if he hadn't." He hovered for a moment, as if waiting for a response. "I never seen anyone move that fast."

I said nothing, and a moment later he, too, retreated to the evening's repast.

Gently, I touched my nose—and a new universe of stars exploded in my vision. I nearly fainted again.

When the pain had subsided to a tolerable level, I tested my nose once more, infinitely more careful this time. I felt around its gross contours. It had swollen up, almost as large as when it had been freshly broken, but was nowhere near as deformed. I crawled over to my bedroll and lay down, my back to the others. That night was a sleepless, pain-filled misery, and I remember little of the next day's march. I barely had the energy to drag myself after our small company. Exhaustion and hunger muddled my thoughts.

That night I slept like the dead.

On the third day, I collapsed.

Since the river, I'd neither eaten nor drunk.

Through a fog I recall Kite crouching over me, trying to force water between my lips. "I don't know what you've done, boy," he said, "or what you think you've done, but you cannot atone for it if you're dead." Behind him, Ali glared.

I pushed the water listlessly with my tongue; it trickled from the corners of my mouth.

I wavered in and out of consciousness, plagued by a recurring dream. In it, an ever-changing monster pursued me. At times it was insectoid, with a chitinous skin and snapping mandibles; at others it was like a stone giant, massive and raging. Sometimes it was utter darkness cloaked in human form. These, and a hundred other shapes. Always, though, it pursued me, and I fled, filled with terror. And always it would impale me, crush me in a stony fist, drown me in darkness. Each time, as I died, there would be Ali, at a distance, watching, her small sword drawn, a shield on her arm. She could save me, I knew. Despite my agony, I could not bring myself to call to her.

I woke in the depth of the night, more or less sensible. Ali hovered over me. She stuck a cup of cold broth under my nose. "Drink."

"Wh . . . why?" My voice rasped, barely audible.

"You'll do me no good dead."

She tipped the cup, and I let the broth trickle down my throat.

I choked. When I stopped spluttering, she tipped the cup again, and this time I was able to control myself.

I lapsed back into a semi-conscious state.

During the night, she returned half a dozen times, each time giving me another small sip.

In the morning, she brought me a crust of bread. I chewed on it listlessly.

"Why did you not kill me?" My voice, though still rough, was much improved. "I would have, if I were you."

She shrugged. "I've better people to kill."

I ignored her sarcasm. "You need me. To get to Rome. But I don't understand why."

She looked away, as if the conversation bored her.

"They will never let you sing, you know."

"Rome," she said distantly, "is more than a choir."

Hearing Ali echo Kite's words took me aback. I essayed no response, though. Truth be told, I didn't want to know. I'd promised I'd keep her secrets, and those we don't know are always easiest to keep.

Kite bid Lark and Ali support me as I walked. I couldn't bring myself to touch Ali, but she grabbed my arm and slung it over her shoulder so vigorously I thought she was going to pull it out of its socket. It was slow going at first, but by midday Ali had abandoned me just to Lark. He huffed and puffed and probably got more than his fair share of exercise. He had filled his pockets with bits of food, and gave them to me, one after the other, all day. At lunch I managed a decent portion of cheese and dried strips of pork. By the end of the day, I felt strong enough that I tried limping along under my own steam.

Kite frowned, whether at my poor efforts or at the delay my infirmity had caused, I couldn't tell. He halted us early that night, and we camped in a clearing with pines pressing in on all sides.

The next morning, Kite woke us all before sun-on; he shoved crusts, each with a thick slice of cheese, at us, and bid us eat as we walked.

I walked on my own that morning. As it turned out, we did not have far to go.

We emerged from the forest at sun-on, and the next Assumption hove into view. It sat on a rocky island in the midst of a stagnant lake, water lolling against one of its alabaster walls. At the base of this wall, a rickety wooden dock clung like a barnacle, and dilapidated stairs switch-backed up the side of the Assumption to a point mid-way to the wall's summit. A raft, poled by a burly Jesuit, struck out from the dock to where we stood on the shore, and then conveyed us across. I felt the Jesuit eyeing my broken nose, black eyes, and the contusions that peppered my head.

As we disembarked, the Jesuit barred Kite's way to the dock. "It is a poor Soldier of God," he said, eyeing Kite's tattered uniform, "who beats his children."

"I am no longer a Soldier of God," Kite said, "and these are not my children."

For a moment the two locked gazes, and I wondered if it would come to blows. But the Jesuit inched back marginally, and Kite brushed past.

As we climbed, I glanced back to see the Jesuit staring at me, his hands on the bottom rail of the stair, ready to follow. I think if I had cried out for help, that man of God would have come to my aid in a heartbeat. I shook my head *no*, to try to tell him things were not as he assumed. I don't know if he understood, but he did not follow us.

An unadorned plank door swung open for us when we reached the last landing. A Jesuit beckoned us in, then led us through a series of corridors, until we found ourselves in the weighing room. Although the fixtures and furniture were different, and some temporary structures had been erected, the layout of the rooms and corridors seemed identical to the first Assumption, as was the weighing apparatus.

Kite proffered his letters of passage to an officious-looking Priest.

A few minutes later, I was rising toward home.

Home

During our Assumption, I searched my memory, piecing together the routes we'd travelled, working out the general direction in which we'd moved through the last two Spheres. I reckoned we were quite a distance from my boyhood home in the Sphere above. However, it was possible that I'd missed a turn, or miscalculated the angle at which two of many roads intersected. There were also blanks where I might not have recalled the bend in a road, for as I said before, what I recall is exact, but my mind does not store every insignificant moment of my life.

I asked the Jesuit conducting us what Parish we'd be in when we emerged from the Assumption.

"*Saint Dominic's*," he told me amicably.

My heart skipped a beat; it was a neighbouring Parish. "Near Abraham City?"

"No. The one on the shore of the Dead Sea."

Although I knew there was nothing for me in this Sphere, I still felt a pang of disappointment when I realized my boyhood home was, as I had estimated, on the other side of the Sphere. I would see nothing familiar.

"Where are you travelling?" he asked brightly.

I'd lost interest in conversing, but Kite surprised me by answering, "Rome."

"Then you won't see much of this Sphere," he said, looking between us. "From here, it's a week's passage on a ship to the Assumption."

I had already determined to see Ali to Rome, whatever her reasons. But had I still hoped to slip away from Kite, on a ship it would have proved impossible. No matter that I no longer had plans to flee, it felt like another door had been slammed and bolted behind me.

"*The Charon*?" Kite asked.

The Jesuit nodded enthusiastically. "Know her?"

"I sailed on her after I was excommunicated."

The Jesuit was taken aback. He eyed Kite, seemed to take in his uniform for the first time. You could almost hear the gears turning in his head.

"When is she due?" Kite asked, as if nothing had changed.

"Fortnight," the Jesuit answered coolly.

Kite asked if there was lodging nearby, and a few other questions about the place, but the Jesuit waved them all away, suddenly consumed by his work and too busy to answer.

The Jesuit had understated how little of the Sphere we would see. Or rather, how little there was to see.

When we walked from beneath the Assumption's outer portcullis, we found ourselves looking out over a vast body of water, larger than any I had ever seen, extending beyond the curve of the horizon. The air, too, was unlike any I had ever breathed, heavy and with a salty tang. Directly below us a small fishing village perched on the sandy shores of the sea; it could have been home to no more than a hundred souls. The few streets were empty. A thin line of intermittent vegetation clung to the coastline, but that was the only foliage in sight. The rest was desert, dune after dune, rolling away behind us. Other than dirt tracks meandering along the coast, there were no roads in or out of the village. The wind gusted; I felt the tick of tiny sand particles across my cheeks and caught a whiff of the previous day's rotting catch.

We picked our way down a narrow footpath from the Assumption, shooing a goat that blocked our way. It was hot, and I was sweating by the time we reached the village.

From the heights, I had seen the finger of a wharf stretching out over the water. Now that we were in the village proper, I saw that it was actually two docks. An older weathered pier stretched over the beach, and I saw by the marks and rusted rings on its pilings that vessels had once moored there. At the water's edge, however, more recent construction extended the dock to a point where there was enough draft for vessels. It was hard to tell how old the newer wharf was, but I'd have guessed the extension to have been built at least a few decades ago.

All the vessels were at sea, save a disused one as weathered as the older dock and keel over on the beach. I scanned the horizon, and thought I could make out a clutch of small, ochre squares I took to be sails. If they were the vessels from this village, they would have put out long before we roused ourselves.

The inn was easy to pick out; it was the only two story structure in the village (save for the Church's spire). It looked small and austere, but well maintained. Over its door was a brightly painted plank declaring it to be the *Widow's Walk Inn*. Though it was well past sun-on, we had to bang several times on the door to rouse the *padrone*, a lugubrious man of indeterminate age. He wiped sleep from his eyes when he saw the shine of Kite's gold popes.

Kite hired two adjoining rooms that were surprisingly well appointed, with real beds, clean sheets, and night stands on which had been laid fresh towels and pitchers of water. I wondered at such luxury here, in this tiny village, then realized that the only guests hostelling here would be those travelling between the Assumptions—Clergy.

Kite and I were to share one room, Lark and Ali the other.

On that first day, Kite picked a flat spot with hard-packed soil just outside the village; stunted trees screened it from all the houses save for the railed platform atop the inn. In the relative privacy of this spot, we resumed our sparring lessons.

Lark and I fought. He was almost my equal now and it was easy to let him win so I wouldn't have to go up against Ali, at least not right away. No doubt thinking the same thing, Ali let Lark beat her. It was well enough executed, and Lark seemed to believe it. Kite would have none of it, though, and paired me off against Ali. I dropped my stick and walked away. Kite made no attempt to stop me.

At a loss for what to do, I walked around the village; no one was about, but I fancied I saw the curtains in a few windows move as I passed. In a few minutes I'd seen all there was to see. I retreated to the inn and searched for a means to ascend to the structure on the roof, thinking to observe the sparring from there. Past our rooms I'd noted a corridor, and I turned down this and found a ladder rising through a trap door to the roof. I clambered up—and found the gloomy *padrone*, leaning on the rail, watching Lark and Ali go at it. "That skinny boy's a natural talent," he said, turning to face me. "Put a bit of meat on him and I expect he'd be a right formidable opponent."

I moved over to the rail. Ali was reining blows down upon poor Lark, who was tripping over his own feet.

The *padrone's* dolorous stare lingered on me. "You're no slouch yourself."

I let the compliment go unacknowledged.

"Not that you're a match for that boy." He spoke slowly, articulating each word as if it was a brick he was laying. "I've an eye for it, you know. My father was a swordsmith, and back of our shop was an area with wooden dummies, so's the customers could test the mettle of their weapons. Often they came in pairs, though, preferring that to the dummies. From the window of my room I watched them practise their noble trade." He sighed for the joy of a lost life. "But now I am here, a humble inn-keeper." He sighed again. "I reckon the way they're going they'll be hungry soon." He lifted himself wearily from the rail. "If you've nothing better to do, you can come to the kitchen and keep me company, boy."

The *pardone* told me to call him Ambrose. Though he spoke slowly, he spoke constantly and so filled up the air with his weighty words. His tales were, without exception, woe filled. I tried to be condoling, to little effect. Why should Ambrose want consolation when misery seemed to have become his way of being? In the hour leading up to our midday meal, he related his sad history—a love of the sea that had seduced him from his home and hereditary trade, a love of a fisherman's daughter that had brought him to this shore, and the illicit love that had spirited her away one night as he slept. It was then that I learned the inn was named for the railed platform on its roof: a widow's walk, so called for the women who'd pace there, staring out to sea when their husband's ships were late returning. Now only Ambrose walked it, standing watch for a wife who would never return.

If I didn't commit every detail of his sorrowful tale to memory, I shall never forget that smell of the chowder he prepared. It wound together with that of baking bread, and my mouth watered uncontrollably. While I waited impatiently for the others to return, he gave me a history of the village's tragedies, as well as a long list of the prominent visitors who'd passed through over the years. Bishops and Cardinals and the like. No Pope, though, for Pius CXXIV had not left the confines of the Vatican since being elected some twenty years ago, the year before Ambrose had made this his home.

"No one much travels these days," he said, sawing off a piece of warm bread and tossing it to me. "You're the first guests I've had in over a month."

At that, I heard the others clumping into the inn and, moments later, we settled down in the common room to the first hearty meal I'd eaten in days. If there isn't something in others' tragedy that piques our appetites, then there is certainly nothing to dull it.

Boredom

Ours was a corner room, and that first night Kite barred the windows before lying on the floor, his heels against our locked door, his halberd next to him. I couldn't imagine what possible threat there might be in this drowsy little village, but if Kite was worried, then who was I to question his instincts? When I snuffed out the candle, we were enveloped in utter darkness, and it occurred to me that anyone breaking into our room would be at a disadvantage until their eyes adjusted to the dark—by which time it would be too late for them. Perhaps this was another lesson.

"You will fight Ali," Kite said, his disembodied voice unnaturally loud in the darkness.

"No."

"He will not improve unless you do."

"Is he not good enough to fend off the priests yet?" I regretted my slander as soon as it left my lips, and silently begged God's forgiveness.

Then I heard a strange sound that took a moment to identify: Kite chuckling. "There's hope for you, boy."

For a time he was silent, then he spoke again. "He *must* improve."

"Why?"

Kite didn't answer my question. Instead he said, "You once told me that I did what I did because I owed Ignatius a debt. Though that is not entirely why, it is true enough." It was the most personal thing Kite had ever revealed. "I can see you feel a similar indebtedness to Ali. I don't know why, nor do I want to know. But you must fight him. And you must try to win. For *his* sake."

"I don't think I can."

"You must, Thomas." It was the first time he called me by my Christian name. "It will be hard. But the more difficult, the more it will balance the scales between you."

He lapsed into silence, leaving me to ponder that.

I knew Ali was not destined for the choir, and it seemed Kite did, too. *She must improve.* But why must she learn to wield a blade so effectively? I didn't ask, nor do I think Kite would have answered. But he never bade us do anything he did not deem essential.

It sickened me, knowing that Kite imagined such violence in her future. It sickened me even more that I must fight her. I tossed and turned, dreading the morrow, knowing I would do as Kite asked, not because he asked, but because I would do anything to help Ali, whether she knew I was doing so or not.

I needn't have fretted as much as I did; Ali engaged me enthusiastically the following morning, and it was all I could do to keep her from beating me senseless. Normally, she was a more careful opponent, preferring to wear me down before launching a relentless, calculated attack. This time, however, she threw herself at me without reserve. Not having time to think, my instinct for self-preservation kicked in, and I parried her thrusts, some of which would have done serious damage had I not. Her eyes blazing, she swung the butt of her weapon at my battered nose and I just managed to get my guard up to deflect the blow. In doing so I stumbled backward and went to one knee. She raised her blade and swung down with a stroke that would have split my skull—had Kite not leapt forward and reached out, her blade smacking into his palm with a sound that made me wince. Kite, of course, didn't blink. He simply stood there, fixing Ali with his implacable stare until the anger that burnt in her eyes receded.

She retreated, allowing me to regain my feet.

After that, she continued to attack me aggressively, but never once swung for my head. As she pressed me, I began to use her reluctance like a shield. I knew she would be swinging low so I crouched and led with my head. The stratagem was absurd. But it worked, and in this improbable pose I was now backing her. I loosed a wild flurry of overhead slashes which forced her to raise her own blade to block, effectively making it useless for attack: as fast as she was, it would be impossible for her to defend high while attacking low. She looked confused as I landed a blow on her shoulder—and she sucked in a sharp breath, probably more in surprise than pain. Abruptly, she adjusted her stance, stopped all counterattacks, and just parried my swings and thrusts. In a moment my aggressive tactics wore me out, as she knew they would, and after she easily deflected a feeble blow, she dropped her guard completely and spun around, kicking a leg out and planting her heel in my stomach. I went down like a sack of bricks, gasping for breath.

"Good," Kite said to her, nodding in satisfaction. "You are thinking." He looked to where I lay crumpled, arms wrapped around my belly. "You both are." He stepped back. "Now Ali and Lark."

We passed ten days in that village, training morning and afternoon.

The small fleet of fishing vessels departed and returned with numbing regularity. There were only four, all of a type the locals called a *Smack*. Ambrose, who'd seemed to have taken a liking to me, spoke at length about the various kinds of seafaring vessels, and their various riggings, after exhausting his stock of woebegone tales. He had told me during one of his orations that these local ships were ketch rigged, meaning they had two masts—a main mast and, abaft of that, a mizzen, which had to be forward of the rudder post. When I had asked why it had to be forward of the rudder, he said, "If it was abaft, then it would be a *yawl*, wouldn't it?"

I caught sight of the local children—of whom there were only five, by my count—when they spied on our training sessions, or followed us through the village, darting between houses, like frightened mice. They seemed to run wild, for I never saw them with adults; but in the evening they disappeared, one by one, into their homes.

Kite continued to sleep with his feet planted on the door. Yet nothing untoward happened. If we had an enemy, it was boredom.

Kite's Past

On the thirteenth day, as we returned to our last evening meal, we found three strangers occupying our usual seats at the inn's table. One wore the same uniform as Kite, that of the renowned *Cent Suisse*, although his was in much better shape; the second man wore a black cassock, trimmed with the purple and amaranth fascia characteristic of a Latin-Rite Bishop; the third was a striking young woman, with flawless pale skin, cascading tresses of blond hair, and eyes the colour of a stormy sea. There was something ethereal about her, something not of this world. I can't be more specific, for it was a quality that defied description, and one I'd never seen before (and wouldn't see again until I ascended to Heaven). She would have been deemed beautiful by any standard.

She rose, and a smile like a thousand suns broke upon her face. "Kite!"

I was shocked to see a small smile distorting Kite's features, too.

In a swirl of skirts, she rushed over and wrapped her arms around him, tattered uniform and all. More astonishing still was that he hugged her back. When they broke their embrace, they looked at each other with genuine pleasure.

"Come," she said, tugging at Kite's arm. "Join us!"

"Meussin." The Bishop (whose name, Ambrose later informed me, was Singleton) had risen. "This is not appropriate."

She laughed aloud. "You should know by now, Peter, nothing is appropriate about me!"

He frowned. "Your father—"

"—knows me and loves me for who I am."

"And if you loved him the same," Bishop Singleton said softly, "then you would heed me."

A cloud passed over her face, and she glanced at the *Garde* who sat at the table, focused on his meal, feigning deafness.

"You are right, your Excellency," Kite said, executing a formal bow to the Bishop. "We will return to sup later."

The Bishop waved away the suggestion. "No need. No need. We are finished. You may have our seats." He nodded at the *Garde*, who was not finished his repast, but rose anyway and retrieved his halberd from where it rested against the wall. "Good evening," Bishop Singleton said, and gathered up his robes with a flourish, walking with exaggerated dignity to the stairs. He held out a crooked arm. "Meussin?"

She looked to Kite, who essayed the slightest of nods, and she let his arm drop. The vestiges of her smile that had lit her face vanished as she took the Bishop's arm. Without another word, the Bishop led her up the stairs, followed by the *Garde* who thumped the butt of his weapon on each step.

We took our seats at the table, and I felt the prickle one gets when being watched; I looked up to find Ali's eyes fixed on me, and realized the whole time she'd been standing next to me, I'd felt that prickle, too. My face coloured.

A few minutes later, the unhappy innkeeper swept away the remains of their meal and laid out a new one for us. We ate in silence, and for a change, Lark kept his opinions on the quality of our repast to himself.

After a silent supper, Kite retreated to our room; Ali, Lark, and I followed in short order. However, after leaving Lark and Ali at their door, I passed my own and continued to the short corridor, clambering up the ladder to the widow's walk. There I found Ambrose, as I expected I would.

He leaned on the railing, scanning the sea, as he did every night.

"Good evening."

"Good evening, boy."

Ambrose—who somehow seemed able to see around the curve of the horizon—said, "There," and pointed to something invisible to me. "If she doesn't anchor this night, she should be here by sun-on."

I peered, but could not make out any vessels.

"You want to ask me about her, don't ya?"

I did, and admitted it to him. He looked at me kindly, perhaps thinking it was an infatuation that motivated me.

"Ask then, and I'll tell you what I know."

"She's been through here before, hasn't she?"

"Aye," he said. "Once a year, every year, since she was a little girl."

"To Rome?"

He nodded.

"To visit her father."

He nodded again.

"He must be an important man, for her to have such an escort."

"More important than some, I'd guess."

I considered for a moment. "Did Kite ever escort her?"

"A long time ago. I didn't recognize him at first. He's changed." Ambrose put a comforting hand on my shoulder. "He is stone, and she was too young to be his lover."

I pretended relief; and, to be honest, felt some. For although I did not desire Meussin in the way Ambrose believed, I suppose I did love her—in the way that a man loves a goddess. My relief was not for my own chances, but sprang from an unassailable belief that she deserved better than Kite.

"You've good tastes, I'll grant you that. But she's not for you."

"How so?" I tried to sound offended, wishing him to continue talking.

"You take me wrong, boy. I didn't mean anything personal by it. Just that she's not for anyone."

"I don't understand. Do you mean to say she's guarded like this all the time? Kept away from suitors?"

"From what I hear, aye. She lives on an estate, surrounded by forbidding walls, and equally daunting matrons. I believe she is lonely, for she has seemed so since the first time I saw her as a young girl. I think she had no childhood, at least the kind most children do, and now that she's come into her womanhood, her father will never let her enjoy society—or the company of men." He shook his head sorrowfully for a kindred spirit. "I believe she suffers terribly."

"Then I will pray for her," I said, and meant it.

"I fear that is all you can do."

He was likely right, but I vowed to myself that I would do what I could, should the chance ever arise.

I squinted at the horizon. "Three masts, with lateen sails. A *xebec*."

"Aye," Ambrose said. "That's her."

We both watched *The Charon* tack against the wind. I said, "If her father has hidden her away, it is for one of two reasons: he fears for her life, or is shamed by her presence."

"She's done nothing wrong!" Ambrose was clearly upset, and I realized that it was he who was infatuated—although his loyalty to his unfaithful wife blinded him to it. "It's not for her sins, it's for those of her father!"

"Her name is Meussin," I said. "In Latin *Meus sin* means 'My sin'." I don't think he'd ever thought of that before, from the look he gave me. I pressed on. "She has a father who sends for her once a year, with no less an escort than a Bishop and one of the hundred. Bishops and the *Cent Suisse* do not do any father's bidding, save one."

He looked at me, mouth agape, knowing I had worked out the thing he'd thought so secret: that we were sharing an inn with Pope Pius's daughter.

The Charon

Meussin and her escorts were gone when we arose.

From the porch of the inn Lark spotted them in a dinghy, well on their way to *The Charon*. The vessel had anchored several hundred metres off shore; she was much larger than any of the smacks, and had twice the draft, so she couldn't tie up on the pier without danger of running aground. Ali seemed bothered by their early departure, and fidgeted at breakfast. Perhaps she feared the Bishop would bribe the captain to leave us behind. Kite, however, was unperturbed. He ate his biscuit and eggs as he always did, methodically and without relish, as if he was merely storing energy against whatever tasks he set for himself that day.

I, too, was unconcerned.

Hours before sun-on, I had woken to find one of our windows open and Kite gone. I tip-toed across and peered out. The exterior of the inn was weatherboard, as it was for all the houses in the village. However, the inn had several large windows on each level, and these all had casings upon which an agile man might make his way with toes and fingers. I scanned the parts of the village that were visible, but saw nothing. Slipping back into bed, I drifted back into a dense sleep. Some time later, with the first hints of sun-on limning the edges of the boards that blocked the same window, Kite shook me awake.

After our meal, Kite paid Ambrose in full, and bade us pack our paltry possessions. At the door, Ambrose hugged me with affection, and, much to my surprise, I found myself hugging him back.

"Take care, boy," he said.

"I will." I shouldered my pack and turned to follow Ali and Lark to the pier—then stopped and looked back to Ambrose. "Would it be presumptuous," I asked, "if I prayed for you?"

"Not at all," he said, smiling for the first time. "As long as you put in a word or two for my wife."

I gladly assented, and hurried after the rest of my company, who'd already started down the pier.

By the time we'd reached the end of the dock, Meussin's party had boarded, and their luggage was being hauled from the dinghy and stowed. I saw the Bishop standing toe-to-toe on the quarterdeck with a gentleman who looked to be the captain. Whatever they were saying was indecipherable at this distance, but by the way he gesticulated, Bishop Singleton was clearly agitated. The captain, for his part, remained unmoved. The Bishop spun on his heel, his robes billowing out behind him in a dramatic fashion, and went below deck. Moments later, at the captain's direction, the dinghy pushed away to retrieve us.

When I asked one of the sailors manning the dinghy, he told me the captain's name was Richardson.

When we boarded *The Charon*, I watched Kite clasp hands with captain Richardson in the way that men do who've reached an accord, and I wondered if their alliance was based on a monetary agreement or a mutual dislike of the Bishop—or both.

Meussin was quartered aft in the Captain's cabin, Bishop Singleton and the *Garde* forward in the cabin beneath the forecastle. These were the only two private spaces on the ship. For himself, captain Richardson rigged a small tarp shelter on the quarterdeck near the wheel, and ate and slept there for the duration of the voyage. We were given hammocks on the lower deck amongst the dozen men who crewed the ship; at Kite's request, the captain contrived to suspend blankets from ropes at the fore of the ship to give us a semblance of privacy. He needn't have, though. The sailors preferred, save when it rained one night, to sleep on the main deck under the stars and a cooling breeze. I would have joined them, too, had Kite not forbid me.

I found I had an affinity for the sea, and enjoyed the gentle rolling of the ship; predictably, Lark's weak stomach didn't, and he spent much of the voyage laid out in his hammock, moaning, or leaning over the rail, retching. Ali, too, initially suffered a touch of sea-sickness, but within two days was climbing the rigging as adeptly as any of the seasoned deckhands.

The Charon was unusually shaped, at least compared to the sketches I'd seen of other ships. She had a long overhanging bowsprit and protruding stern, and was narrower than other ships of her size, making her lighter and more manoeuvrable. She sported six cannons a side, and ballistas fore and aft. Her lateen rig was raked back, allowing for the ship to sail close hauled to the wind. An advantage, Ambrose had told me, in pursuit or escape. *Of what?* I had asked. Ambrose looked at me as if I was daft, and said, *Pirates, of course.*

Despite the confines of the ship, I was never bored. Kite continued his sparring sessions on the main deck as best he could, and it was not uncommon for those men off-duty to watch and cheer us on. Indeed, one of the crew members, a pock-faced young man who couldn't have been eighteen, crowed about his own prowess until Kite let him have a go—and though the young sailor was taller by a head and heavier set with muscles knotted like rope, Ali handed him a humbling defeat without breaking a sweat. The old tars guffawed at the young man as he picked himself up from the deck, and skidded in his own blood. He scowled and cursed them roundly, challenging them to step up.

None did.

Our choral lessons resumed, too, even though I could see them serving no purpose save for Lark—and to maintain Ali's pretence. There was to be no privacy, so I suggested on the first day that if Ali and Lark wished to sing, it might be best to do so in the early evening while most of the sailors took their meals below. But it wasn't long before the men brought their food above, and arrayed themselves around us, eating while they listened. I stopped and begged their pardon, but they insisted we continue. And so we did. Even Bishop Singleton wandered out of his cabin, nodding approvingly as Ali and Lark's twinned voices rose in praise of God. After our practise concluded, and just before sun-off, three or four sailors, as was their habit, played upon instruments carved from wood or whale bone. As if on cue, the Bishop returned to his cabin. Shortly after, those sailors not playing rose and danced wildly, thumping jigs that vibrated through the planks of the deck. It was music and celebration of a wholly different kind from the rarefied spirituality of the Masses, and although I felt a twinge of guilt, I have to admit I found deliberate abandon a welcome tonic.

Our voyage lasted ten days.

In that time I saw Meussin emerge from her cabin only four times, and always in the company of the *Garde*. She'd stroll about the deck for a few minutes, and lean over the rail lost in thought for as much as half an hour. Then she'd retreat to her cabin. Sometimes she'd open a small window that overlooked the main deck, when Kite held our sparring sessions; at other times I noticed the window open when we sang. Never, though, could I make out her face in that dark rectangle. On the few occasions I saw her, she did not seem distressed by her isolation; on the contrary, she seemed to bear it with the patience of one used to such solitude.

And perhaps she wasn't as bereft of company as she appeared. For in all of this it hadn't eluded me that Kite had ample opportunity to speak with her, had he wished. At the inn he could have easily stepped from casing to casing until he was outside her window. And on the ship there was no lack of ropes and spars by which he could have conveyed himself along the hull to where the aft windows of the captain's cabin opened onto the sea. It would have been difficult for an ordinary man to do so unobserved, but Kite was no ordinary man.

I would have liked to have had some private moments with Kite, too, for I had been doing my own musing since we'd departed the inn, and had questions I wished to ask him. However, my questions were displaced by other concerns that last day at sea. It was early evening, and only Lark was singing that night, Ali having begged off because of a sore throat. All of us assembled heard a cry, then a rush of footsteps on the companionway. The young sailor with the pock-marked face burst onto the deck—with Kite hard on his heels. In three strides Kite caught him and pinned him against the rail, then quickly drew his blade across the arteries in the boy's neck. As blood jetted in two thick streams, Kite heaved the body over the rail and it pinwheeled into the sea.

Rumours of War

Below deck, next to the galley, was a cage with iron bars and a heavy brass padlock in which the more precious victuals were kept. Here Captain Richardson had Kite confined while he decided what was to be done. I stood outside the bars; within, Kite sat on an overturned rum case, picking at the modest meal I'd brought him. Behind me a grizzled sailor stood, arms akimbo, one hand clutching the hilt of his cutlass. I couldn't blame that sailor—I, too, would have kept my weapon at the ready after witnessing Kite's cold-blooded execution.

Looking up from his meal, Kite licked his fingers and said, "I wish to talk to Thomas here in private."

The sailor shook his head. "Cap'n ordered me to stand watch, and that's what I'll do."

"Did he order you to stand watch this close?"

The sailor spat. "I never liked that boy nohow. Lazy as a sloth, and always causing discord. I've no doubt he did as you say."

What Kite had said was that the young sailor had waylaid Ali with the intention of violating him and likely killing him in retribution for the humiliation he'd suffered. Had it been anyone other than this boy—on his first voyage, poor at the work they set him, and poorer at finding friends—Kite might well be dead, too. But the majority of the crew shared the grizzled sailor's view; the boy's death was neither here nor there for them. If anything, his absence would make their lives easier. No doubt Kite had reasoned all this out, too, before he pulled his knife.

The sailor retreated enough to allow us a quiet exchange.

Kite leaned as close as the bars would allow. "Thomas, I cannot tell how all this will play out. But here's what I need you to do. First, you must stick to Ali to make sure no more harm befalls him. You can trust Meussin to help there."

We'd found Ali laid out below deck, unconscious, her skin ashen, blood pooling from a large gash on her forehead. I had stood there stupidly. Uselessly. But Meussin (who'd emerged from her cabin at the commotion) had torn a strip from the hem of her skirt and pressed it to the wound to staunch the bleeding. She held it thus as she had the *Garde* convey Ali to her cabin.

Kite gestured for me to move closer. "I think they don't mean to kill me. If, however, things go ill for me, you must—"

"No."

It's was the first time I'd ever seen Kite looked startled. "*No?*" He gave me a look that made me wish I had my own cutlass.

"I have done murder with you, and witnessed you murdering another without cause. I cannot—*will not*—bear responsibility in more."

"He near killed Ali."

"God will be his judge, not you."

"He intended rape, Thomas."

My face burned, but I managed to control my voice. "There was no need to kill him."

Kite lowered his voice even further. "He had her pants down around her ankles when I found them. He knew, Thomas." I was shocked that Kite said this so matter-of-factly, as if we'd both shared Ali's secret for some time, even though a moment ago he'd called Ali *him*. Had she told him? Or had he worked it out on his own? "Do you think I could have persuaded that boy into keeping his tongue?"

Kite was right, but that didn't excuse murder. I said so.

"It had to be done."

"Why?" I wanted a reason, needed a reason, as much for myself as for Kite. When I'd heard what the boy had tried to do, I felt murder in my own heart, too.

"I cannot tell you. Leastways, not yet."

I turned, and Kite reached through the bars and snagged my arm, pulling me back. Our faces were centimetres apart. "There is war brewing, Thomas."

War? Was Kite justifying his murder as an act of war? There was no conflict, had been none for a generation. Not since heretics had challenged the doctrine of infallibility. But, as the *Third Addendum* documented, their improvised army had been shattered, and the few *Fallists* that had survived had been castrated and banished—with all of their kith and kin—to the Spheres of the Lesser Apostles.

Kite, as always, seemed to anticipate how the wheels of my mind turned. "Not the *Fallists*."

"Then who?"

He hesitated, and I pulled back, ready to walk away. "Lower Heaven makes ready."

The Angels were preparing for war? The idea was absurd. Lower Heaven stood apart from the affairs of man. And who would be audacious enough to defy the Angels, and in so doing, God? The *Fallists* had tried to overthrow the Holy See, never Lower Heaven. Indeed, their greatest heresy was in claiming the one true God for themselves.

"I speak the truth, Thomas. The Angels are less than you think, and there are men who believe themselves more than they are."

I recalled the refugee camp; how easy it would be to lose faith there. Their numbers were great, and growing—along with their desperation. "*The Meek*?"

Kite shook his head. "They're weak and disorganized and poorly armed. If they figure into the struggle, it will be as pawns."

If it was not a resurgence of the *Fallists*, or the new found desperation of *The Meek*, then—

"The Church."

Kite did not respond; as usual his expression gave away nothing— and confirmed everything.

The Church at war with Lower Heaven. The monstrosity of the idea made me reel. I staggered away from the cage. Somehow, I managed the ladder. No one tried to stop me when I entered Meussin's cabin. Ali was abed and unconscious, sweat bathing her pallid face below a bloodied compress. She looked barely alive. I fell into a chair by her side, and took her cold, limp hand between mine.

And you will hear of wars and rumours of wars. See that you are not alarmed, for this must take place, but the end is not yet.

Could such madness be upon us?

Perhaps it was my agitated state, but only then did I realize I had neglected to ask Kite the most important question of all: had he murdered that poor boy for the sake of the Church—or at the behest of Angels?

An Impromptu Trial

I've been told that trials at sea are usually speedy affairs, regardless of the outcome. And so it was with Kite's. However, before the trial commenced, the better part of the morning was spent wrangling over issues of jurisdiction. In civil matters, lay judges ruled; in all else, Clergy. Crimes of a venial nature were presided upon by Parish Priests and, for the lesser offences, Deacons, while crimes that endangered the mortal soul were judged by Bishops. As far as I knew, this jurisprudence applied everywhere, save in Heaven and at sea where only a captain's absolute authority could maintain order. So it was only after a heated debate that two chairs were placed behind a table where ordinarily there would have been only one. Here sat both Bishop Singleton and Captain Richardson. As was the custom, the trial took place on the weather deck, for God and all to witness.

It was a cloudless day, and the wind barely plucked at the sails. The Captain scowled, irritated with the tepid wind, as well as with necessity of the trial; yet not so irritated that he was willing to cede authority to the Bishop. For his part, the Bishop, unused to such open proceedings, endured the warm day beneath his heavy robes, and perspired heavily.

The trial was relatively straightforward. Kite told his story, and was then cross-examined by the judges who probed for inconsistencies, of which there were none. When Kite stepped down, the Bishop said in a sonorous voice, "Are there others who will bear witness?"

None did.

In the absence of other witnesses to contradict his story, Captain Richardson declared himself satisfied that events transpired as Kite has said. The Bishop was not convinced, however, rendering the two judges deadlocked.

In the end, the oldest form of sea justice prevailed: it came to a vote. It went in Kite's favour, ten to one. The captain, in what seemed an attempt to simultaneously placate and nettle Bishop Singleton, still fined Kite a silver bishop for the loss of a working crew member, and in a spate of generosity earmarked it for the family of the deceased. Kite proffered a second, and asked that it be divided amongst the crew as compensation for the extra work that had fallen to them. I thought this unwise for two reasons: it further irked the Bishop, and I noticed that Kite's purse, once fat with coin, now seemed to weigh next to nothing. Nevertheless, I knew Kite always had his reasons, so I brushed away my misgivings.

By noon, the wind had picked up and we made good time; shortly, a tip of land hove into view. Well before sun-off, we made anchor close by a fishing village not unlike the one from which we departed, except that it did not fall under the shadow of an Assumption and here desert had given way to sere terrain. Captain Richardson bade us depart first; I suppose he did this to give Kite a chance, should the Bishop try to gain sole authority and overturn the verdict once ashore. I did my best to help as the crew rigged pulleys so that Ali, who remained unconscious, might be lowered to the dinghy on two planks secured with rope. When Kite disembarked, the captain did not shake his hand.

In short order, Kite had hired the only pony and cart available in the village, and we set out for the Assumption, which lay inland several kilometres. As we crested a hill just outside the village, I looked back to see Meussin leaning on the taffrail of *The Charon*, following our progress. (Years later, when I witnessed the Christening of a recently constructed vessel, I startled when I saw a figurehead on the prow that matched Meussin's pose and visage so closely it could have been her twin, and I wondered if perhaps it had been carved by one of the sailors who crewed *The Charon* that day.) Below Meussin, on the weather deck, the Bishop seemed as discomfited as he had been ten days earlier as we'd waited to embark, for he was alternately railing at the Captain and individual members of the crew, who seemed in no hurry to assemble and transfer their party's considerable number of bags and trunks to the dinghy.

The villager, whose cart we'd hired, never spoke a word on the journey; when Kite paid him the agreed upon amount, and then an extra brass deacon to take his time returning, he tipped his cap. "Godspeed," he said.

Carrying Ali on her makeshift litter, we passed beneath the portcullis and into the gloom of the Assumption.

Rome

"He'll be back."

Lark looked hopeful at my words, but the Jesuit merely shrugged. "You wouldn't be the first boys abandoned here—nor, I fear, the last."

We had been waiting for Kite in the upper ante-room for near an hour. But that was only a guess. Like all Assumptions, there were no windows, and so no way to accurately gauge the passage of time.

"We're going to be in the choir of the *Cappella Sixtina*," Lark said, apropos of nothing. "Ignatius promised."

The Jesuit raised his eyebrows, giving us the once over. "You ought not tell lies, boy." He looked irritated, perhaps at having to keep an eye on us.

"We *are*," Lark insisted.

"The *schola cantorum* does not take boys unheard," the Jesuit said. "It is rare for them to grant an audition, and rarer still for them to accept a boy. As best as I can remember, they have taken only two new boys in the last five years."

Lark looked crestfallen. But this didn't concern me, knowing that I wasn't for the choir; I was more anxious about how close on our heels Bishop Singleton might be. I knew Rome to be a large, complicated city; even with Ali's litter, once away from the Assumption it would be easy for us to disappear into the labyrinthine tangle of streets. I trusted Kite—up to a point—and I'd no doubt he had a much better idea how soon the Bishop would arrive. Even so, I couldn't push away my worry. What if something had happened to him? I realized I was tapping my foot, and that the Jesuit was watching me do so. I stopped. For his part, Lark looked on the verge of tears. I was trying to think of something reassuring to say to him, when, from the corner of my eye, I thought I saw Ali stir on her litter. The light in the room was poor, and when I looked directly, she lay as motionless as she had since the attack. I had to stare for a full minute before I detected the slight rising and falling of her chest that confirmed she still lived.

Lark began sniffling.

Compassion must have overridden the Jesuit's irritation, for he said to Lark, "Perhaps he just stopped for an ale...."

I was about to suggest that I go in search when there was a pounding on the door. The Jesuit shuffled over and opened it. Kite strode back into the room. Without a word, he handed me his halberd and scooped up Ali. We followed him into the ante-chamber.

"And what am I supposed to do with this?" the Jesuit shouted after us, waving his hand at the abandoned litter.

"Whatever you wish," Kite replied, and I heard the Jesuit blow out an exasperated breath before slamming and barring the door.

We crossed the room to the inner portcullis. A *Garde* posted there shouted up an order, and the portcullis was jerked upwards, the rasp of iron on stone deafening. A moment later we passed under the second portcullis and I blinked at the light, a shock to my eyes even though it was now dusk. And so we emerged from the Assumption, passing between two more *Gardes* stationed outside, and into the glorious tumult that was Rome.

I have been in a good many cities, both large and small. Up to that point, *Los Angeles Nuevo* had been the largest. Though no official census exists, I feel fairly confident in saying, based on its extent, that it was home then to no less than a hundred thousand souls. Rome had ten times that number—and perhaps more. There were people everywhere, and with them the jostling cacophony of their lives. The murmur of conversation subsumed us, mixed with laughter, voices raised in anger and, now and then, the jolt of an anguished cry cutting through it all like a knife.

No one paid the least attention.

I thought it equally strange that no one gave us a second glance, Kite carrying Ali, her head wrapped in a bloody dressing, and I struggling with a halberd twice my size, its butt dragging across the cobbles of the street. But I didn't know Rome then.

Kite pushed on, elbowing relentlessly through the crowd; Lark and I trailed in his wake. I found it hard to keep Kite in sight, for I was looking up as much as ahead, struck by the height of the buildings. I craned my neck, gawking, as I'm sure all visitors unaccustomed to such sights do, for

I'd never seen lay structures so high. Whereas most cities boasted edifices no more than a few stories (and those always dwarfed by Cathedrals and Church spires), many of the buildings here had half a dozen or more floors of apartments. And these *were* indisputably lay structures, for at the base of each building awnings covered all nature of dry goods and foodstuff laid out on painted boards, the vendors hawking their wares incessantly, the bustle of commerce unmistakeable. Smells, too, assaulted my senses, a hundred novel odours battling for attention. The swirling richness of it all stupefied me.

Kite turned down an alley so narrow we had to walk single-file. Once, we had to turn sideways and press ourselves against the wall as a group of revellers brushed past us going in the opposite direction. We stuck to narrow lanes until the sky had darkened. Rising on either side now were geometric patterns of yellow squares as lamplight bled from windows. We came to a large building that stood detached from others and boasted rows of arched windows. It was also more lavish, made of a kind of stone I'd never seen before, grey and veined with white, smooth and cool to the touch. (I later learned this was marble, and as far as I am able to determine, Rome is the only place in the world where such stone is to be found.) Kite led us around back. I wondered if Lark and I would be sleeping in a stable, and if Ali was to be hidden there, too, like so much excess baggage.

I needn't have worried.

Kite hustled us around the clamour of a cart filled with caged chickens, and through a broad back door into the steam and chaos of a massive kitchen; he exchanged nods with a fat man in an apron who seemed to be choreographing the mayhem. We followed a passage away from the bedlam and climbed a narrow set of stairs up several flights, emerging in a quiet, beautifully appointed corridor, decorated with stone pillars and paintings depicting all the stations of the cross. Between the paintings, on either side of the hall, were numbered doors.

Kite took us to the one labelled 512. Holding Ali with one arm as women hold infants, he pulled a large key from his pocket, slipped it into the sturdy lock, and led us in. In the front room there were two beds; another room in the back held two more. A third, smaller room, contained a washbasin and copper tub large enough to fit us all.

It was an inn, of course. I did not recognize it right off as such, having never seen one so magnificent, nor expecting that we would be staying in a princely place like this. I did not yet know that, as nice as it seemed to me then, this was merely one of a hundred such indistinguishable places to be had in Rome.

Kite laid Ali on a bed; then, more gently than I would have believed, undid the dressing over her wound. The gash, although it had ceased bleeding, looked awful; the flesh gaped, wrinkled along the edges, revealing the sheen of skull beneath. I sat on the edge of the other bed and watched Kite expertly change her dressing—and noticed that aside from towels and linen, a supply of fresh dressings had also been laid out in the bathroom.

Not long after that, a furtive-looking man in a black overcoat knocked on our door and Kite let him in without hesitation. He must have been a doctor, for he carried a doctor's kit—and a sick call cross. I had seen these crosses before and knew they usually held two candles and a small bottle of holy water used in the Sacrament of the Sick liturgy to anoint the dying. He placed bag and cross on the bed next to Ali, then pulled back the new dressing and took a quick look at Ali's wound. He must have noticed my agitation, for he picked up the cross and said, "I always bring this as a precaution," then handed it to me. "I won't be needing it today. Please put it on the table by the door so I don't forget it." I did so, with great relief, while he washed up.

I watched as he pulled open her lids and examined her eyes, then palpitated the wound with dexterous fingers. I guessed (and found out later I was correct) that he was checking for cracks or depressions in the skull that would signal more serious trauma. He tilted her head first one way then the other, looking behind both her ears, though for what I couldn't say. At one point he leaned forward, and squinted at the side of her head, as if he'd found something odd, though whatever he might have been staring at was nowhere near her wound. When he had finished his exam, he nodded to himself as if satisfied, and set to stitching up Ali's wound. After applying a fresh dressing, he cleaned himself up, reached into his bag, and handed Kite a bottle containing a cloudy ointment.

"Change the dressing twice a day, and each time spread this unction on it so that it covers the wound." He pulled a small vial from his bag, and handed it, too, to Kite. "Wait a day or two. If the boy does not come round, try this. It produces a powerful odour that sometimes shocks the spirit to wakefulness."

The doctor packed up his things and stood. "There's a circular scar on his temple. An old one." He stared at Kite, and I wondered if this was his way of enquiring about his patient's medical history.

"He joined our company recently," I said, wanting to be helpful. "He's an orphan, and was reluctant to speak about his past."

"I can imagine," the doctor said.

Kite looked troubled. "This old wound presents no danger?"

"It's not a wound, but the vestiges of a surgical procedure. A trepanning, to be precise. A circular section of the temporal bone was cut out, and then replaced with something harder and smoother. A silver Bishop, would be my guess." He made a small circle with thumb and forefinger to show its size. "The scar is clean and barely visible, and the skull beneath has knit extremely well."

"Then why mention it?"

"Because this kind of surgery is a last recourse for those possessed—if the devil cannot be ousted any other way."

"I do not believe in the devil," said Kite, "and I've no interest in the boy's past."

"Nor I," answered the doctor. "But many do not survive such a procedure. And those who do often find their faculties severely impaired. Yet this boy, as you've told me, is in every respect normal. I'd also have expected his scarring to have been more severe. *Much* more severe." He shook his head, as if in disbelief, then looked at Kite expectantly. "I would consider it an honour," he said slowly, "to meet a surgeon of such skill."

When Kite said nothing, the doctor sighed. "Too bad." He snapped his bag closed. "Well, then," he said, "I will take my leave."

Kite followed him to the door and thanked him. Withdrawing his purse from his pocket, Kite upended its contents into his palm: two silver bishops and a single brass deacon. He offered it all to the doctor—who refused. Kite continued to hold out the coins and the doctor as steadfastly refused to look at them. A history of debts, too long and convoluted to untangle, seemed to hang between the two.

"Even if things go well, it could take several weeks for a full recovery," the doctor said, pushing Kite's hand away. "And we both know nothing in Rome comes cheap."

Lark roused me the next morning and dragged me to the front room where I found Ali sitting up in bed, sipping from a pewter cup. She glanced over the lip of the cup when I entered, but said nothing.

Kite handed Lark the brass deacon, and instructed the two of us to fetch something more substantial. "Thomas will know where to go," he said, which surprised me, though it shouldn't have. Kite would have noted my capacity for remembering things, and known that I could easily find my way to the forum where I'd seen the food stalls—and then guide us back.

I had no idea how much anything cost in Rome, but was a quick study, stretching our deacon to three meals, and in doing so learning it should have been five.

Ali left her bed the third morning; Kite supported her as she wobbled around our apartment, until she briefly found her legs. That afternoon, Kite had me resume Ali and Lark's vocal training, with Ali sitting on the edge of her bed. This was not ideal, for the diaphragm cannot drop properly as your lungs fill with air. I found it awkward assuming the role of her teacher again, and worried how she might react, particularly when I began chiding her for slouching; although she took my advice without comment, she often didn't comply.

Three days later, when Ali had become more or less ambulatory, Kite recommended light sparring matches. I thought it premature, but came to realize that Kite intended it as much for its therapeutic value as he did for polishing her fighting skills. And it did seem to speed her recovery. During this time, Kite rarely left the room, and Ali not at all. Lark and I ran whatever errands were necessary—but always during the day, never at night when darkness swallowed the narrow streets, and the city yielded itself to footpads.

After a few days, I became adept at bartering with the vendors, and struck up a relationship with two of the more honest ones who seemed to appreciate our trade. I told them my name was Matthew, and that I was new to Rome. I made it known that my master had instructed me to return to the market each day for the next few weeks to purchase our victuals. To entice us, the first one added an extra bun to my bag; the next time, the other added two. Often, when I confessed I did not recognize a certain item of food, they would cut or break off a small sample for me to try. It was in this way that I discovered what an astonishing and complex variety of flavours the world held—several vendors sold what became my favourite, a flat round of bread topped with cheese and olives and onions, spiced with a sauce they called *garum*, made from fish that had been left to rot in the sun for several days.

A week passed thus, and it was on the first morning of the second week, as Lark and I returned from the market, I caught sight of two figures emerging from the entrance of our inn: a woman and her squat manservant, a gunnysack on his back. I didn't get a look at her face before she melted into the heavy midday crowd, but her flowing carriage and graceful dignity recalled Meussin. Kite said nothing of her visit, and I was half-convinced I had only imagined it—until I realized that the three short swords we had acquired in the Postulants' camp, all roughly the length of the bag the manservant had been shouldering, were nowhere to be found.

Questions and Some Answers

It was at the end of the second week that, for the first time since his trial aboard *The Charon*, Kite and I were alone—Kite had sent Ali and Lark to the forum market. He positioned himself on the edge of the bed, bringing our eyes level. "You have questions."

I acknowledged I did.

"Ask."

"You gave Lark and Ali your last coin this morning." I'd been carefully counting as Kite had doled out his money. "How are we to buy food tomorrow?"

Kite shrugged.

"You didn't answer."

"I didn't say I would."

I suppressed my irritation. "Is it because we audition tomorrow?" Other than an angry red gash on her forehead, Ali had recovered, and her voice was in fine form.

"Yes."

"What will happen?"

"You will audition for the *magister capellae*. If he likes what he hears, then he will put you forward as a candidate to be examined by the whole *schola cantorum*."

"That's not what I was asking."

"Don't blame me, boy, for your poorly thought out questions."

"You know I can't sing, and you know Ali could never be a member of the choir."

He conceded it was so.

"And you don't think much of Lark's chances, do you?"

"*You* don't think much of his chances—and in this I value your opinion above mine."

I smarted at his suggestion, and at his knowing how I felt when I'd never shared a word of my concern. "Yet you've arranged an audition," I said. "You've no money left, and no hope of a commission from the Church. Why proceed?"

"I think you've already reasoned it out, Thomas."

I had—at least part of it, only I wanted confirmation. "Ignatius sent word about us, didn't he?"

Kite nodded. "They are expecting three boys. One with a *voice that would make Angels weep.*"

I felt my cheeks colour. "Since I can no longer sing, can I assume Ali and Lark are here to maintain that pretence?"

"Yes," he said, "and no."

I let his latest ambiguity pass unchallenged, for I wanted the '*and no*' part of his response to be true. I'd feared Lark and Ali were mere window dressing, to be dispensed with the moment Kite had achieved his purposes. But Kite's training regime and his negation suggested otherwise—at least for Ali. "You need Ignatius's letter, and us, to get inside the Vatican."

"Yes."

"Why?"

He shook his head in a way that made it clear he would not answer this, or any other question, about his intentions.

"You do not trust me."

"I have faith in you—much as you have faith in God."

"Then why won't you tell me?"

"Faith is not an absolute, Thomas. It exists only in relation to doubt."

I wanted to object to this, but realized it would only lead us in circles. So I changed tack, hoping to catch Kite off guard. "Did you arrange the ambush?"

A terrible cloud darkened Kite's face; he clenched his hands so hard his knuckles went white. Then, as quickly as it had manifested, the storm vanished. "No," he said, his *sang-froid* restored.

I said before that I had no way of knowing if anything Kite told me was true; yet, I believed him in this. Which meant it likely that he and Ignatius had conspired together. But for what cause? Though you may think it odd, I had not pursued an opportunity to speak to Kite about the question of his allegiance or on his assertion that war between the Church and Lower Heaven was imminent. I had several good reasons for this: first, I had no faith in any answer he might give, nor hope of determining the veracity of what he said; second, his actions thus far shed no light on his loyalties, and an equally compelling case could be made for his support of either the Church or Lower Heaven; third, knowing the truth would have changed nothing for me, and so it would be safer for me to reserve judgement, and to act from that ignorance rather risk being caught in a falsehood (for, as my father's inquisitor had said, I made a very poor liar). I could see no advantage to my knowing.

Despite this, I asked.

"On the side of the Angels," he said. "As best I can tell."

Although I'd expected this answer, his proviso vexed me. "How can you not be sure?"

"Causes are an illusion. Things change."

"Morality doesn't," I said, and meant it, not knowing any better back then.

"And who determines what's moral?"

"God."

He laughed. "Tell me, boy, do you believe the Angels are intermediaries between Heaven and Earth?"

"Yes."

"And that they are our Guardians, anointed by God?"

"Of course."

"And do you believe in the infallibility of the Magisterium and the Pope, as promised by Christ?"

"Yes." As soon as I said it, I understood what he was trying to make me understand: if the Church were to war with the Angels in Lower Heaven, then on whose side would be virtue? God seemed to have blessed both.

"Choosing sides wisely is a tricky thing," Kite said.

Still, I could not accept his assertion. If I did, then there was no moral compass. "Everything proceeds from God," I said, thinking aloud. "Since the Angels are closest to Him, shouldn't the righteous stand with them?"

"If virtue were as easy to catch as the clap, you'd be right."

"But God created the Angels—"

"And us, too, Thomas. Only he made *us* in his image, not them. We are flawed, but so are the Angels. Or have you forgotten Satan?"

I had no answer to that.

"You are not asking the right questions. You concern yourself with whose side is most virtuous, and you haven't even asked me the why of it."

He was right; I had been avoiding the question. So I asked: "Why?"

"The Church is starved, and there's no more to be wrung from the lower Spheres. Drought plagues all the lesser Spheres, and each year worsens. Crops wither, people die. Not just in *Los Angeles Nuevo*, but everywhere. Even in Rome. You may not see it, but hunger is here, prowling the back alleys."

"But not in the Kingdom of Angels?"

"When you are starving, it's hard to see past the feast on another man's table. And make no mistake, Rome is starving. When the Cardinals look up, all they can see are the Angels, who are rumoured to number less than two thousand, yet are the sole occupants of the greatest material Sphere. They see the glory of the Celestial Gardens, while vast tracts of surrounding land lie fallow; they see pristine streams and rivers and lakes, while deserts bloom in Spheres below; and they see magnificent palaces, each for the benefit of a single Angel, while the Vatican's Chapels fall into disrepair."

"Then," I said, "they have the right of it."

"Perhaps. But there are Angels who would say it's the cause of the drought that needs to be rectified, not its symptoms. Lower Heaven may look green to the envious, but its Gardens wither, too. If there is abundance, it is the consequence of the Sphere having so few inhabitants. Ceding part or all of Lower Heaven to the Church will change that, and although it might make things better for a time for the few lucky souls the Church anoints, it will do nothing to stave off the inevitable."

"The inevitable?"

"Plague, war, famine, death," he said, casually naming the horsemen.

I was incredulous. "God would never let such a thing happen."

"You forget your Bible."

Still, I shook my head in disbelief.

"The Jesuits have been keeping records for a millennium, Thomas. The droughts grow worse, more some years, less others. But always worse. If God were going to act, don't you think he'd have done so by now?"

As loath as I was to do so, I accepted most of what Kite said as true. Yet I could not accept the cruel or indifferent God he posited. "You said you were *on the side of the Angels*. If you believe all is hopeless, then why are you here, doing their bidding?"

Kite looked at me as if I'd missed the obvious. "Because," he said, rising from the bed, and signalling an end to my questions, "the Angels pay up front."

I didn't believe him then, and I don't now. I thought better of Kite— better, I suspect, than he thought of himself.

Audition

Before we departed the next morning, Meussin appeared. My heart buoyed as I saw her breeze past Lark, who'd opened the door. The same manservant I'd observed before followed her into our apartment. He seemed of middle age, yet was no taller than me, although he was much broader, from his wide face through his barrel chest and down to his stumpy legs. Throughout, his frame rippled with hardened muscle. In our travels, we'd once encountered two similar men at an inn. Ignatius had told me they were from the heathen Spheres, where people tended towards such a physique. He added that ignorant people found their shape grotesque and believed it to be a punishment for their unrepentant natures. If this were true, then this particular man was more unrepentant than most, because God had squashed him even flatter than the other two.

The meeting must have been prearranged, for immediately Kite handed over his halberd and morion to the servant who withdrew, pulling the door closed. In exchange, Meussin gave Kite a letter folded in three, which he tucked into the breast of his uniform. They said nothing, Kite and Meussin, but only looked at one another, she burdened with the ache of sadness, and he without expression. I knew Kite was a hard man, cynical and embittered, but I could not understand how he didn't falter under that affecting gaze. She raised a hand as pale as the vellum of Ignatius's letter and laid her fingers, one after the other, on Kite's ruddy, scarred cheek. Then she turned, and fled our apartment, leaving an emptiness that seemed both profound and irreversible.

We gathered our few paltry possessions.

As we pushed out into the bustle of the narrow, jumbled streets, I confess my mind was in turmoil about many things; curiously, though, what bothered me the most wasn't Meussin's perplexing visits, or an audition that wasn't an audition, but that the four of us had set out, for the first time in months, unarmed.

We arrived at *Porta Santo Spirito,* the imposing concave gate at the southern limit of *Stato della Città del Vaticano.* Kite produced Ignatius's vellum and the letter Meussin had given him. As he unfolded the letter, I could see it had been freshly inked and that it bore a wax seal with the crossed keys of the Holy See. The *Garde* waved us forward after only a cursory glance. And so we passed between the strangely truncated columns that flanked the gate, our footfalls echoing in the passage under the massive wall that ringed the Holy City.

The hurly-burly of Rome fell away immediately. Few people were out, and most of those were robed Clerics. All moved at a subdued pace, save a troop of *Gardes* who marched past us double-time, halberds shouldered. (From the corner of my eye, I noted Kite's hand twitched ever so slightly.) We walked on a cobbled street between stately buildings, more ancient than any I had ever seen, and constructed of materials and in ways for which I had no word. The structures evoked in me a sense of ponderous tranquillity and, more than that, of displacement, by which I mean they *felt* as if they were from a place—or time—outside our own. I suppose this shouldn't have been surprising since, as the *Primoris Addendum* to *The Bible* recounts, when our world was young, God Himself created Vatican City, and placed it here, in the Apostle Peter's Sphere, that we might feel closer to Him. I didn't; rather, I felt cowed, as if by a baleful power I had betrayed. I lowered my head and hurried forward.

We followed the street to where it intersected an expansive avenue of brick, then turned left—and I caught my breath, as any person must on first witnessing the facade of the *Basilica di San Pietro.* No one could possibly doubt this was God's work. Saint Peter's was impossibly large, larger than I had imagined any structure could be, and flanked by massive colonnades on either side, sweeping out like welcoming arms. Atop the cornice, statutes of Saints watched over the square. Above it all hovered the sublime dome of the Basilica. So overpowering was the impression of this vista, and as prepossessed as I was in trying to take it all in, that it wasn't until we were hard upon the *Piazza San Pietro* that I realized the immensity of the square—and that it was a hubbub of activity. It overflowed with thousands upon thousands of soldiers, dressed not in the uniform of the *Gardes*, but in black, loose-fitting jackets and trousers. Each company was comprised of several hundred men in parade formation, and there were perhaps a hundred companies. All stood at attention facing the great facade of Saint Peter's.

"They are waiting to be blessed," Kite said. "For all the good it will do them."

He veered right when we reached the edge of the square and had us follow that arm of the colonnade toward the Basilica; we picked our way through officers taking advantage of its shade, many of whom cast us curious looks, as if we were the ones out of place. Reaching the end of the colonnade, Kite abruptly turned right and led us up to the entrance to a small Chapel. Its arched double doors were secured with a rusty hasp and padlock, but to the side of the Chapel a smaller, unassuming door stood slightly ajar, and it was through this we walked into an antechamber. On a bench, sat two of the famous *Cent Suisse*, Kite's former peers. They rose, and Kite, knowing the drill, held his arms out. One *Garde* frisked him, never once exchanging a word or meeting his implacable gaze, though he must have known him—how could he not when the One Hundred lived, trained, and fought together? Yet he wouldn't meet his eyes, and it was as if he was searching a lifeless mannequin. When he finished his search, the *Garde* indicated that we should all leave our rucksacks by the door. When we had done so, the other *Garde* rapped on an inner door, and I heard it unlatched from the other side. They permitted us to pass, not asking for our documents, and by this I surmised they both knew Kite and had been informed of our appointment. Inside, we passed another two *Cent Suisse*, standing at attention on either side of us, eyes forward, as if we were invisible.

We were in a broad corridor adjacent to the Basilica, and to our left was a series of doors leading to offices of various Church functionaries. To the right was a single door which bore a brass plaque reading *Capella Musicale Pontificia Sistina*. Kite knocked loudly, once.

"*Come.*"

We entered a compact room; behind a carved desk sat a Priest with a sour look on his face; at his side were small tables, each holding scripts of vocal music. He peered at us over the rims of his spectacles disapprovingly.

"These the boys?"

"Yes, Father Jean," Kite said.

I was surprised Kite knew the Priest, but shouldn't have been. Despite its size, the Vatican was home to less than a thousand permanent residents, and given Kite's intimacy with Ignatius, it is likely he was well acquainted, through contact or by reputation, with all who served this office.

The priest gestured towards a door behind him so small even I would have to stoop to make it through. "The choir-master waits in there."

Lark, uncertain, looked at Kite. But Ali strode over to the door and pushed it open. It gave onto the Chapel whose locked doors we'd passed outside.

"Not you." Father Jean's bony finger pointed at Kite, who hadn't stirred. "Only the boys."

Kite shrugged. "As you wish." He put a hand on my shoulder. "Not Thomas, who's been unwell. His voice is not fit for singing."

"Thomas, you say? Isn't he the one Ignatius—"

"Yes."

The Priest pursed his lips for a moment. "Then perhaps," he said slowly, "you should return when Thomas is better prepared."

"The others are ready."

"A strong recommendation from a disgraced soldier."

"It is true that I am no judge," said Kite, brushing away the slight. "However, Ignatius said so."

"Ah, well, if a disgraced Jesuit says so, too . . ."

Kite *looked* irked—I say looked, because I'd never really seen him discomposed, save when he deliberately did so for effect. "They can audition or not as you please," he said sharply. "And by the talent of the other two you may judge whether or not Thomas should return. However, if I leave now, with these two unheard, my pride would force me to barter elsewhere."

The Priest snorted. "Your pride?"

"Then call it the *exigencies of my circumstance*, if you will." The Priest blanched at these words. Kite stepped nearer, towering over him. "Perhaps you may find some empathy for my situation, Father, as I know you've had your own *exigencies* in the past."

The Priest looked as if Kite had just made him swallow poison. "Yes, well," he said, hesitating, licking his lips while he weighed his options. He glanced at me and Ali, likely wondering if we could be trusted with what Kite might reveal. "Perhaps the two today," he said, "and we will see about the third."

"As you wish," Kite said, motioning Lark and Ali to the door.

But Lark froze, as frightened as I have ever seen him, even though of the three of us he'd been the most enthusiastic to get here. Ali took his hand and pulled him through, Lark misjudging and barking the top of his head on the frame. In the next room I heard someone order them to shut the door, which they did. All we heard was the murmur of a soft voice until they sang, first Lark, then Ali, then both together. It was hard to say how well they performed because the door, though small, was thick and closely fitted to its frame, effectively muting their high voices. As best I could tell, Ali did a credible job, likely as good as I had heard her sing, while Lark, easily discombobulated, faltered, warbling in and out of key, as I feared he would. Soft words followed, questions from the choir master, if I read the intonations correctly, and answers from Lark and Ali. The door swung open. Ali stuck her head out. "He wishes to see Thomas," she said to Kite, "and would speak with you, too."

Kite looked at Father Jean, who waved a contemptuous dismissal. So I ducked under the door. On the other side I straightened to find myself in the choir at the side of a chancel; Ali and Lark sat in a pew at the front of the nave. Directly in front of them, on the altar steps, stood an elderly man dressed in a black cassock, a gold cross on a chain around his neck. On his head he wore a Cardinal's red *zucchetto*. He smiled benignly. Behind me, Kite prodded me to move out of his way. I did so—and realized on either side of the door through which Kite was passing, stood two more *Gardes*, halberds at the ready. As soon as he was through, they barred the door, then escorted Kite to the altar rail. It struck me that they treated him more like a prisoner being brought to the gallows than a petitioner to the altar. I followed meekly, and sat myself next to Ali. The Cardinal waved the *Gardes* back a step, blocking my view. I sidled over so I might see better.

"*Commandante*," the Cardinal said, "how nice to see you again."

"And you, Cardinal Adolfo," Kite replied. "But not *commandante*. Just Kite now, if you please."

"Of course." The Cardinal looked contrite. He raised his hands in *mea culpe*; jewelled rings glittered on every finger. "Please, forgive me if I offended, Kite."

"You did not, your Eminence."

"Good. Yes." He let his hands fall to his sides. "I would like you to know I took no pleasure in your censure. But I could not back away from my duty, nor my obligation to the Ecclesiastical Court."

"A Minister of God could not have done otherwise."

"Thank you for saying so," Cardinal Adolfo said. "I have already offered my prayers for Ignatius. May I add my condolences?"

Kite nodded stiffly.

"He was a great *magister capellae*, and set a standard that I fear I shall never equal." The Cardinal paused, as if waiting for Kite to disagree, but he didn't oblige. "Yes. Even in death Ignatius contrived to send us these wonderful voices," the Cardinal continued. "No small thanks to you, Kite. And for that we are grateful."

Kite essayed a short bow.

"There is no question they both have talent enough. The one," he nodded at Ali, "is ready. The other lacks control—or perhaps confidence. But I can hear what Ignatius must have heard in his voice." He rubbed his chin as if in thought, then nodded to himself. "Yes, I will recommend both to the *schola* for examination." Then, he looked at me. "They told me, Thomas, that after Ignatius's death you took over their tutelage. Is this true?"

"Yes," I answered in a raspy voice, then coughed for good measure. That I had been perspiring freely only strengthened the illusion of my illness.

"Remarkable," the Cardinal said. "They also told me your voice exceeds theirs in every regard."

Perhaps it was only false humility, but I was taken aback at the compliment. "I wish it were so, your Eminence," I said without a word of lie.

"Humility, too." The Cardinal clasped his hands behind his back. "I will advance all three to the *schola*. Yes." I wondered if the Cardinal's habit of agreeing with himself were a purposeful affectation. "Now then, Kite, on the matter of your compensation . . ."

"Ignatius shared the terms of your agreement, your Eminence."

"Ah, well, there's the problem, yes? It was a contract with Ignatius, not you. And circumstances have changed. The Vatican's resources are stretched perilously thin. Every piece of gold is now counted."

Kite didn't feign anger as he had with Father Jean, probably because he knew the Cardinal was better acquainted with prevaricators. He merely said, "Your Eminence?"

"The Church would look upon it kindly if you were to forgo the fee you believe you are owed. Think of it as an offering, the sort a good Christian might make. It wouldn't hurt you any to build up some credit with God, would it?" The Cardinal smiled beatifically.

"God gave us free will so that we might *choose* to do right," Kite said. "I suggest you pay me so that I might have the chance to earn that grace myself."

The Cardinal laughed, and I have to admit I liked him for that. "If we had someone with your good sense in the treasury, we might not be in such a predicament." He extracted a purse from his robe. "The boys will remain in Vatican City until Thomas is ready for examination," the Cardinal said. "If any boy fails to be taken up by the choir, you may retrieve him and see about finding him a place elsewhere."

"Yes, your Eminence."

The Cardinal tossed the purse at Kite and, as he snatched it from the air, the *Garde* to my right plunged the tip of his halberd into his back. Kite grunted and staggered forward against the communion rail; the second *Garde* then thrust his halberd into Kite's side for good measure.

I have heard people describe similar moments in which they think time slows, so much so that later, they claim to be able to describe the minutia of what transpired. However, I believe this to be the trick of a mind struggling to make sense of things. This has never been my experience. I see what I see, and I can play it back a thousand times. It never fades, but never grows any clearer.

I did not see Ali falling upon the first *Garde* from behind, nor her planting a dirk in his back. His startled cry, however, drew my attention, and so I saw her withdrawing the blade, then sticking him twice more directly behind the heart, as Kite had taught us. He fell away still clutching his halberd, and, with a sucking sound, its point pulled free of Kite's back.

Lark shrieked and threw himself to the floor.

Kite, all colour drained from his face, absurdly gripped the shaft of the other *Garde*'s halberd. At first I thought he was trying to pull it out, but then realized he was, with a monumental effort of will, struggling to keep the *Garde* from withdrawing it. Ali flew past me and flung herself onto that *Garde*, seizing his collar and pulling her knife across both the arteries in his neck, exactly as Kite had done to the young sailor. She sprang away nimbly as the *Garde* collapsed, blood jetting from his wounds. As he twitched on the floor, Ali wiped the knife on her trousers, stuck it in her belt, and looked at me. "Close your mouth," she said.

Two *Garde* lay dying at my feet, and Kite, leaning on the altar rail, slowly withdrew the halberd from his side and let it clatter to the floor.

That he was still standing defied understanding. Pressing his hands over both his wounds, side and back, he croaked, "Where is he?"

Ali pointed.

"Help me."

We did, Ali taking one arm, and I the other. As we mounted the altar steps, I heard the clack of wood across stone, and I saw that Ali had picked up the halberd Kite had dropped and stuck it under her arm, the end of its shaft now tapping on each step.

Behind the altar we found the Cardinal, scrabbling desperately at the trim on the wainscoting.

"Your Eminence," Kite wheezed through clenched teeth.

The Cardinal turned, his expression oddly blank.

Ali let go of Kite's arm, and I sagged as his whole weight settled on me. Placing both her hands on the shaft of the halberd, Ali lunged, driving its point clean through the the Cardinal's chest and into the dark wood behind, pinioning him. Jerking it free, she let go the shaft; the impaled Cardinal fell to the floor, eyes glazed, lips moving wordlessly, looking for all the world like a speared fish.

Kite tuned his head to the panel the Cardinal had been pawing, and croaked, "It's us."

There was the snick of a lock, and a narrow, man-sized panel swung inward on hinges; from the opening Meussin emerged, carrying a small lantern. She lost what little colour she had when she saw Kite's wounds. Rushing over, she helped me sit him, crossed-legged, on the floor.

"Quickly," Kite hissed, "move the Cardinal there." He pointed a bloody finger at the passage.

Ali and I dragged Cardinal Adolfo over and laid him across the threshold; he didn't stir, though I think he might still have lived.

"Wipe the blood from the flags, and any marks you left dragging him."

We did this, too, I stripping off my shirt so that we might use it as a rag. Through bleary eyes, Kite examined the scene.

"Halberd," he said, and Ali laid it across his thighs. Then she pulled her knife and dropped it in his lap, too. Kite stared at it, looking confused for a moment; then he nodded. "Of course." He shook his head, as if at his absent-mindedness. Then his shoulders slumped and his head sank. He muttered something that sounded like, "Go."

Meussin did not; instead, she cradled his head. As she had that day at the inn, she placed pale fingers on Kite's cheek. This time Kite raised a trembling, bloodied hand away from his wound and covered her fingers. Meussin leaned over and kissed him once, on the crown of his head. Kite's hand fell. "Go," he said again, only this time there was no misunderstanding his intention.

Meussin released him, and Kite swayed but managed to hold himself upright. She picked up her lamp. Turning, she lifted her long skirts, and stepped lightly over the Cardinal's body as if she were avoiding an inconvenient puddle. Within the unlighted passageway she paused and turned, beckoning us to follow.

Flight

Throughout the Vatican there exist kilometres of ley tunnels and secret passages, and it was through these we fled. Meussin led, holding the lamp aloft. Most of the corridors were less than a metre wide, and so we were forced into single file, Meussin's body often occluding the light from the lamp. If it was difficult for Ali to be sure of her footing in the chaotic, churning shadows, it was worse for me, for I was at the rear, that much farther from the lamp and contending with two interposing bodies. I found I had to focus on my feet, every bit of my attention on not tripping on uneven flags or displaced bricks. I was slowing us; Meussin and Ali paused several times to allow me to catch up. After proceeding thus for perhaps ten minutes, I realized Ali must have been aware of my predicament, for whenever she encountered the lip of a dislodged flagstone or a brick that had tumbled from a wall, she would straighten her arm to point at the obstacle as she passed over it, though she never once said a word or looked back. It was hard, at first, to trust her eyes more than my own, but as soon as I did, our pace quickened—

—until I stopped dead in my tracks.

I turned, and peered into the pitch of the corridor behind, trying to visualize the way back.

A hand clasped my shoulder. "Thomas," Meussin whispered, "we must continue."

"I cannot abandon him," I said.

"It is what he wished."

"Not Kite," I said. "Lark." I had promised myself I'd see him to Rome, and so I had, but to desert him under these circumstances . . .

"He will do better without us," she said. "We are poison now."

She was right, of course. Ali had murdered two *Gardes* and a Cardinal, all within the heart of the Vatican. And I had knowingly abetted her crimes. I was convinced this had been their plan all along; that the Cardinal had the presence of mind to strike first changed nothing. If taken, it would go poorly for us—and for anyone found in our company. Lark, however, was an innocent and could reveal nothing, as any competent inquisitor would quickly realize (or so I tried to persuade myself). There was another less worthy reason, too, that weighed in favour of leaving him: I had a debt to Ali, and our chances of escape improved without Lark slowing us. Though I knew it to be true, it only made me feel the worse for thinking it.

Meussin put a hand on my shoulder and turned me. "We had good reason for what we did, Thomas. Adolfo would have Rome go to war with Lower Heaven. By silencing his voice, there is a chance reason will prevail in the College."

"And so we leave Lark to his own devices and Kite to die?"

"If the scene we set is to be believed, we must." In the light of the lamp I saw all the melancholy of the world in her face. I thought then about Kite, head hung and sitting cross-legged in the Chapel, dying or perhaps already dead, and understood something of her sacrifice and pain. My own guilt paled in comparison.

Kite had contrived to make it look like an act of vengeance. It was why he'd had us move the body, and clean the blood, and Ali surrender her weapons. And who would not believe it? First Kite's disgrace, and the death of his lover at the hands of bandits, ones likely in the pay of Rome. Then there was Cardinal Adolfo, who presided at the Ecclesiastical Court that had tried Ignatius and Kite, afterwards taking for himself the honour of Ignatius's post. Kite had more than enough cause to seek retribution, and the Cardinal made a suitable object for his outrage. Still, I did not understand why we had to leave both behind, and I said so.

"For two reasons, Thomas. First, carrying a gravely wounded man through these passages would have been near impossible."

This I could not dispute. I also believed, wounded or not, Kite would never have left that Chapel.

"Second, if we were to try to spirit Kite away, their pursuit would be relentless. And we'd likely be taken, too."

I have said before I do not think myself brave, and I knew that if I were to undergo the tortures my father had endured, I would easily be broken. "You fear your fiction will come unravelled."

"Knowing that our act was a strike against the Church, Adolfo's death would be used to rally those Cardinals still undecided."

"Surely they are intelligent men. Some will suspect."

"Let them," Meussin said. "As long as there is uncertainty, it will make them more cautious."

I had already worked out most of this for myself, and hoped hearing her say it aloud would make it more palatable. It didn't.

Meussin must have read the indecision on my face. "It is up to you, Thomas. I will not compel you forward, nor will I aid you in returning." Having said that, she turned, brushed past Ali, and set off again, leaving me the choice.

Ali didn't move, and with a sinking feeling I realized she would accompany me; my choice would be for us both.

I watched Meussin's light dwindle; Ali remained resolute.

When her lamp was barely a speck, I followed.

We caught her up at the top of a steep staircase; had she not waited, I believe Ali and I would have tumbled down the flight. Without a word, we descended and entered a tunnel. At regular intervals, other tunnels intercepted it; here and there were doors or darkened arches leading into unlit subterranean chambers. Sometimes I felt an opening rather than saw it, dank, telltale breezes wafting across my face. We climbed a second flight of stairs and stopped, finally, at what appeared to be a *cul-de-sac*, and I wondered if Meussin had lost her way. But she pressed something I couldn't see, and the wall in front of her gave a few centimetres. She peeked through the crack, then swung the door wide, revealing a broad, gloomy corridor, light coming from leaded windows overhead. She pressed a finger to her lips, then swept across the corridor to a bas-relief of a recumbent lion—a mirror image of the door through which we'd just passed. Reaching behind its mane, she pulled on a catch, then swung the secret door away from the wall. She motioned for us to come. We did, but before I crossed, I pushed the first door closed until I heard a *snick* as its latch caught.

For an hour we travelled more lightless tunnels and corridors, turning first one way, then the other, rising and descending stairs, sometimes passing through chambers (one so big that the lamp illuminated neither walls nor ceiling from which our footsteps echoed) until I thought it impossible that anyone might track us. Finally we entered a short corridor terminating in a wooden door. Meussin pulled a chain from around her neck; on it was a single gold key. This she fitted to the lock and, turning it, pushed the door inward. And so we entered the hidden apartments of the Pope's daughter.

A barred window, high on the opposite wall, weakly lit the room. She extinguished her lamp, then shut and locked the door behind us. The room contained a settee and two oak chairs arranged around a low table; on the tabletop was a tray with the crumbs from Meussin's last meal. In one corner stood a shelf holding a ceramic pitcher and bowl, some towels and sheets, a large stoppered bottle of lamp oil, a tinder box, and other sundries required for her stay. Aside from the door through which we entered, there were two other interior doors, both on the same wall and both ajar. Through one I saw the corner of a bed, while the other appeared to be a toilet. The room we were in was small, but comfortable enough with the three of us; a fourth and it would have been crowded.

Meussin bid us sit. Taking a wooden box from the shelf, she placed it on the table and opened its lid, revealing a cache of food—bread, apples, oranges, and an assortment of hard cheeses and cured meats— enough, at least, for several days. "My appetite is small, and they bring more than I can eat. If we share that, and what I've managed to put aside, we won't starve."

Starve? I wondered how long we were to be here.

"Twenty-five days," Meussin said, as if she'd read my thoughts. "The balance of Lent."

Lent

There was lots more I wanted to know, both about Meussin's role in what had just happened, and her circumstances here. So I resolved to extract what explanations I could. My resolution, however, was unnecessary. In her small sitting room, she spoke at length and, I believe, with candour. As I said, I need be in most people's company only a few days before I can discern their lies; I was at close quarters with her for twenty-five, and remained convinced she was forthright in all she said—and nothing I have seen or heard since would give me cause to think otherwise.

Meussin confirmed what Ambrose had told me, that each year Bishop Singleton and a *Garde* escorted her to Rome. From Ash Wednesday to Easter—the duration of Lent—she occupied this secret apartment. As best as she could tell, no one knew of this place save for those two men and the Holy Father. Leastwise, she'd never seen anyone else here, nor was there ever a sign that anyone else had inhabited these rooms during her absence. Except for a new layer of dust, her things were always as she'd left them.

Even so, it is hard to keep secrets in Rome, making it impossible to say how many Cardinals might have guessed of Meussin's existence. But she was certain Bishop Singleton, who'd been charged with her care from the day of her birth, had been diligent in his silence. She told us the Bishop, before becoming Meussin's guardian, had acquired a reputation for tact and discretion, as well as cultivating an intimate knowledge of the secret passages of the Vatican. It was not surprising that he became the Pontiff's eyes and ears—and it was inevitable that he'd become the steward of the Pontiff's secret shame. When she was thirteen, the Bishop confided to Meussin that he thought the visits madness, and could not see the need for them. Meussin, however, thought she could: she believed that risking discovery was part of her Father's self-imposed penance.

When I asked why she had such trust in the Bishop, she told us he was, in fact, a Cardinal *in pectore*—that is, a secret Cardinal. Meussin believed the honour had been bestowed as a way of ensuring his silence. Such Cardinals were appointed by the Pope, and known only to him. They did not sit with the College, nor were they allowed to wear a Cardinal's vestments or exercise any of the privileges of the Cardinalate—until publicly named by the Pontiff. Should the Pope die before doing so, however, the elevation expired with him. This, according to Meussin, was Bishop Singleton's greatest fear.

As for Meussin's time at the Vatican, it ran with a predictable regularity, measured in the tolling of bells for Canonical Hours. Each morning, before sun-on, her Father would arrive, always with the same *Garde*, who would stand at attention outside her door and never spoke; then, forty-five minutes later, when the Holy Father emerged, the two would return to less secret places in time for the celebration of *Matins*. At *Sext*, and again just before *Vespers*, the *Garde* would return alone, bearing her meals on a tray. Although her Father never entered her bed chamber, and the *Garde* never entered her apartment at all, she thought it best that we absent ourselves at these times rather than try to hide within.

That first day Meussin took us out into the maze of surrounding dark passages, guiding us some distance to a place that was at the juncture of two corridors. She walked us there once, and asked me to lead the way back, which I did unerringly. She then sent us alone to do it again, without her lamp. In the absolute dark, Ali stumbled into me twice, before I took her hand and placed it on my shoulder; my heart seemed to stop when I did so, for I feared she might pull it away in anger, but she didn't—her grip, however, was fierce. We moved slowly as I felt my way along, trying to match what was under my feet or beneath my fingertips with what I had seen on our first trip. It took perhaps three times as long, but we found what I was certain was the junction.

"Good," Meussin's disembodied voice floated to us through the dark, and I realized she'd been following us all along, without a sound. "Now back."

We repeated the trip twice more, and each time my confidence, and our speed, increased in measure. Back in her apartment, Meussin told us where each of the corridors at the junction led, in case we should ever need to flee.

Then she bade us go one more time, as *Sext* was approaching.

Meussin waited until we returned, then shared out her noon meal, supplementing it from her store. We ate in a gloomy silence. She seemed unconcerned about pursuit, but I was on edge, listening for the sound of footsteps in the corridor outside. I picked at my food, my appetite lost. There were several other things bothering me, too—things that had occurred to me while we'd been sitting at the dark junction of the corridors. When I put my uneaten portion back in her store, I said as much to her.

She bid me ask.

"You don't think they will pursue us?"

"No."

"Why not?"

"If they interpret the scene as we intended, they will believe Kite was bent on vengeance, and that two scared boys panicked and fled into the secret passages. Since there is nothing to implicate you and Ali, no one will give you a second thought, except to wonder if you managed to escape the Vatican tunnels—or met your end in darkness and despair."

"Yet the Cardinal knew."

"Not *knew*, suspected." Meussin sighed. "We were so bent on creating a plausible context for Kite's vengeance, it didn't occur to us that Adolfo might anticipate the act himself—and strike first."

"Yet you barred the door, as if you knew he'd have a chance to flee. I'd have had more faith in Kite, and wouldn't have thought of such a contingency."

"Nor did we," she admitted. "Barring the door only occurred to me when I heard the commotion."

"Then you were there for another reason?"

"To do what I did: to keep you from the hands of the Inquisitor."

"Because of what we knew?"

"In part," she answered. "But if that were the only reason, having Kite kill you would have been simpler, wouldn't it?" She said this matter-of-factly, our lives weighing little against their secrecy.

"Then you have plans for us."

"Not I," she replied. "But that, by itself, is a disingenuous answer, and I would like to be as honest as I can. So a better answer would be that, yes,

I know there are plans for you, but I have not been told what they might be, nor do I want to know."

We fell silent for a moment, and I considered the possibilities.

"You said there were several things bothering you, Thomas."

I did, but was hesitant to ask it of the Pontiff's daughter. "Why Cardinal Adolfo? Why not the Pope Pius?"

"He is weak," Meussin answered. "And Cardinal Adolfo would likely be his successor."

I suspected this was not the only reason, but decided to leave it—for now, at least. "Was Ignatius part of this?"

"It was his plan more than anyone's," Meussin answered.

"And Bishop Singleton?"

"No. He is faithful to the Church. It is his life."

"So he knows nothing of us?"

"No."

"In that case, I have one more question."

She nodded.

"You told us that the Bishop, more than any man, is acquainted with the Vatican's secret ways. If they were to search for us, would he not be given charge?"

"It is probable."

"Then he could lead them to us."

"He would prevent any search here, for fear my Father's shame be exposed."

"And perhaps his own," Ali said. The two women locked eyes, and something passed between them that I didn't understand.

"I hadn't thought of that," Meussin answered. "But, yes, that is likely."

The Bishop's shame? I recalled the times I'd encountered the Bishop, and could remember nothing out of the ordinary—save that first time when we'd taken him unaware at *The Widow's Walk*. There had been something odd in his comportment towards Kite and Meussin, and in the way Meussin had addressed the Bishop. And just now Meussin had shared the Bishop's private thoughts and fears. I cursed myself for being blind to what had been obvious to Ali: the Bishop's conduct that day had been more suited to a jealous paramour than a chaperone. Meussin was his *inamorata*.

I don't know what she saw, or thought she saw, in my expression, but Meussin said, "You will learn these things are not so important, Thomas."

I felt my face flush. Ali laughed, and my embarrassment turned to anger. "Will we have to absent ourselves during his *visits*, too?" My words were out—and I was stricken, for Meussin had done nothing to deserve my scorn.

"No," she said, not stung by my question; rather, she cast me a look of pity. It made my boorishness seem all the worse.

Meussin said more, perhaps to soothe me. I don't remember. Not much of it, anyway. I burned inside, preoccupied no longer with shame of the Pontiff or the Bishop, but with my own.

There is one more thing worth telling about that first day: after sun-off, Meussin surprised me by insisting we all share her bed.

I protested I would be fine on the floor of her sitting room, until she pointed out that both her father and the *Garde* possessed copies of the key, and that, in the event of an unexpected visit, we at least had a chance of concealing ourselves in her bed chamber. Ali accepted the arrangement with equanimity, as she had much of what happened since that day at the river. I can't say why, but this bothered me, more than if she had balked. For my part, I'd have felt uncomfortable—even ungallant—at sharing a bed with the two women under any circumstances, but it was all the worse with these two women, particularly after our conversation earlier that day. I couldn't see any way around the logic of Meussin's suggestion, and reluctantly agreed, with the proviso that I might still sleep on the floor.

"The mattress is far more comfortable," Meussin said. If nothing else, she was practical, no matter what anyone else might think, even in matters between the sexes. I admired her for that, largely because I couldn't claim to be so sensible.

Meussin and Ali proceeded me into the room, leaving the lamp with me; I delayed, making noises about cleaning up anything that might betray the presence of extra occupants. I wasn't anxious to join them, and thought it best that I give them time to make whatever preparations they would, so that I could discreetly enter after they were in bed. Even though I was sure there was no trace of our presence, I meticulously went over everything again, looking for stray crumbs and plumping the cushions to remove any sign that they'd been used by anyone other than Meussin. After completing this, I did it again for a third time, before I picked up the lamp, and went into the bedchamber.

As I'd hoped, they were both abed. I placed the lamp on the floor next to where I thought to stretch out—and froze. Against the two walls not visible from the sitting room rose floor-to-ceiling shelves packed with books. There had to be a thousand or more, a library of books. Large and small, thick and thin, bound in leather dyed in dark, rich colours, all with titles stamped in ink or gilt lettering on their spines. None, as far as I could see, were *The Bible* or its *Addenda*.

I had never thought to see such a thing; I was astounded.

I took a step towards the nearest shelf and reached out, running my fingers over the ridged spines, to convince myself of their reality. I wondered if on these shelves might be any of the books my mother had so much loved, and for which my father had died.

"Do you like to read, Thomas?"

I pulled my hand away like it had been stung. I turned to her, and saw on an end table next to the bed a small stack of books, flagged with slips of paper. "I don't know," I said, truthfully. Then added, "My mother did."

"I do, too." Meussin was sitting up in bed, a book in her lap, Ali a shadow next to her. The light from the lamp seemed to cling to Meussin, and as ethereal as she sometimes appeared in the day, in this light she seemed like a radiant spirit. "It helps pass the time."

"It is a sin."

Meussin laughed, and it was like a small bird had flown into the room. "I am the Pope's daughter. I was conceived in sin. How much worse can possessing these books be?"

I thought, then, of my father. "The Church will try you for heresy."

"Then they will have to try themselves," she said dismissively. "From whose libraries do you think I stole them?"

I was taken aback; it had never occurred to me the Church might ignore its own edicts. Yet, all around us was proof.

"Go on," Meussin said. "You will learn much from them." She lay back, and the light in the room seemed to diminish.

With a trembling hand, I pulled a volume from the shelf, and placed it on the floor next to the lamp. Opening it, I read, *"Well, Prince, so Genoa and Lucca are now just family estates of the Buonapartes."*

I did not understand much of what I read in that book. I did not recognize the place names, and the setting was wholly foreign to me, both country and city. Despite my gift of memory, which had also given me a considerable vocabulary, I did not know many of the words I read.

Numerous elements of the work seemed fantastical, inventions of a wild imagination, and I knew by this that it must be a piece of fiction, a novel, wherein such things may be drawn, whole cloth, from the author's imagination. But despite the strange new world, the thread of the story was familiar, for it was about people of various stations swept up in war.

I drank from that book like a man dying of thirst.

When Meussin shook me before sun-on, I lifted my face from the cold, stone flags and rubbed my eyes, the last tendrils of my dream evaporating. In waking life, my memory is perfect; but my dreams evanesce as readily as the next man's. I struggled to retain what I could in our hurry to depart before the Pontiff's arrival. But I lost it all, save for a single echo: that of me as Napoleon, standing in front of my pavilion on the banks of the Niemen, surveying a world I made ready to conquer.

We Come to an Arrangement

I was infected by stories.

In those twenty-five days Meussin harboured us in her chambers, I read without pause, giving in only when exhaustion took me. The second morning I woke on the floor with my face pressed into the pages of an open book, and had to gently peel the paper from my damp cheek. On the third, I awakened to find myself atop the austere sheets of Meussin's bed, her arm draped protectively over me. I know I hadn't crawled in myself—I hadn't the nerve. Which meant that she'd carried me to the bed. I lay rigid, my heart thudding, while Meussin's breasts pressed against my back, and her deep, warm breaths tickled my neck. I found it impossible to sleep. Some time later, Meussin gently shook my shoulder, for the Pope's visit was nigh. Ali stirred and sat up, rubbing the sleep from her eyes—and looked, at first shocked to find me on the other side of Meussin. She said nothing about it, not then or later, but glared at me throughout the day, making her displeasure clear.

That night, and the next, even when Meussin roused herself to try to convince me otherwise, I stayed on the floor, and wondered how could one arm, draped so casually over me, contain all the love in the world?

The novels I read, I quickly realized, contained an idealization of truth. In real life, the truths are still there, but they are never quite so clear. That's why people in stories always act in *character*—the good remain good, and the bad remain bad. If there is any change, it is small and hard won. Why is this so? Because we, as readers, demand it. Real people, however, are messy and complicated. We act out of contradictory motivations that even we ourselves are frequently at a loss to explain. Even stranger, we create our own fictions about who others are and how they will act. And when they do something incongruous to the character we've built for them in our heads, we believe they've deceived us and think nothing of rewriting them entirely. Good becomes bad, or vice versa. And so it was with Meussin for me.

On the fifth night, I opened a slim volume that began, "Adelrune's earliest memories were of finding the *Book of Knights*, hidden away in the attic of the four-story house of bricks where his foster parents lived." I had closed the bedroom door, as I had on the previous night, so my light wouldn't disturb Meussin and Ali's sleep. I was drawn out of my book when I heard them talking quietly, earnestly. To tell the truth, I was relieved, for Ali hadn't said two words since we'd taken up residence. She'd also taken to wandering the tunnels by herself for long periods of time. It worried me, and I could tell it worried Meussin, too. I had my books for solace, and I suppose they distracted me from my guilt and shame. But, in the absence of action and in our confined space, Ali had nothing else to distract her. I wanted to believe that in unburdening herself to another woman Ali might feel better—but I also dreaded what Meussin might think of me if Ali did. Nevertheless, I was glad they were talking, and hoped it helped Ali.

I have to admit I fought an urge to creep over to the door, to try to overhear; instead, I focused on my novel, and after a few minutes their conversation faded into the background of my consciousness. I don't remember when their words tailed off, but they had, for a completely different kind of sound shattered the silence: a gasp of pain. One that was remarkably akin to the last sound that had passed from between the Bishop's lips. I jumped to my feet, thinking one of them had taken ill—or been grievously wounded, though I didn't want to consider the latter possibility. Dropping my book, I snatched up the lantern, and tore over to the door and flung it wide.

Ali and Meussin were both naked. Ali lay on her stomach, rigid, legs apart, and moaning. Meussin, who knelt behind her, turned as I entered. One of her hands lay on Ali's buttock; the other held a piece of glistening wood shaped like a phallus. She waved me out of the room with it.

I was so dumbfounded, that I stood there staring at them stupidly for a few seconds; then, when my wits returned, I withdrew quickly, closing the door. I stumbled over to the chair and dropped into it, heart hammering, and burning with—

—with what? It took me a moment to recognize it as jealousy. Of Meussin mostly. But also of Ali. Of the intimacy they shared. I was young and still naive in the ways of love. Yet, when I recall those moments, those feelings seem truer, and stronger, than any I've had since. If I've loved anyone, it was those two women.

In the next room, Ali's moans of pleasure intensified; my consternation deepened in equal measure.

Ali prefers women.

Strangely, this didn't come as much of a surprise.

But when I brought the image of Meussin to mind, the soft, subtle curves of her pale body against the sinewy duskiness of Ali's, I felt sickened. Worse, I felt betrayed.

I was furious with Meussin, and blamed her for making something unwholesome and messy all the worse. *She is a whore*, I thought, *who thinks only of her own selfish pleasure.* In that moment, I hated her as much as I've ever hated anyone. Though I didn't realize it at the time, I hated her with the intensity we can only muster for the few lucky souls whom we love.

"I know you are angry, Thomas. But you will get over it."

After we'd broken our fast in silence, Ali, as was her wont, had vanished into the tunnels of the Vatican, leaving me alone with Meussin. She sat on the settee with her book, and I took my usual chair, immediately burying my nose in a book of my own.

"If you grip the covers any tighter, you will deform them."

I placed the novel in my lap, and glowered at her. "How could you?" I said, knowing how trite my words sounded as soon as they left my mouth.

"I did what she wanted," Meussin answered. "What she needed."

"It's a sin!"

"If you believe in God, Thomas, you must also believe he made us this way, to feel this kind of pleasure. How can such pleasure be a sin?"

I'd heard these arguments before, or very similar ones, from Ignatius, to justify his own excesses. "There are Laws. The Bible says—"

"The Bible?" She seemed amused. "It is an ancient text of second-hand stories."

"So you do not believe in the Word of God?"

"If the Word of God is in the Bible, it is too obscure and contradictory for me to understand."

"Interpretation is the role of the Church, of the Magisterium."

"I no more believe in the Magisterium's ability to interpret that Bible than I do in my father's infallibility—particularly since both those privileges were granted *to* the Church *by* the Church."

"The Law is the Law—we cannot live without it. If everyone forsook it, there would be only chaos."

"I cannot speak to that, Thomas," she said. "Though I doubt it. I rather suspect things would be less chaotic. In any case, I have my own rules. Sometimes they are the same as the Church's, sometimes not. But my rules are as consistent as I can make them, and so I can give you good reason for anything I might do. Can the Church say the same?"

"Did you have good reason for seducing Ali?"

Meussin blinked, perhaps not expecting the vehemence of my response. "I did not seduce her. It was her idea. I could see no harm coming of it, at least not for her or me. And maybe some good." She paused, looking grave. "But I can see now that it has hurt you. And for this I am sorry."

"Do not apologize to me," I spat back at her. "It is God's forgiveness you should seek."

"I have forsaken God," she said. "It frees me to enjoy this life, instead of worrying about the next."

My anger got the better of me. I stood and took a step towards her, my hands balled into fists. I am ashamed to admit it, but I wanted to strike her. "You had me believing you loved Kite." Her face creased with the sadness of a fresh wound.

"I do," she said, eyes averted, voice suddenly distant.

"Then you betrayed him."

"He would not have thought so." She looked at me. "Just as Ali would not believe she betrayed you last night."

My throat went tight and I couldn't catch my breath; I began shaking as if palsied. Meussin stood, pulling me into her arms, and I collapsed against her, gasping for air.

"It's all right, Thomas."

Tears welled in my eyes and, for a time, I wept.

Meussin was tall for a woman; and she was more than a head taller than me. When I'd regained some control of myself, she cupped my chin in her long, pale fingers and raised my head, then kissed me, full on the lips, as a woman kisses a man.

When we broke, she smiled sadly at me. "We are more alike than you might suppose, Thomas. I think you love me. Perhaps not in the same way you love Ali." She put a pale hand on my cheek, just as she had done when she'd said goodbye to Kite. "And I suppose I love you well enough, though not in the way I love Kite." She took my hand, drawing me towards temptation. "Perhaps we can find some comfort in each other."

I loved, and still love, those two women above all others.

Not once did we speak of our arrangement, and we carried on as if nothing was amiss. Yet it was always there in the room with us. Each evening, after sun-off, I'd read while Ali and Meussin repaired to the bedroom. Sometimes I heard them making love (more quietly now than that first time), and I waited until the sounds subsided before I extinguished the lamp and crept into the room; on other nights, when I heard nothing, I nevertheless waited the interval decency demanded before entering the bedroom. In the mornings, as soon as she finished her breakfast, Ali would always abandon the apartment for the tunnels, leaving Meussin and me alone. When I'd depart the apartment before the *Garde* brought Meussin her lunch, I'd always find Ali waiting at the dark cross-passages Meussin had shown us that first day. And so it went, the folly of our passions carrying us relentlessly forward.

There was one more aspect to our arrangement that bears mentioning. As Meussin had said, the floor was anything but comfortable. I found it cold, hard, and unforgiving. So that very night I crept into bed on Meussin's side. I didn't do it to provoke Ali, or so I like to think. But who knows? Others have proven better at unravelling my motives than me. Meussin, for one. And since she raised no objection, and Ali wouldn't break her silence to do so, I considered the matter settled. From that day, the three of us slept together in Meussin's bed in that secret apartment beneath the Vatican.

On judgement day, what would God make of us?

The Pontiff's Atonement

After Meussin and I became lovers, we shared stories of our childhood.

Until then, I had thought memories cheap and easily acquired, but Meussin taught me that no more valuable gift could be given. I treasure hers—as I hoped she treasured mine—and would not wish to dishonour her by recounting things spoken of in the privacy of her bed. Nevertheless, I believe a few are essential to the truth of this memoir; as painful or embarrassing or banal as they might seem, they trace back the idiosyncrasies of our adult personalities to their roots in our childhood, and so explain how we became who we are.

I have already told something of my father's inquisition, and of my time at the orphanage at *San Savio*, but said little of my life before, for it was largely uneventful. Meussin's was equally routine until the age of five, when she was first conveyed to Rome. There, Bishop Singleton locked her in a small, windowless cell beneath Saint Peter's. It contained a mattress and a chamber pot—but no lamp. She supposed they'd been afraid she might set fire to the mattress—or herself.

More confused than afraid, she didn't cry the first day. When she did on the next, her sobs went unheard.

She saw no one, save the silent *Garde* who brought her meals—and a stooped Priest who entered her room each day, the light from his lamp waking her. He never spoke to her, only to God. In silence he would gather his cassock and, tucking it beneath his knees, kneel on cold stone flags; then indicate she should do the same. Side by side, they would pray for forgiveness.

For what, she had no idea.

The Priest would then leave her to the darkness.

On her third visit to that squalid cell, when she was eight, she discovered the cell harboured its own secret. Sitting in the far corner as the *Garde* opened the door to deposit her meal, she felt a draft tickle her legs. It took her two days, and four more meals, for her to locate its source: two small holes that had been bored in a stone near the base of the wall. She'd assumed these holes had been made to anchor chains. But when she put her fingers into them, they didn't end in rough stone or a stub of iron, but in pieces of wood that gave slightly to the touch. Pressing hard on both at the same time, there was a *click*. It took her only a few more minutes to learn that if she pulled back with her arms while pushing the slats with her fingers, the stone could be canted forward. That first time she pulled too hard and too quickly to get out of the way, and the stone fell forward onto her arms. After a moment's panic, she managed to wiggle free. In the excitement of her discovery, she forgot about the painful bruises rising on her forearms; feeling around the opening created, she realized it was the entrance to a crawlway.

The space was cramped, big enough for a small man perhaps, but still too small for her to turn around. If she went forward, it would be difficult to return. Fortunately, it wasn't far to go; within a few metres the crawlspace gave onto a full sized corridor tall enough for a man and wide enough for two. Thus Meussin found herself at large in the secret passages beneath the Vatican.

She crawled back to her cell and carefully returned the stone to its place.

In the weeks that followed she slowly mapped the secret corridors near her cell by touch. On Good Friday (if her reckoning was right) the *Garde*, as usual, unlocked her door and set her meal down—but did not retreat. She blinked in the light from his lantern set down in the corridor behind him; it shrouded him in darkness, and it was a moment before Meussin realized he was holding something out.

"Take it," he said. Though she'd seen him upwards of forty days each year for Lent, and another twenty in their travels to and from Rome, those were the first words she'd ever heard him speak.

She reached out with trembling hands and drew what he proffered from his shadow: a small lamp, filled with oil, and a tinder box.

"I will bring more oil, as I can."

She stood there, trembling, too surprised—and afraid—to say anything.

"Do not hide it in your cell, and do not light it near here," he said. "The smell will raise suspicions."

She clutched his precious gifts to her chest. "Thank you . . ." She stopped, because she didn't know his name.

"Kite."

"Thank you, Kite."

"It's nothing, Meussin," he said, before locking the door of her cell.

That several years passed before she understood the stooped man who came to her cell each morning was her father should not be surprising. In her other life she was isolated; she had no contact with anyone save her governesses and Bishop Singleton, both of whom spoke to her only when necessary, and never answered any of her questions. How could she have known? Meussin thought herself content on the estate, where her governess generally let her be, and so reconciled herself to her yearly sojourns to the Vatican as the price to be paid for what happiness she had.

Her fourth year in Rome, growing more confident, she extended her explorations, finally stumbling upon corridors that admitted cracks of light. She discovered hidden galleries with spyholes overlooking dusty chambers; sometimes she would chance on a meeting of Clergy, sitting around tables and speaking in hushed tones. Within a week she found her way into the Vatican's unacknowledged library—and stole her first book. She found a crypt containing the bones of long-forgotten saints, in which several inscriptions baffled her (for they spoke of canonizing miracles that helped make the world—but how could men have existed before there was a world?). Here she would sit with her back against the cool stone of her favourite sarcophagus—that of Saint Viktor, the blessed architect—and read for hours. As she finished them, she placed the books upon the flat lid of his coffin, and so grew her collection.

Toward the beginning of her fifth Lent, she found herself lying inside a space within the arch of a ceiling, looking down upon a group of aged Cardinals at a large oval table; in this secret cavity, the sounds from below were somehow amplified, so that every word was clear, even the mumbling of the most elderly. They spoke in Latin, and having had no schooling in the language, she did not comprehend what was said. But she did recognize a voice, that of the Priest who attended her each morning—only now he wore the vestments of the Holy Father.

When Kite laid her meal on the floor that evening, she said, "He is the Pope."

Kite paused, a hand on the door, and nodded affirmation.

"Why does he bring me here?" But she knew the answer before she asked the question; it had been given to her in the books she read, in the sins of the men and women whose lives they considered. Their morning prayers were part of his atonement, Meussin knew, for the iniquity of being her father.

She wept and, for the first time, Kite held her.

The year she reached menses, and grown into the promise of her beauty, Meussin seduced Bishop Singleton on the journey home. From her books and observations, she had learned something of men's desires and the guilts they engendered. She put this knowledge to work to the desired effect: when Singleton brought her to Rome the next year, it was to new chambers, those in which she would hide us years later. By standing tiptoe on a Bible placed on a chair, she could see out the window and into *Giardini del Vaticano* and sometimes catch a glimpse of the birds that sang there. Although she now had a bit of natural light and had been given a lamp, as well as other small conveniences that had hitherto been denied her, she was once more captive. On the second day of her stay, Kite brought a key. The next, after having slipped from her chamber to learn her new surroundings, she returned to find, in her bedroom, several neat stacks of all the books she'd ever stolen. In the paltry illumination of the first small lamp Kite had given her, the pile had always seemed trifling; in the natural light of these rooms, she was taken aback by the number she'd read.

Her new quarters were far from her old, and another two years passed before she stumbled across a familiar corridor and found her way back to the library. Nevertheless, her collection grew. For the rest of that Lent, and in the year following, each meal tray Kite brought would hold a new book under the neatly folded napkin. They never spoke of those books. Or of anything else.

When she told me all this, I felt a pang of jealousy, and admitted as much to her. I knew she loved him, but from what she said, I couldn't be sure he felt the same way. So I asked her directly if she believed he'd loved her.

"Yes." Naked, she rose from the bed and wandered with effortless grace to her bookshelves. I watched, rapt by her melancholy beauty, as she ran her finger lightly along the spines of the books.

"He told you so?"

She hooked a finger around the top of a book and angled it out of the shelf. As she handed me the volume, she smiled. "In each book he chose for me."

Sanctuary

Clinging to the outside wall of the Holy City was the *Albergo Roma*, an inn catering to the endless procession of pilgrims. In its undercroft, where temperatures were more or less constant, twelve oaken casks rested on stout stands, six on either side of the narrow vaulted cellar. Eleven held various vintages; the twelfth, however, was always empty. Through this barrel, on hands and knees, Ali and I crawled out of the Vatican tunnels and back into the city of Rome.

Meussin's squat manservant waited for us.

The last day of Lent, the last day of Meussin's penance, she told us she had arranged for us to be conveyed safely out of Rome—but that she would not accompany us. "I must play out my role here," she said. My heart sank, even though I knew it would be folly to not make use of her position so near the Pontiff and the College. She told us that, if we should wish it, there were those who would harbour us until we might learn what the Angels wanted of us. And should we not wish it, then we would be left outside the city to make our own way. Given how casually she'd brought up the notion of Kite killing us to preserve their secrecy, I regarded the second option with suspicion. Not that I believed Meussin was capable of such a thing, but I knew there must be others in the service of Angels who were. As always, she sensed my apprehension.

"If you choose to strike out on your own," she said, "I give you my word you will not be harmed. But if you do, I ask you to remember that you carry my life in your hands."

I had not wanted to agree under threat, but now that she'd assured our safety, I didn't hesitate in agreeing. It wasn't that I felt so much the Angels had the right of it; to be honest, I had no idea who did. Very few people usually do, and those who claim otherwise are often fooling themselves. No, I agreed for two other reasons. The first was that I liked it better than the alternative (that is, Ali and I trying to make it on our own in an unfamiliar Sphere); the second was because Ignatius, Kite, and Meussin had taken up the cause, and I was willing to trust their judgement. After I had declared my intentions, Ali followed suit. I suspected she had already pledged as much to Kite before we'd even reached Rome, and I was both right and wrong on this count—later I learned Ali had indeed pledged her service, only long before we'd ever met Kite.

We followed the manservant up a crooked set of stairs at the back of the cellar and out into an alleyway, and thence onto a narrow street where dozens of other inns, indistinguishable from ours, stood cheek by jowl. Moving through back lanes, we made our way to the the outskirts of the city. Here, in a street of merchants, we entered a Liturgical shop; it was filled with dusty reliquaries containing artifacts of a dubious origin. At the end of the store's sole aisle, a balding proprietor rose from a stool, where he'd been fanning himself.

"Good day and God bless," he began, squinting at us. "Is there something—" Then stopped as he took in our guide. "Bator," he said, "come to collect your goods?"

The squat man nodded.

The shop owner walked behind one of the displays and hoisted the gunnysack containing our weapons onto the counter.

"Pay him," Bator said, his voice pitched surprisingly high for someone so barrel-chested.

Ali did, extracting a silver Bishop from the purse that Cardinal Adolfo had flung at Kite. I didn't see Kite drop it, nor had I seen Ali pick it up, but there it was all the same. The proprietor's eyes lit up.

"Too much," Bator said, sticking out his thick palm. "Give back six deacons."

The proprietor balked, and it appeared he was weighing his options; but when Bator narrowed his eyes and took a step forward, his hand still extended, the owner returned the difference at once.

Bator and I stopped at a second merchant's to replace the rucksacks we'd lost at our audition, and then at two others to provision ourselves; Ali, meanwhile, visited several other merchants, entering and leaving each empty-handed, until she finally emerged from an ironmonger's shop carrying a chisel and hammer. She stuffed them, without comment, into the backpack we'd bought for her. I couldn't imagine what those tools might be for, yet thought it best not to ask.

From the street of merchants, it was half an hour's march until we passed over a busy bridge and left the city proper. We found ourselves in the midst of a steady stream of travellers on a broad, well-maintained brick road. There were stone walkways for pedestrians on either side, which proved a good thing, for the central lanes were travelled by large, heavily laden carts and drays rumbling past in either direction. I noticed that each wagon, no matter the size, had at least one armed passenger in addition to the driver. When the second prison wagon (and its reek of stale urine and feces) passed us mid-afternoon—filled to capacity with sullen-eyed prisoners, their backs pressed against the bars—I recalled what Kite had told me about the troubles reaching here, to the highest of all man's Spheres.

Houses gave way to estates, and these to fields. We continued straight, while many others turned left or right at the numerous junctions, and it wasn't long before the walkways petered out and we had to take to the road. The cart traffic had thinned somewhat, although there was still a steady stream, and occasionally we were forced to the side of the road by larger wains. As the day progressed, the traffic diminished, until at last there was only a single wagon far ahead of us. Then we were alone.

Just before sun-off, when the road entered a forest, we followed a narrow path into a glen, where we settled for the night. Ali made a fire, and Bator cooked us stew; I think it was good, but I was too distracted to enjoy it. We ate in silence, each lost in our own thoughts.

I delayed when the others spread out their bedrolls, waiting for them to settle for the night. When they had, I opened my backpack and drew out Meussin's parting gifts: the small lamp Kite had given her years ago, and a black, leather-bound book. The gilt lettering declared it to be *The Bible*. I'd thought it odd when she gave it to me, only later to discover that a different text was hidden inside. I lit a small stick from the dying embers of the fire, and used that to light the lamp. Then I opened the book and began to read: *When he woke in the woods in the dark and the cold of the night he'd reach out to touch the child sleeping beside him.*

We marched along that highway the entire second day. In the afternoon, the road broadened, and changed from brick to rectangular stones embedded in mortar. Though the road was still as wide as it had been just outside Rome, weeds had eaten into its margins, cracking the mortar and canting the stones, so that now there was a lane only wide enough for a large cart. The number of travellers on foot had dwindled to nothing; the wheeled traffic had fallen off, too, so that for long stretches no carts were in sight. As sun-off approached, we turned right off the road, and descended a deer run into an unpopulated valley; we halted when our path crossed a disused stone road, not unlike the one on which we'd been travelling that morning. Only this one was unserviceable, its entire surface cracked and askew, weed-choked, impassable save for those on foot. We followed Bator down this ancient highway for a kilometre or so, until we entered a clearing next to the rocky shores of a brown, slow-moving river. On either side, and in the middle of the river, were stone pilings and piers, the remains of a long-gone bridge.

Bator threw off his rucksack, and Ali and I followed suit, then set about gathering fuel for a fire. As soon as we had coaxed some flames to life, Bator pulled a square of paper from his shirt, and unfolded it to reveal a map. He placed it on the ground in front of me.

"Can you see?" he asked.

The sun was nearly off, and some of the smaller words were hard to read, but in the unsteady incandescence of the fire I thought I could make them all out, and said so.

He held a stubby thumb and forefinger about five centimetres apart. "Ten kilometres. Get it?"

I nodded.

He crouched and stabbed his index finger near the bottom of the map, on a line representing a meandering river. A second line, added in pencil, intersected the first beneath his fingertip, and I assumed this was the ancient road on which we stood. A shaky hand had labelled it *Vetus Via*—the Old Road. "We're here." He ran his finger along the pencil line to the upper edge of the map where someone had scratched a small X in charcoal. "Where you want to be."

The distance looked to be roughly a hundred kilometres, as the crow flies. Between our location and the X, the general direction of the rivers and lakes suggested a series of intervening valleys. On a maintained road this would have been no more than three days' travel; but on this dilapidated highway, with several rivers to ford, it would take at least twice that. I noticed a line, this one labelled *Novus Via*, that represented the road we'd been on earlier; it was about ten kilometres distant, and ran roughly parallel to the *Vetus Via*, but curved in at the top of the map where the two met just before the X. I asked him why we couldn't take the New Road.

"Not safe," he said. A string of circles had also been drawn on the map along the *Novus Via*, the first a few kilometres from where we'd turned off. He tapped them, one after the other, all the way to a cluster near the X. "Church pickets," he said, speaking with the pride of someone who'd spent time mapping them out. "Most at bridges. No one passes—unless bearing a letter from the Holy See." He pointed across the river to where the *Vetus Via* bored into the gloom of the forest. "No one watches the Old Road."

I was confused. "Meussin said you'd guide us to a sanctuary. If it is here," I tapped the X, "it makes no sense that the Church should have sentry posts along the route."

Bator lifted his broad shoulders in a shrug. "Meussin said you would understand when you got there."

I stared into his broad face, but could detect no hint of deception; I was sure he believed what he told us. Still, I was uneasy. "Why does no one watch this road?"

"No need," he said, his smile exposing yellow teeth as wide as the nails on my fingers. "Chimeras." He sketched a square on the map that was bordered on the left by the *Novus Via*, and on the bottom by the river in front of us. He tapped in the centre of the square. "They hunt in here."

Belief in such mythical creatures was a sin, and I told him so.

He pointed across the river again. "Tell them."

I couldn't be certain, but where the road swept into the trees, the shadows seemed to shift.

I almost jumped when Ali spoke; I hadn't heard her approach and squat next to me. "They won't cross the river."

Bator nodded his agreement.

"Why not?" I asked.

"Bones of the Saints," he answered, pointing to the opposite shore. It took me a moment to realize he was indicating a series of steles, each about a metre high, strung along the bank. They looked like nothing so much as miniature obelisks. I had taken them to be the remnants of the bridge, but the last two in sight were too far from the bridge to serve any functional purpose. On the map, Bator traced the outline of the box again. "They won't come near the bone fence."

I considered as the three of us crouched around the map in a semi-circle. I didn't believe in Chimeras, nor in any kind of monster, save for the demons of *The Bible*. But those were spiritual creatures, not blood-and-bone animals, and I was now sure there *was* something in the shadows over there, pacing back and fourth, on four long legs.

"And what's to protect us when we cross?"

Before Bator could answer, Ali said, "My Angel."

Incredulous, I looked from her to the squat man and back. Chimeras, Saint's bones, and now an Angel. Not to mention a sanctuary guarded by the Church.

Bator clapped a wide hand on my shoulder. "Boy," he said, "it's the Old Road or back to Rome."

I looked at Ali. "If I choose to go back to Rome, what will you do?"

She was staring across the river and into the black tunnel where the road entered the forest; her eyes, always better than mine, could probably make out more. "Keep on."

"Then so will I." Having said that, I lifted the map and slid it into the fire.

Bator raised his eyebrows in surprise, and for an instant his fingers dug into my shoulder so hard I let out a gasp. The pressure of his grip relented. I saw a flicker of distress on his face as the edges of the map darkened and crumpled, but he didn't make a move to retrieve it. I knew he took pride in his scouting, and likely had spent weeks, perhaps months, mapping out the sentry posts. I also guessed that this wouldn't be his only copy; and as I now had my own copy in my head, carrying his would have served no purpose other than to implicate us should we be taken.

When the last bit had turned to ash, he released my shoulder, and rose to prepare our meal.

The Old Road

That night I couldn't focus on my book; after reading and rereading the same page, and not remembering a word of it, I gave up and stretched out on my bedroll. I drifted into a restless sleep, waking three times.

The first, I sat upright from a dream in which unnatural beasts had backed us against the river. Ali was waist-deep in the water behind me, while Bator stood in front, sword drawn. Horrified, I watched a grotesque creature—with the body of bear and the head of a vulture—fall upon him, clamping one claw about his shoulder, while its beak tore mercilessly at his eyes and the flesh of his face, stripping it off the bone. Bator's shrieks threw me out of this horrific dream.

Around the periphery of our campsite, the bushes rustled, and at first I thought that behind every movement was a slavering animal. But it was only the gusts of a wind that had arisen. I looked to my companions to reassure myself. Ali slept on, undisturbed. But Bator, and his things, were gone. I wondered if he'd never intended to take us farther. Or whether he'd just run off. I hoped it was the former. Briefly, I considered waking Ali, but could not think what it would accomplish other than to disturb her sleep, so I lay back down.

The second time, I awoke confused, thinking for a moment I was back in Meussin's bed, lying between her and Ali. I was careful not to move, for fear I'd disturb them. Then the sound of the river and the rustle of the trees drew me back, and I remembered where I was. Yet I lay completely still; when this became unbearable, I turned very slowly under Ali's arm lest I disturb her. She mumbled something in her sleep, the warmth of her breath spreading across my neck like a balm.

The third time cold drops woke me.

"We must go." In the first light of day, Ali knelt next to me, naked. From her short hair, water dripped onto my face. "It comes up to my neck in the middle, but only for a step, and the current isn't too strong."

I gathered my things, and waded into the dark water where Ali waited, hand shading her eyes, scanning the opposite bank. However, whatever had stalked the shadows last night was gone. We stood thigh deep, but the bottom was already lost in the clouds of silt our feet had stirred.

Ali had slipped her sword through the harness on her backpack to keep it dry, and I had done likewise. Unlike her, I removed my shirt but kept my pants on—my shame prevented me from doing otherwise. Despite my best efforts to not look at her or think about her, I had become aroused. Even so, when she turned, my trousers failed to conceal my state. She stared unabashedly, and her lips curled in disgust. Then she turned and slogged deeper into the water. Red-faced, I followed, feeling relief as the chilly water washed around me, extinguishing my ardour. When the river rose above Ali's breasts, she lifted her backpack and balanced it on her head. I followed suit.

The current was mild, as she said; but Ali was taller than me, and near the middle, where it was up to my chin, I slipped on a rock. With the extra weight on my head, the insistent tug of the current drew me under. Almost immediately I felt her grab hold of my hair and drag me up. I sputtered and coughed for a moment, but was otherwise fine.

One-handed, Ali dragged me to a point where I could regain my footing, then waded to the shore and dumped her gear; she squinted in the dim light, watching something in the river. I pulled myself out of the water and, following her gaze, caught sight of my backpack as it, and Meussin's gifts, floated serenely downriver, sinking lower and lower. I made a move towards it, and Ali grabbed my arm and shook her head. We watched, until my backpack dipped under the surface as it rounded a bend. Then Ali splashed back into the water and, after diving three times near where I slipped, came up with my sword. When she handed it to me, she said, "Wipe it as best as you can, and don't return it to its scabbard until both are dry."

My clothes were, of course, soaked, so I used dried leaves, though they didn't seem to do much good. I laid the blade on a flat rock; then I took off my belt and hung the scabbard from it, looping the whole thing over my bare shoulder. While I was doing this, Ali pulled out the hammer and chisel she'd bought, and made her way over to one of the obelisks Bator had indicated the previous night, a few metres from where we'd climbed from the river. From the other side of the river, the steles appeared featureless; on this side, however, I could see each had been etched with a cross within a circle just below its pyramidic cap.

I watched as she slipped the chisel into the bottom of the cross, and realized the thin black lines of the cross were not shadows of an etching, but were, in fact, slits. She swung the hammer smartly against the chisel, driving its blade a centimetre deep. Tapping the shaft of the chisel, she wiggled it free, then repeated the process on the two arms of the cross. When she hammered it into the top of the cross, there was a distinct *snap*, and the circle of stone, containing the cross and her impaled chisel, fell away from the post and onto the rocky shore.

She reached inside the hole thus created and pulled out something; she tossed it to me.

I snatched it from the air, and opened my hand. It was the size and shape of a robin's egg, but its surface was ebon and smooth as glass, and it exhibited none of the delicacy of an egg or the brittleness of glass—it was hard as stone. Warmth emanated from it, as if somewhere inside a tiny fire burned. When I closed my fingers around it, I felt a slight tingling, like the sort one feels when striking a tuning fork. Yet there was no sound.

I looked up to find Ali watching me as she buttoned her shirt.

"What is it?" I asked.

"Put it in your pocket," she said. "And keep it close." She picked up the circular piece that had fallen, and pulled her chisel free. Then she stuck the piece back in the post where it seated with a *click*, and the post looked exactly as it had before. She put the chisel and hammer away and, hoisting her backpack, started up the *Vetus Via* towards the margins of the forest—

—and five of the largest dogs I'd ever seen.

Only they weren't dogs, because they were half again the size of any dog I'd ever seen, and their coats were an unlikely grey. Their heads were also broader at the top, tapering to long, blunt muzzles, and powerful-looking jaws. When the animal in the front flicked out his tongue, I caught sight of large teeth and long curved canines, the sort you see on predators. Even so, I was slightly relieved, for they were real and looked nothing like Bator's mythical creatures. Rather, they matched a description I'd once read, of an animal I'd never seen: *canis lupus lupus*—a wolf. All sat on their haunches, regarding us impassively with pale, grey eyes that reminded me of nothing so much as Meussin's.

They rose as one as Ali drew near. The largest animal raised its head and bared its canines; the fur on its back rose, and it growled, a deep, feral sound that vibrated through my bones. I snatched up my sword and dashed after her.

Then, an amazing thing happened: the wolves tore off into the forest, scattering and yelping as if the ferocity of my charge had panicked them. I knew better than to credit this, and stopped next to Ali, letting the tip of my sword fall onto an old paving stone, perplexed. She grabbed the wrist of my free hand and raised it; I uncurled my fingers to reveal the strange egg she'd tossed to me.

"It makes a sound they don't like," Ali said. "One we can't hear. Now put it in your pocket and stay close to me."

I did as she asked, then stumbled after her into the forest. For the next two hours I checked all sides; but I seldom saw the wolves, save when one would trot across the trail ahead or behind. However, I heard the crunch of leaves and the snap of twigs on both sides of the road as the pack paced us. Still, they kept their distance, as Ali had said they would, never coming closer than twenty metres, which seemed to be the range of that strange egg.

My obsession with the wolves was distracting, and it wasn't until an hour or so later that I realized my upper body was covered with hundreds of mosquito bites. When Ali noticed me scratching, we stopped and she began unbuttoning her shirt; I turned and pretended to scan the forest for the wolves.

"Here," she said, tossing me the vest-like garment she'd been wearing to conceal her breasts.

Though it didn't protect my shoulders and arms, it was better than nothing. I laced it up, only it was small on me, and impossible to close the gap at the front. When I'd finished, Ali said, "Let's go."

I shook my head.

She stared at me, frowning.

"How did you know about this?" I pulled the egg from my pocket. "Who told you how to get it out of the post?"

"An Angel," she said wearily, as if this was the most obvious thing in the world. "As I told you."

Yesterday, I thought her answer absurd; now, I wasn't so sure. I asked her about the second thing that had been bothering me: why she hadn't used the same process to liberate an egg for herself.

"If we had two," she said, "you might wander off, thinking yourself safe. This way we have to stick together."

In my desperation to make some small amends, I had promised myself I would protect Ali to the best of my abilities. She had recognized this, and knew I would do my best to keep the egg close to her. She was using my guilt—so that *she* might be nearby to protect *me*. I had known this on some level, but couldn't admit it to myself: everything she had done since Ignatius's death had been to prepare herself to be my bodyguard. I felt foolish. And not a little unmanned. Worse, though, I felt a profound sadness that the one small thing I had tried to do to atone for my sins had meant nothing to her.

It took us not a week, but ten days to make the journey. The reasons were varied.

Perhaps the biggest delays occurred because we'd lost half our food with my backpack, so we had to ration what Ali had, and it quickly became apparent that to have enough energy to march a reasonable distance each day, we'd have to find alternatives. Ali knew something about setting snares, and we managed to catch a squirrel and two chipmunks—but that required an entire day. So we fashioned spears from fallen branches and tried our luck at fishing. It took us another full day, through trial and error, to learn both the concentration and patience required to catch our first fish. But after that it became much easier, and an hour's work each day yielded at least one trout, smallmouth bass, or darado, all of which were plentiful in the rivers we crossed.

As I had feared, none of the bridges on the Old Road were extant; indeed, at least two had been torn down purposefully, for we found stones stacked on the shore instead of having fallen into the river as they would have had the bridge collapsed on its own. The scattered stones were worn by many years of rain, and whether natural decay or human intent had brought the bridges down, their destruction had taken place a long time ago. The lack of bridges meant fording the rivers, and four times we had to leave the road and push a significant distance through chaparral before finding a shallows to cross.

Through all of this, the wolf pack tracked us, night and day. I began to distinguish between them, noticing a torn ear on one, the bent tail of another. My memory served me well, and by the fifth day I'd counted twenty distinct individuals in the pack, though I never saw more than half a dozen together at a time, and this only when we emerged from the gloom of the trees into a rare, but welcome, glade. I suppose while the few tracked us, the rest were out hunting smaller prey. Twice I saw unfamiliar wolves who tried to join the hunt, but these interlopers were set upon violently by the pack, and the one that didn't escape was quickly torn to pieces. Even so, I became accustomed to their presence—at least as much as one can—and after a few days I picked a favourite: the runt, with a pronounced limp, who seemed to eke out an existence on the margins of the pack. When the opportunity presented itself, I tossed him my scraps, and I fancied his tail drooped a tiny bit less at those times. There was one thing, though, that I would never become used to: at night their eerie howling crawled up and down my spine, and deprived me—and Ali, who stirred restlessly beside me—of much-needed sleep.

Shortly after breaking camp on our tenth morning, we crossed the penultimate river on the map, a dried creek bed with a dirty trickle at its centre. As we crossed the thread of water and climbed back onto the Old Road, a gleam of white caught my eye. "Wait," I said to Ali, but she followed me to the road's margin anyway. The white was that of bone, and before us were the remains of a man; save for a forearm, the skeleton was whole, although some of the thinner bones had been snapped and most were scored with the teeth marks of large carnivores. All the internal organs and muscles were gone, but here and there ropy threads of dried sinew clung stubbornly to bone. The poor soul's ankles were shackled and joined by a short, rusting chain.

I reached into my pocket and touched the egg, to convince myself I still had it.

"Let's go," Ali said, starting down the road again. After half a dozen steps, she paused, waiting on me.

Ignoring her, I began searching the ground for the man's missing arm. But it wasn't anywhere to be found. So I walked back to the river bank and carried back a sizable stone. Ali watched me drag back half a dozen more before she pitched in. It took us the better part of an hour before we had enough to make a decent mound. I placed a small makeshift cross at its head. Father Paul had once told us that God does not hear the prayers of those in a state of mortal sin: *He that turneth away his ears from hearing the law, his prayer shall be an abomination.* I hoped God might hear mine on his behalf.

We resumed our trek.

By my estimation we were a few kilometres from our goal. For most of the journey we'd been mantled by overarching branches, unable to survey our surroundings, so when we crested the next rise, I suggested I climb the tallest tree adjacent to the roadside and survey the valley ahead. Ali shrugged agreement. So I handed her the egg, and clambered up. I managed to pull myself to a spot where the foliage thinned, and inched my way out onto a branch. When I'd secured my perch, I turned to survey the road before us—

—and almost lost my grip.

In the centre of a broad valley before us, amidst the ruins of a devastated city, stood a tower of colossal proportions. It rose to span the gap between this, the highest of all human Spheres, and the realm of Angels. The size of it took my breath away; and its audacity made me cringe—and fear for the souls of all men. I knew that its construction could serve only one purpose: to provide a bridge across which the Church might launch its attack against Lower Heaven.

The City and Tower

"How far?" Ali asked before my feet even hit the ground.

I was surprised at her question, for I'd expected her to ask about what I'd seen, and not how far away it might be. "Five kilometres, perhaps. But we can't—"

"Five to the tower?"

She knew. As she'd known about the strange posts that fenced in the beasts. If I was to accept that Angels spoke to her, why wouldn't they tell her about the tower, too? However, as much as the Angels might have vouchsafed to reveal to her, they hadn't told her everything, for after I nodded affirmation to her question, she asked me to describe what I'd seen. I did so, trying to do credit to the immensity of the structure and its odd conical shape. From base to summit the tower was constructed of diminishing levels of supporting arches, all opening onto interior darkness, giving the impression the tower was hollow inside. Its massive base was ten times larger than the largest building in the city, and an inclined road spiralled up its exterior, like the thread on a fat screw. Specks that were men crawled along that helical road in both directions; more clung to scaffolding that girdled the summit.

It was, I told her, a monument to man's arrogance and an affront to God.

She asked about what lay between us and the tower.

"A city," I said. "It looks to be uninhabited. Some of the buildings are no more than rubble, and others have only the remnants of broken walls. Many roofs are fallen in, and where they haven't vegetation has overrun them."

"If the city is uninhabited, there must be a camp."

I nodded. "There is a cantonment, with rows of canvas tents. I counted smoke from twenty-three cook fires. It's impossible to see the design from this distance, but the flags sport the colours of the Holy See."

"Where does the camp lie?"

"Between us and the city."

"And the river?"

The map had shown one last river. Yet I hadn't seen a cut in the trees to betray its presence. Then I realized there would be no gap; where there were trees, the river ran parallel to the *Novus Via*, then swung towards us as the trees fell back, demarcating the change from forest to the fields circling the city. "Three kilometres from the tower, two from us." On the other side of the river there were the remnants of a raised aqueduct that once fed the city, and the faint traces of the Old Road to the outskirts of the city. "The road gives unto a cultivated field just outside the encampment."

She chewed on her bottom lip, the way she always did when considering things.

"There are troops everywhere," I said, "and men labouring in the field." She didn't seem to hear me. "There is no sign of sanctuary."

She frowned impatiently at me, as if I'd missed the obvious. "Sanctuary, Thomas, is above."

It took me a moment to grasp her meaning, and when I did I shook my head in disbelief. Ali wanted to secure asylum in Lower Heaven, amongst the Angels. Men never rose to this Sphere—save after death, when the souls of the worthy ascended. Worse, I knew how she intended to get there. "You mean to climb the tower."

"After sun-off."

"And when we get to the top, what then? Will there be Angels to welcome us with open arms?"

"I . . . I do not know. I only know that if we are to be safe, that is where we must go."

It was folly. "We can't—" My voice faltered. "*I* cannot." I was not thinking of the impossibility of making the tower, let alone achieving the summit, or even of the unforgivable blasphemy of entering Lower Heaven uncalled should the opportunity present itself; rather, I thought of my sins. And even though I believed I served the Angels, if I were to be judged now, the outcome wouldn't be in question. "Lower Heaven," I whispered in self-abasement, "has no place for me."

"There is a place for everyone, Thomas," Ali said, wearily massaging her temples, as if this conversation had made her head ache. "Even me."

In my concern for my own soul, I'd forgotten the blood on her hands, and that she had as much to fear as I.

She shouldered her pack and set off down the road; to either side, the underbrush rustled as the wolves followed. She knew my guilt would compel me to follow, and in this she was right. But what she didn't know was that I'd have followed her regardless. Though I could not have told her, and though she would not understood it if I did, I loved her and would have followed her anywhere.

Clutching the egg, I hurried after her, afraid of what she'd have us do, and fearful this would be another black mark upon our souls. Yet, even as I thought this, I felt strangely heartened. If we were to be judged, we would be judged together—and whether for Heaven or Hell, only God would say.

The Unrepentant

We hid in a thicket at the forest's edge, the row of steles that warded off the wolves a few metres in front of us. Across the river were the tilled fields, and half a kilometre farther the camp began. In the fields, dozens of men methodically dug tubers from the dirt and dropped them into sacks they dragged along furrows. All wore ragged clothes and were unkempt, and when they moved, they shuffled slowly, hobbled by shackles with short chains. It took me a moment to locate the single *Garde* who, from the shadows of a distant, jury-rigged canvas, had been charged with overseeing the prisoners. He lay on the ground and looked to be asleep. With the chains, and the wolves blocking the only way of escape, I suppose there was little to watch. To our left, the last bridge stood intact; this was an unexpected blessing, for the river was deep and swift in either direction as far as I could see. However, the railing was low, and in crossing there would be no way to conceal ourselves from the men working the fields, or, indeed, from anyone on the periphery of the camp who chose to look in our direction. So we retreated into the forest to wait for sun-off.

Our plan was, of necessity, simple: cross the bridge and make for the city. The fields surrounding the camp offered little concealment; however, there was a series of ditches that skirted field and camp, running to a cluster of crumbling buildings on the margins of the city. We had no idea what was in those ditches, but no one had entered or left them in the time we'd been watching, nor had anyone been working on them, and if they were as deep as they appeared, they would provide ample cover. We'd be exposed as we dashed from one to the next, but we saw no alternative.

We waited, Ali sharpening her blade in that same slow, meticulous way Kite had. From time to time she'd test it on a leaf; once, she drew it delicately across the back of her own arm, drawing a thin line of blood, then looked at me, as if I was somehow to blame.

Long after the men retired from the fields, and the cooking fires were reduced to embers, we made ready to chance the bridge. We fixed a last, cold meal and packed away our gear. Ali tied a rope to her pack, then threw the other end over a stout branch several metres above the ground; hauling on the rope, she hoisted her pack off the ground high enough so the food would be out of reach of the wolves, or any other large animals, then tied the loose end around a second, smaller tree. We wouldn't need the gear or food for the trip to the tower—but, it would be invaluable should we be forced to return. We kept our swords, which we strapped to our backs.

Around midnight we crept up to the bridge. It was difficult to see anything; all lay in shadow. When, after fifteen minutes, we had detected no movement in the camp, we scuttled across the bridge, throwing ourselves behind a mound of earth to the left of the roadway. For a moment we both held our breaths, listening to see if an alarm would be raised. When none was, Ali touched me lightly on the shoulder—at which, I admit, my foolish heart seemed to flop in my chest—then lifted herself from the ground and began edging to our right, toward the lip of the first ditch.

"Be caught for sure."

Ali spun around, pulling her sword from its sheath. I reacted, too, albeit more slowly, rolling onto my back, and peering into the shadows at the footing of the bridge.

"There's other ways. Better ways." The voice was sonorous, and the words spoken slowly, as if the speaker gave careful consideration to each one.

"Show yourself!" Ali hissed, scrambling back to my side.

Silence. Then the rattle of chain as a tall, cadaverous figure shambled from the shadows. His skin was drawn tightly over his face, his cheeks fleshless and collapsed, the contours of his skull pronounced. Even his lips looked shrivelled, drawn back in a permanent grimace over a mouthful of broken and discoloured teeth. "Expect you're wanting the city."

"What we want is no business of yours," Ali said.

"True," he conceded, then fell silent, staring at us as if we had accosted him.

"You wish something," I said.

"No," he answered, lowering his eyes. "Not really."

"You saw us earlier today, then hid under the bridge, knowing we were waiting for sun-off to cross."

He contemplated the ground in silence.

"Answer!" Ali said, raising her sword. The emaciated man tried to dance back a step, but his foot caught on a rock, and he sprawled to the muddy ground, scuttling backwards to the edge of the river, eyes wide with fear.

I like to think Ali only wanted to frighten that miserable wretch and had no intention of slaying him, but I'd learned that I was not always the best judge of her intentions. Unwilling to let her add another sin to her burden, I stepped between them. "We won't harm you," I said, and then turned to Ali. "Will we?"

She didn't answer, but after a moment, let her sword down.

"There," I said, "you see?" I moved towards the man, and he cringed, raising his hands as if to fend off a blow, though he didn't try to move away. I helped him up, feeling bone beneath the loose folds of skin on his arms. Though he was nearly a metre taller, he couldn't have weighed much more than me. "I am Thomas," I said when he'd regained his feet, "and this is Ali."

The man blinked, looking at both of us, as if taking us in for the first time. Then he seemed to come to himself again. "Samuel," he said. "Sam to them who know me."

"You wish to show us a safe way into the city, Samuel?"

"Sam. You ought call me Sam. Reckon you know me as well as any living man—since them who knew me better is all dead now." His mouth twisted into a rictus, which I took to be a grin.

"Sam, then," I said. "Can you show us a safe way into the city?"

He nodded, a slow dip of his head.

"And in return you want us to show you how you might escape."

"Seen you. You came through the woods." He placed a hand on my shoulder, and kneaded my skin lightly, as if convincing himself I wasn't a spectre of his imagination.

"We did." I pulled the egg from my pocket and held it so he could see it. "This offers protection against the wolves. It makes a sound they don't like, one pitched to high for us to hear." I tossed it to him.

Ali cried out, and stepped past me, backing Sam into the water up to his shins. But she must have thought better, for she stopped, and glanced back at me.

"As you can see, Sam, Ali values what you are holding in your hand. Enough that she would kill you for it. I might, too—*if* we were going back into the woods." I looked to Ali. "But we're not."

Sam clutched the stone tightly in his fist.

"As you guessed, we're headed for the tower and have no further need of it. That's why I gave it to you, Sam. Consider it a down payment." As I spoke, Ali relaxed her stance ever so slightly. "Go ahead," I told him. "Take a good look at it."

Sam looked to me for assurance, and I nodded. He opened his hand and squinted at the egg. To my surprise, he popped it in his mouth and held it there for a moment, before spitting it out. Then he looked at me expectantly.

"There is a backpack in the woods, Sam. In it is a chisel and hammer you can use to remove your shackles, as well as food and a flint, and maybe some other things that might be handy, too. I will tell you how to find the pack, and then how to make your way back to Rome. In return, you will guide us to the tower—and answer some questions truthfully."

He rolled the rock around in his hand for a moment, then stuck it in a pocket in his filthy clothes. "Done." He needlessly spat on a palm already covered with his saliva, stepped forward, his ragged pant legs dripping, and stuck his hand out.

I spat on mine and we shook.

"Now I'll put my first question to you, and I want an honest answer, as you promised."

"Shook on it," he said. "Ask."

"Can we trust you?"

He mulled it over for a moment, then said in his slow, careful way, "S'pose. Least as far as I can trust you."

"A fair answer." I pointed at his shackles. "The men in the field wear chains. And though I couldn't say for sure because of the distance, many of those ascending the tower walk as if they are, too."

"They wear chains."

"When we were on the *Novus Via* I saw a prison wagon filled with men in the same sort of chains. Are prisoners being brought up here to work on the tower?"

Sam nodded. "For as long as they can."

"When they can't do heavy labour any more, they're sent to the fields?"

"'Yes."

"And when they can't work the fields any more, what happens?"

He pointed. Because of his height and the bank of earth between us and the camp, I couldn't see what he was indicating, but it was in the general direction of the ditches.

"Are they graves, Sam?"

"Them mounds between are. T'others ain't graves. Not yet, anyhow."

"A reasonable man would say that the Church would never make men labour to their death, and against their will, no matter what they might have done."

"We're dead men afore we were brought here."

"You've been condemned to death?"

"Every last soul—save for them what guards us." He shrugged. "A hole in the ground is a hole in the ground, here or in Rome. It's all the same to them what's put into it. Only in Rome, I'd a been planted a lot quicker."

I considered this a moment. "You have not repented. Nor have any of the other men here."

His eyes widened in surprise. "How'd you know it?"

"I didn't. I guessed it. What did the Priest tell you?"

"It were the Bishop, back in Rome."

"The Bishop, then."

"Told us any who would *not* repent, that the Church in its mercy would allow them souls to live a bit longer, so they might serve the Lord and so see clear to coming into his graces. Heard good men, those what prayed each and every night, repudiate the Church and their Saviour and blacken their souls so they might live a bit more—to come here."

I wish I could say I was surprised by what Sam told us; but I knew that men, even those of the Cloth, would bend reason beyond repair to justify their vanities. No matter how convinced one might have been of the necessity of the tower, no one could look upon it and not know in his heart it was a blasphemy. And if it was, then putting men to work on it would be akin to putting their souls in jeopardy—which itself would be a mortal sin. But if those who laboured on the tower were already in a state of mortal sin, and unrepentant, there was no risk to them, or to those Clerics whose orders they followed. "They don't allow you to speak when you're on the tower, do they?"

Sam shook his head. "Them that does is sent to the Cross." He leaned in, as if to share a secret. "Call it the Babel Tower, only not out loud, on account of them Priests don't like to hear it called that."

I asked Sam about the construction of the tower. He confirmed it was hollow on the inside, and that the ramp, on which four men might walk abreast, was the only means of ascent. When I'd first seen the tower, it appeared to span the gap between the Apostle Peter's Sphere and Lower Heaven; however, the firmament was the same uniform colour, making it impossible to judge exactly how close the apex of the tower came to the Sphere above. And the scaffolding near the summit suggested it hadn't yet been completed. Sam confirmed this. "It were close to finished when I was last there, a fortnight ago. And them that's still working on it says it's all but done."

"How many men guard the entrance to the tower at night?"

"Two," he said. "Don't need no more. *Gardes* don't like coming near it, and none will set foot on it save when they must. Guess they reckon it's a sin. Only I'd say they ought not worry so much about that and think more on the sin of how they treat them what do their dirty work."

I nodded my agreement. As young as I was, I'd already worked out that men often punish others to assuage the guilt of their own crimes. Looking now at the immense shadow of the tower, at how it must loom over every thought and action in the valley, I could think of nothing that might engender more guilt. "Then I've only one more question, Sam. How will you take us there?"

Samuel pointed again, this time under the bridge. "Other side, there's a waste pipe big as a man."

Of course. Where there was an aqueduct, there'd be a sewer. When we'd left the road, we'd moved into the woods upstream of the bridge and surveyed the encampment from there; a large pipe, close to the bridge and emptying into the river downstream, would have been hidden by the structure. Still, I felt stupid for not having thought of this.

"Show us," Ali said.

Sam turned and strode into the dark beneath the bridge, following a strip of mud; I hustled to keep up, Ali in my wake. Just as he said, half a dozen metres beyond the bridge was the black maw of the sewer. A thin stream of brackish water ran over its lip and crawled down to the river. Sam had called it man-sized, but he'd have to hunch, while Ali and I could walk upright. We peered inside; the dark was absolute. A dank breeze wafted from the opening. I had feared there would be the stench, but the pipe had clearly not been used to flush waste for a long time.

"I could fetch our kindling for torches," Ali said. Her voice echoed inside the pipe, and there was a scuttling in response.

"No," I said. "You'd have to cross the bridge again and risk being seen. There might also be pockets of gas in the sewers. We'll take it slowly. Go by feel." I turned to Sam. "Do you know the tunnels, Sam? Good enough to find your way in the dark?"

He shook his head. "No. But I seen grates in the streets big enough for a man. It's dark outside, but there's still enough light to see you by. So I reckon inside it should be easy enough to see a way out when we pass one."

"You said *we*, Sam. Do you mean to come with us?"

"Said I'd take you there. Know the streets. Leastwise, most what leads to the tower."

Something occurred to me then. "You know we hope to find our way into Lower Heaven?"

"Thought as much."

"And you know you can't go with us?"

He shook his head. "An' I wouldn't want to, if it's all the same to you. Ain't ready to be judged. Not yet, leastwise." He pulled the egg from his pocket. "There's a man I wronged. Mean to make amends in this world first."

I nodded, wishing I had the same luxury. "Thank you for your honesty, Sam."

He shrugged, putting the egg away. "Deal's a deal."

"Then let's make haste," I said, suddenly aware of the minutes of the night that had already crept past. I turned to Ali, and pointed at her sword. "Put it away. It will only slow us down."

She did so, sliding it into the sheath on her back. Then, like rats returning home, we scuttled into the thickening darkness—Sam, his long arms extended to touch either wall, leading the way.

A Lie in the Dark

In hermetic darkness we walked, seeing nothing and hearing only the irregular drip of water, the unnaturally loud scrape of Sam's chain, and the *tap-tap-tap* of his foot as he tried the way. I found I was having trouble keeping my equilibrium; so I stretched out my arms, as I'd seen Sam do, but the diameter of the pipe was too great for me to touch both sides at the same time. So I swung my arms up until they were almost vertical and I felt slick stone. I held my arms thus for a time, until my shoulders ached so badly I could hold them up no longer. After that, I alternated, one hand at a time. Surprisingly, there was less debris to stumble over than in some of the Vatican tunnels. I had no idea what calamity had befallen the city that would make the former inhabitants abandon it— the nature of decay I'd observed suggested it had been abandoned, rather than destroyed by strife or natural disaster. But whoever had made this sewer had expected the city above to still be thriving.

We felt our way along for perhaps fifteen minutes.

Although I had said nothing to Sam or Ali, I was dubious about how far we might get in the sewer. I suspected the pipe we had entered might be the sole point of discharge for the entire city, which meant that if we did not find an egress from this pipe, then we would be forced to search down smaller and smaller branches. I also wondered if we'd even be able to see any of the grates Sam had mentioned, for rubble from the buildings, or lighter debris like leaves, had likely accumulated on most, rendering them invisible from within. Yet I'd felt a breeze, and Sam had said he'd seen grates, so some, at least, were not blocked. How many, though, and whether or not they were directly above this pipe, worried me.

I had another worry, too. It had occurred to me that Sam might have been lying. He admitted, after all, to being a condemned man, who'd spent time in prison and here, with other condemned men. Even if he had scruples before, it would have been hard to keep them in such company. I wondered if perhaps his abjection and self-abasement were merely an act, one designed to lure us into the sewer. Here, our weapons would have been less useful. And, for all I knew, Sam might have confederates lying in wait. I listened closely for the telltale clink of other men's chains. What I heard instead was the drag of Sam's own chain, and his tapping, abruptly stop.

I froze, and felt Ali's hand tentatively touch my back. "Sam," I said, placing my hand on the hilt of my sword, "what's the matter?"

"Floor gone."

"Can we—" I jumped when cold metal pushed against my ankle. There was a basso chuckle. "That only Sam," he said, and I realized he had prostrated himself, so he could lean over the edge to test its depth. "Can't touch no water. No bottom I can reach, neither." I heard a pebble tick against brick, then a small splash. "Water, though, down a ways."

Relief—at least as much as was possible in this situation—swept through me, and I let go of my sword. "Are the bricks broken at the edge?" I asked. "Or is it finished, like it was made to end there?"

I heard him running his hands over the brick. "Finished."

"Then it must be a catch basin or cistern," I said. "If it is, there's likely a way on one side or the other to skirt it."

I heard him scrabbling for a moment. "This side."

"Which side, Sam?"

He laughed at himself this time. "Left." His chain, which was still against my leg, pulled away. "Narrow. Wall curves. I can manage." I heard him shuffling forward, the clink of his chain multiplied by more confounding echoes as he entered the larger space of the cistern. "Hands and knees for me. Easier for you, I'd reckon."

Leaning on the left wall, I moved forward, found the brink with my right foot. I edged around the bend onto the narrow walkway that ran around the cistern. The wall here curved inward over the cistern, pressing against my shoulder and bowed head; it seemed to be trying to force me off. I decided it might be best to follow Sam's example and go down on all fours, and suggested Ali do the same. In the absence of light it was impossible to tell, but I don't think she took my advice.

Crawling along that edge was unnerving, not knowing what lay a few centimetres ahead, and made worse when I imagined ragged men with good-sized rocks in their hands, waiting patiently at the other end for us to crawl around the corner. When I'd crawled perhaps half a dozen metres, I was seized with a sense of vertigo much more disorienting than what I'd felt when walking upright, and had to pause to collect myself, lest I veer off the edge. I meant to lean against the wall—and experienced a flash of panic when my shoulder didn't encounter brick. Or at least not where I expected it, for here was a indentation in the wall, two bricks wide and perhaps two deep, into which I'd leaned.

"Other side." Sam's voice drifted back. "Not too far now."

He must have missed this notch, or it was unimportant to his scheme—had that been a note of anticipation in his voice? "Hold up," I said over my shoulder, to keep Ali from stumbling on my heels. "I've found something."

I felt around the indentation, discovering that it rose vertically along the wall, and that horizontal iron bars had been set into it at regular intervals. I grabbed one, and hauled myself to my feet. The cut continued along the curve of the wall, up and out over the basin, at least as far as I could reach. Letting myself down into a crouch, I turned, eager to peer into the depths of the cistern.

"Sam, Ali. Look down, into the centre of the basin." I waited for a moment to let them do so. "Can you see anything?"

"If my eyes are not playing tricks," Ali said, from a metre or so behind me, "I think I see a small grey square."

After a moment, Sam said, "Same."

"Me, too. But I wanted to be sure. I think it's the reflection of the light from above." I heard Ali shift behind me. "I can't see anything above."

"The ceiling is domed," I said. "But the dome does not reach the street. A manhole must lead from the apex of the dome to the street above. We can't see the opening directly because it's centred over the cistern and the ceiling blocks our view." I stared into the darkness, believing I could make out the faint scallop where the roof of the dome intersected the vertical tunnel.

"If it's true, it will do us no good," Ali said. "We have no way of getting there."

I turned to face the wall, grabbing hold of the farthest iron bar that I could. I put a foot on a low rung and started climbing. "There's a ladder of sorts. I think it runs up the wall to the access tunnel."

I heard Ali shuffling forward, as I knew she would, to try to stop me, but I had already pulled myself out of her reach. I dragged myself up another couple of rungs and, leaning back at an acute angle, nearly lost my footing. I realized that if I wished to stay on the ladder, I'd have to simultaneously push down hard on the rungs with my feet while holding most of the weight of my body with my arms. Moving up each rung would become increasingly difficult.

"Thomas!" Ali's shout echoed madly in that domed space. "Don't be a fool!"

I took another two rungs and paused, my arms already shaking, my fingers slipping—and immediately knew I shouldn't have hesitated. So I clambered up as quickly as the awkward angle would permit, until I reached out for a rung and my hand closed on air. At the same instant my eyes were dazzled by the weak light from above, so much so I had to avert my gaze. I gasped, all my weight on my left arm, and swung my right back wildly, slapping my palm against the wall of the access tunnel above, until my fingers closed on a rung just as my feet slipped free. I swung my other hand up and gripped the rung higher. My arms were on fire, my legs dangling in mid-air. It was all I could do to haul myself up one more rung. I raised my knees almost to my chest—and my feet found purchase on the last rung in the access tunnel.

My heart hammered, and my arms shook uncontrollably, but I'd made it around the bend. I rose, grasping higher bars, and was grateful to straighten and let my legs take my weight.

"Thomas?"

The access tunnel was narrow, and I found I could lean back against the wall and still hang onto the ladder. I did so, and took a moment to catch my breath, looking up, blinking until my eyes adjusted to the light leaking through the grate only a few metres above my head. The grate's ironwork did not have the regularity of those in Rome, but appeared ornate, like the wrought iron grilles I'd once seen as a boy in the gardens of our Parish manse, decorated with leaves and tendrils of climbing plants. I wondered what kind of place this had been, that would have such elaborate sewer covers.

"Thomas!" Ali made no attempt to hide her exasperation.

"I'm okay."

Her curses echoed madly in the chamber below.

"The ladder runs all the way up," I said. "Don't climb yet. Best wait until I make sure we can get out."

I paused, half expecting to hear her climbing the ladder anyway; for once, though, she seemed to heed my advice. I climbed. When I was close enough to push against the grate, I discovered it wasn't a grate at all, but a mat composed of the twining stems of a grape plant. I sliced through them easily with my dirk, and poked my head out the opening.

I was on what once must have been an affluent street. Large, multistory buildings lined both sides. For the most part their facades had been overrun by climbing vegetation. Where bare wall showed, the facade was cracked, in some places broken away, the substructure of rough brick exposed. Debris from crumbling fascia littered the road; here and there patches of weeds had burst through the avenue deforming its once smooth surface. And brooding over all this abandonment was that massive, soulless tower, a shadow darker than night. The skin on the back of my neck prickled.

Placing both palms flat on the ground, I rolled forward and out of the hole. I crawled back to its lip. "We can get up this way," I whispered down to Ali as loud as I dared. "Don't stop when you're coming up. Climb quickly. And push down hard on your feet, or you'll slip off the ladder."

I heard them conversing, but could not make out what they were saying. Then Ali's voice drifted up: "I'm coming."

Quicker than I thought possible, her head hove into view, and she swung herself nimbly—and with more agility than I could ever manage—around the bend. She looked fierce clambering towards me, and I scuttled backwards, as she vaulted out of the hole, and landed, cat-like, on her feet. She looked up and down the street, perhaps to see if the commotion had roused anyone. But I knew the place was deserted, save for those two *Gardes* huddled near the tower. We were far enough away that I doubted they had heard us; even if they had, they wouldn't abandon their post in the dead of night to venture into these cursed streets. No doubt satisfied we were unobserved, she glared at me, and my simple heart lurched at her dreadful beauty.

"Christ's blood!" she shouted, and kicked me squarely in the stomach.

Doubled over, I fell to my knees, clutching my gut, gasping for breath.

She swore again, and through my tears it looked as if she was making ready to kick me again. But she didn't. Instead she drew her sword and placed its cold point against my neck. "Swear you will not act again without first asking me." She pushed a little on her sword, perhaps expecting me to pull back, but I stayed rigid. I felt blood run down my gullet, and wind its way onto my chest. "*Swear it!*" she shouted, rage flaring in her eyes.

"Will you kill me if I don't?"

Whatever possessed her fled; almost casually, she flicked her sword up, so that it nicked the back of my jaw. "You know I won't."

"In that case," I said, "I will do whatever you wish."

She stared at me as if I was insane, and I suppose I was. Or had been momentarily. "Will you swear it?"

"Yes," I said. "On my faith and in God's name."

She said something odd then: "And if you lose faith?"

The question took me aback. Why would she pick this, of all times, to question my faith? *Perhaps*, I thought, *she is trying to bait me*. If that's what it was, I decided to ignore it. "Then I swear on my heart and my life."

She pulled a leaf from a nearby plant, wiped my blood from her blade, and sheathed it. "Let us hope that in your rashness you do not lose those, too."

Sam's distant call echoed from the pipe, startling me.

"You forgot about his chains," Ali said.

I hadn't. I'd known there was no way he could climb the ladder. His chain was too short to permit it. But I pretended I had not realized this, and scrambled over to the hole and leaned in. "Sam, don't try to climb the ladder!"

Ali grasped my shoulder and pulled me back from the brink. "He won't. I convinced him to stay put. At least until you speak to him."

I leaned over the edge to shout down, but Ali dragged me up again. "No. Climb down the ladder. But do not descend into the dome. Speak quietly. I will watch here." With that, she stepped lightly over the ruin in the street and faded into the shadows of a portico of the closest building. I swung my feet into the manhole and let myself down, counting the rungs until I hit the last one.

"Sam?"

"Here."

"Ali said you wished to speak to me. I suppose it's about how to find the backpack?"

"No, sir," he said. "T'other boy already told me. And how I should follow the Old Road."

I wondered if he was going to try to lure us back down into the sewer. "Then what is it you wish?"

"To settle our debt."

"We've lived up to our end of the bargain, Sam."

"That you have," he said. "My end is what worries me."

"Your end?"

"Said I'd take you there, and that's what I intend."

"You have. We can't miss the tower from here."

"Man of my word," he said, in that measured way of his. "Nought left but that."

I wondered if lack of food and illness had addled his wits. Or if maybe I'd misread him completely, and he was the most honourable man I'd ever met. "You can't climb the ladder, Sam. The rungs are farther apart than the length of your chain. You'll fall into the cistern. If it's not deep enough to drown right away, its walls will be at least as slick as those of the tunnel. You'd never be able to climb out."

"Might, if I reach high enough."

"Don't be foolish."

There was a moment's silence. "*Foolish*." He said it just as I had, with the same inflection. "Ain't that what your friend calls you?"

I wish I could have disagreed. But I felt doubly foolish now, for taking the risk on the ladder, and for hoping to use it to abandon Sam.

"Might be," he said slowly, "I'm just as foolish."

His chain rattled then, and I feared he'd already begun climbing. "If you fall," I said quickly, "then so will I. I'd try to save you, Sam, as any good Christian would, and we'd both likely drown." It was a lie, but a well-intentioned one, the sort I like to think God overlooks.

The noise of his ascent ceased. Then I heard him sigh. "Can't say I'd feel good about that."

"By not climbing the ladder you'd be saving my life."

"And mine in the bargain. Another debt to owe you."

"I expect there's no way to talk you out of a thing when you've set your mind on it."

"None can."

"I believe that." I decided to take another tack. "Sam, you told me you wanted to escape so that you might make amends. For a man to say that,

I expect he feels he owes someone a large debt. Larger, I'd guess, than the one you think you incurred here. An honourable man would repay that first, before endangering his life, wouldn't he?"

There was another moment of silence, and I knew he was thinking on what I'd said. Then: "Spoke too soon."

"About what?"

"When I said 'None can'."

"Here's what I think, Sam. You should make your amends first. Once that's done, then you can pay me back whatever you believe you owe, if you still want to. But you don't have to, because I think you fulfilled your part of the bargain already."

"Given you haven't left much choice, it's a deal."

"Good," I said. "Deal."

The clink of his chains echoed up to where I had wedged myself; but this time I knew it for the sound they made as they were dragged along the brick floor.

"Sam?"

The noise of his movement stopped. "What?"

"I do not know why the Church believes you sinned, and I do not want to know. But you seem to me a good man."

"Not always. But thank ye for the thought."

"No one is all good," I said. "It's being good on balance that's important."

I believe he would have agreed with me, had his humility not prevented him.

"I will pray for you, Sam."

"Likewise." This time it was hard to make out his words, for he spoke over the echoing sound of his passage. Likely he was already outside the cistern and back in the sewer pipe. "Luck," I think he said, and I heard no more, save the fading scrape of his chains.

I climbed back up the ladder and Ali materialized at my side, an apparition of the night.

"Let's go," I said, anxious to be away. Although I now believed Sam as good as his word, I feared he might still have a change of heart. If he did, I didn't believe I could face him when he climbed from that hole; and, more to my shame, I did not want to hear the scream and splash should he tumble from the ladder, and so be caught in another lie.

The Babel Tower

There was a two-man watch at the base of the tower. One man patrolled while the other sat in a small camp chair in front of a sentry shack, fastidiously sharpening his halberd. Both wore breastplates and shoulder guards over the distinctive uniform of the *Cent Suisse*. From our vantage in a thick clutch of grass, we watched one *Garde* walk the same route around the sizable *piazza* several times, disappearing for a dozen heartbeats at the far side of the square behind logs stacked to twice a man's height. He reappeared, then completed his circuit by marching past windowless structures built of rough timber and about which were scattered idle wheelbarrows, carts, and hods.

We retreated along the narrow lane in which we'd been crouching, and slipped through the back door of a building whose face leaned precariously over the street. Inside, the dark was almost as complete as it had been in the sewer.

"We can circle behind," Ali said, pulling a dirk from her boot. "When the *Garde* is at the farther corner, out of sight behind the logs, we will take the other unawares."

"No." Though I didn't want to say so, I was determined not to kill again. Which would leave Ali to deal with both men by herself. As good as she was, she was much smaller and lighter than either of the two, and her short sword would be useless against the reach of a halberd. Even if she managed to sneak across the twenty metres of open ground and take the first guard by surprise, she would almost certainly have to face the second toe-to-toe. I thought her chances poor at best.

"*No?*" She looked at me as if I was the most cowardly of creatures. "What would *you* have us do?"

"Kite would not have been so rash, nor have killed men when there was no need."

She looked like she was about to say something dismissive, then seemed to think better of it. "I suppose you have a better plan?"

"Samuel told us the *Gardes* do not like to set foot on the tower."

"So?"

"The sentry post is not near the ramp to the tower, but a good distance away—maybe two hundred metres. I think that's because they are not so much worried about someone ascending the tower as about the prisoners stealing tools—hammers, chisels, picks, and so on. Things they could use to free themselves from their shackles."

I saw by her expression she hadn't considered this. She nodded. "Go on."

"Now suppose you are one of those *Gardes*, and you see a man dash up the ramp. Would you follow him? I wouldn't. He has nowhere to go. And there are hundreds of arches on the way up, so you'd have to check each one to make sure he wasn't hiding in their shadows, perhaps with a knife at the ready. No, if I were the guard, I would just wait at the foot of the ramp. At least until sun-on, when it would be much more difficult for the man to hide—and after more *Gardes* arrive with the workers."

"There are two, making it easy to check the arches."

"Only one would follow. The other would have to stay back to guard the tools."

"One, then," Ali said. "Suppose one is thick-headed enough to chase us?"

"They each bear a cuirass, shoulder armour, a morion, and a halberd. That's got to be at least twenty kilograms, maybe more. I did a rough calculation in my head, and I figure the ramp, if its inclination is a bit less than ten degrees, to be at least two and half kilometres. It will be tiring for us, hustling uphill for that distance. But for the *Garde* it would be exhausting. We could outdistance him easily, and still have plenty of time to see what there is to see at the summit."

"And if we can't figure out what to do before he reaches us?"

"Then I will stand next to you, and at least we will have three advantages we would not have had before: we will have to fight only one man, that man will be winded, and we will hold the higher ground."

Ali chewed on her lower lip for a moment, mulling it over. I'm sure she could have raised several objections to my scheme; I certainly could have. But she didn't. She knew that, as shaky as it was, my plan had one great strength: it was simple. And when a plan was simple, there were fewer things that could go wrong, a lesson Kite had oft repeated.

When the *Garde* was on the last leg of his rounds, at the farthest point from the tower, we broke from cover and tore across the *piazza*. We were halfway when the thump of our steps roused the guard by the shack. He leapt to his feet, and shouted a challenge, but stood his post—as I had hoped. A moment later the second *Garde* appeared from behind the tool shed, halberd now clutched in two hands, as he ran back to the sentry post. There was a brief exchange between them, but I couldn't hear what they were saying over the pounding of our feet and my heart. Just as my toes touched the first stone at the base of the ramp, the *Garde* who'd been patrolling set out after us.

Ali and I raced up the ramp, which was smooth and wide enough for six men to walk abreast. The arches were massive, larger than I had thought, and there were countless rows, built one atop the other, to support the tower. Inside I glimpsed a cubical structure around which the tower was wrapped. There were no rails at the edge of the ramp, so I ran as close to the arches as I could, quickly losing sight of both *Gardes* as we rose; when we'd made the opposite side, we were already a good fifty metres above the *piazza*, and that difference grew by another fifty as we completed our first circuit—there were half a dozen more to the top. The sentry shack was far enough away that I could still see the *Garde* at his post, neck craned to watch us; but the other *Garde* was nowhere in sight. If he was on the tower as we were, or standing near the base of the ramp, I would have had to move to the edge to see him, which I didn't dare do, not running full out as I was. I've never been overly fond of heights, though I can stand them well enough. But Ali seemed to have no fear, for she darted away from the tower wall and ran dangerously close to the lip, her sandals slapping within a few centimetres of the edge. Without breaking stride, she pointed down, and I took that to mean the second man had followed us up the ramp. I tried to pick up the pace.

The sentry shack came into sight again as we completed our second circuit; Ali, who'd opened some distance between us, slowed to a trot to wait for me to catch up. By my calculation we'd already run well over a thousand metres, and risen about two hundred. Running on an incline was harder than I had anticipated. My lungs were already burning, I was soaked in sweat, and my legs and thighs complained in ways they never had before. I struggled after Ali as best I could.

Ali paused at the end of the third circuit and laid herself down to peer over the edge of the ramp; I collapsed behind her, clutching at the stitch in my side, gasping for breath. Almost immediately, she sprang up, scanned the tower above us, and set off again, saying over her shoulder, "He gains," as if she'd known all along that my plan was doomed to failure. She set off with an odd, elongated gait, and counted out each stride to herself. With a grunt, I pushed myself to my feet and struggled after her.

As we circled for the fourth time, we passed scaffolding, wooden tubs, paddles for mixing cement and mortar, and bags of lime the prisoners had stacked near the edge of the ramp as a makeshift rail. I knew we must be near the top, and so looked up. Directly above the summit of the tower there were small differences in the firmament—the hint of an edge, a shadow that should not have been there—all invisible from the ground. For a moment I felt a strange sense of vertigo, as if I was looking down instead of up, and that the top of the tower plunged into a hole. Then everything snapped into place in the same way a line drawing of a vase suddenly becomes two faces, and I knew the tower had been built into the upper chamber of an Assumption.

Ali stopped and leaned over the bags of lime, and I followed suit. The *Garde* was nowhere is sight; I couldn't even hear the thump of his steps. While I peered into the dark, Ali rolled the bag next to me over the edge; her lips moved, counting soundlessly to four before the bag hit the ramp below. Then she dragged me down into a squat behind the bags.

"Stay out of sight." She poked her head over the bags to peer down to the ramp below. "When I tell you, heave the bags in front of you over the edge with whatever strength you have."

I heard the slap of sandals on the ramp below. I stood. "He believes he's doing right. I—"

"*Now!*"

I did not do as she asked; I did not want to kill that innocent man.

But what I was reluctant to do, she accomplished on her own. In a few seconds, she heaved three bags over the side. Her first was premature, and thudded down in front of the *Garde*. The second would have missed, too, had he not skidded to a halt. As he looked up, the second bag hit him square in the face. I heard the sound of the impact and two nauseating snaps of bone as the concussion drove him down like a nail being hammered into wood. Absurdly, his halberd, the butt of which he'd planted on the ramp, stood on its own for a fraction of second, before it fell slowly out from the tower, toppling over the edge of the ramp and clattering from sight.

As I began mouthing a prayer for both his soul and Ali's, she slapped my face. I staggered backwards, and might have toppled over those bags to my death had she not grabbed my shirt and steadied me. "Do not pray for my forgiveness," she said. "Look to your own salvation first."

Releasing my shirt, she turned back to the bags of lime, and pushed another four over in quick succession. I didn't look, but some, at least, must have hit their mark, for Ali appeared to be satisfied. "Let's go," she said, setting out at an unhurried pace.

I followed numbly, a hand on my stinging cheek.

We circled the tower for the last time, moving above suns, and I realized those black oblongs had turned to grey. Dawn was upon us. We climbed farther until we rose past the lower edge of the Assumption and were surrounded by its featureless walls.

At the peak of the tower the ramp levelled, then jutted out so that it seemed to hang over nothing; at its brink was a raised wooden drawbridge. I looked to where the bridge, when lowered, would meet the wall of Assumption, but there was no sign of a doorway. Drawing her sword, Ali slashed the thick ropes holding the bridge aloft, and it swung ponderously down to the horizontal, where chains secured to its end snapped taut, arresting its progress centimetres from the wall. Seams split the wall where the bridge met it, and a door, no different than the doors in the other Assumptions I'd travelled, swung inward, framing a darkness as black as an unrepentant soul. Ali turned to me, beautiful and frightening in the sombre light. "Heaven waits."

I confess I never thought we'd make it this far. And I had little faith that if we did, we'd find a way into Lower Heaven. Meussin had told us she believed the Angels had plans for us; and Ali had told me the Angels would grant us sanctuary. Yet I found myself faltering on the doorstep. My sins were many and weighed heavily upon me; I knew my soul was not prepared. If I were to enter Heaven now, I thought it likely I'd have no chance for redemption. Crossing that threshold seemed to me akin to stepping into eternal damnation.

I turned; the point of Ali's blade hovered centimetres from my throat. She backed me onto the bridge. "I know what you are thinking,

Thomas, and you need not worry. If you enter Lower Heaven, you will not be judged. There will be plenty of time for more hand-wringing about your sins. Or, if you prefer, I can kill you right now and let God judge you as you stand."

She was right about my fears, but only partly so—there were other reasons I was reluctant to enter Lower Heaven, ones which I'd rather not share with her.

"What's it to be?"

I liked neither choice she gave me. Or a third she hadn't: I could cast myself from the bridge. I would still be judged, but at least Ali would not have the stain of another murder on her soul. I turned and walked to the door. At the other Assumptions, there had always been lit torches and Jesuits waiting. Here, only undifferentiated black. Without looking back, I said, "I'm sorry for what I did."

I waited, but she said nothing.

Unable to bear her silence, I swung around. Her sword was still raised, only she stared at me not with the hated or scorn I'd expected; rather, it was a look of pity. "You needn't be sorry," she said, "I don't blame you. If I had, you'd have been dead long ago."

I don't blame you.

Why is it that we desire most what we can't have? Or is that the crucible of desire itself? I desired Ali, more than I'd desired anything. Meussin had told me flatly my feelings would never be reciprocated. Yet, in the novels she so loved, there was no lack of spurned suitors who ultimately won over the object of their desire. I know now how naive this must sound, but it gave me hope, even though I'd already realized that, like the *Holy Book*, these fictions told us what we wanted to hear. In the Bible is evidence of an all-seeing father, one who loves us, and forgives us, despite our flaws. How could one not want such a father? And so I convinced myself there was hope with Ali, and built my case on the slimmest evidence—a look, a word, a casual gesture—something, anything, to show she might harbour some latent affection for me. And when one looks this scrupulously for a sign, one is bound to find it, whether it is there or not.

Perhaps that's why I said, "I love you."

Ali's face contorted into equal measures of astonishment and disgust, and I felt my heart plummet as if it had been torn from my chest and cast over the side of the bridge. She lowered her sword until its tip rested on the deck of the bridge. "Christ Jesus, save us," she said, then straight-armed me.

I staggered backwards and tumbled into oblivion.

Heaven

Experience is ofttimes the better teacher, and such was the case with the Jesuit's lesson: *Your body has grown in the context of a certain gravitational acceleration, and so its systems depend on this to move your fluids. Changing the gravity too quickly would disrupt the flow of these fluids and cause you to lose consciousness—or worse.* In crossing the threshold into the greatly diminished gravity of Lower Heaven, I'd fainted.

Opening my eyes, I saw the shadowy arch of the Assumption's corridor looming over me. I tasted bile, and my head throbbed cruelly. I don't think these were entirely the effect of the sudden change in gravity, for as I lifted my head from the stone flags, a spike of pain emanated from a single spot on the crown of my skull; I touched the place and felt the stickiness of blood. *Ali*, was my first thought: she must have struck me as I lay prone. With my addled wits, it took me a moment to realize this would have been impossible. She, too, would have lost consciousness as she stepped through the doorway. The momentum from her shove had done the damage.

I lifted my head slightly higher—and the corridor wobbled around me. When the sickening movement of the world dwindled to a slight rocking, I saw Ali next to me, out cold. Her breath was uneven and her face looked pallid and puffy. I placed my fingers on her throat (something I'd never dare do if I thought her conscious) and was rewarded with a steady pulse.

I was incredulous. Somehow, we'd passed into Lower Heaven and were not dead.

But what Lower Heaven had not taken, the *Gardes* would. I looked around the gloomy corridor. The door was wide open, and outside, the deck of the bridge was in shadow as the light of the sun shone up from the last Sphere of men. I knew that I had only a few moments to shut the door before the *Gardes* arrived. I had an idea about who had opened the door—and if I was right, I also knew it wouldn't shut unless I sealed it myself.

I tentatively pushed myself into a sitting position; a fresh wave of giddiness washed over me, but passed more quickly this time. Girding myself, I gained my legs. My head spun and my stomach wanted to heave its contents, but I managed to cling to the wall. I felt incredibly light, as if I could float away. My muscles, attuned to a much higher gravity, might easily fool me into stepping too far or too high, overshooting the mark, and a fall here would just as likely result in broken bones as it would in the lower Spheres since my mass was the same. I touched my head lightly, where it had hit the stone flags.

Dragging my feet along the floor, not daring to lift them, I fought the temptation to move faster; even so, my progress kicked up a pall of slow moving dust that quickly coated the back of my throat, tasting of an age of disuse.

This, I thought, *is not the Heaven I expected.*

Reaching the threshold, I cocked my head to listen. There were no sounds of pursuit, just a high-pitched ringing that seemed to have taken up permanent residence in my ears. I pulled Ali's legs clear of the door, then touched it where I had seen the Jesuits touch it. The black panel swung shut and sealed itself, choking off all light. The air did not stir, and in a moment of blind panic I fancied myself suffocating. *Calm yourself,* I thought. *Even if there is not much air to breath, you can open the door anytime you wish.* This comforted me, but I still couldn't help wondering if I'd just sealed us in a tomb.

Feeling my way along the wall, I moved back to where Ali lay, then let myself slide down next to her. I thought of how I had dissuaded her from fetching the lamp before we'd entered the sewer, and recognized myself twice the fool for it now.

I considered our situation, and saw only three options: I could leave Ali here and look for help; I could carry her and seek help; or I could wait for her to regain consciousness. I decided to carry her. Until now, all the Assumptions I'd been in had the same layout. If this one did as well, I should be able to navigate the darkness. I crouched, carefully worked my arms under Ali's shoulders and knees, and lifted her with remarkable ease. As light as she was, carrying her was sometimes awkward in that confined space, and I worried that her head or feet might strike some object invisible to me; so I moved sideways, her feet in front, and my back scraping along the wall, to keep my balance in the vertiginous dark.

As in the other Assumptions, this corridor led directly from the platform to a weighing room. My fear had been that the door between the two would be barred from the inside, like it had been in Rome, but it was wide open, swung back against the inner wall and canted on a slight angle, as if it had been torn away from its top hinge. My confidence buoyed; in the other Assumptions, there was only one more door we needed to pass through to reach the outside gates, and that door had always been barred from the side we were now on. The gates, however, would be a different matter. The Assumption was clearly neglected, and if either of the portcullises were down, and the winches inoperable, it might not be possible to raise them.

I worked my way around the edge of the room until I found the door. It was closed, but not barred. I laid Ali on the floor, lifted the latch, and pulled.

Blinding luminescence flooded the room, and fresh air rushed past me into the crypt of the inner Assumption. It took my eyes a moment to adjust. When they did, I saw an inhumanly tall figure, stooping beneath the iron spikes of the raised portcullis. It was naked and hairless, with a massive, distended chest that ran from shoulder to pelvis, and its limbs were thin and elongated. Here and there on its pallid body were long, red ulcerations and patches of discoloured skin, like those I'd seen on the diseased beggars in the streets of *Los Angeles Nuevo* and Rome. If it had a sex, I couldn't tell, for where its reproductive organs would have been hung a flap of skin, like a loincloth. On the left side of its skull was a large, distended growth, which no doubt accounted for the peculiar position of its head, cocked like a bird's. It regarded us implacably through milky white eyes, which had no irises. What was most remarkable of all, however, was that rising above the figure's head, and visible behind the latticed grill of the gate, were the curves of its great folded wings.

It held aloft a lamp in which burned a trinity of unnatural white flames. They were round rather than tapered, and did not jump or flicker, unlike the bright yellow flames of every other lamp I'd ever seen.

"Zeracheil!"

Ali must have crawled from the weighing room, for she was on her hands and knees beside me, swaying. "I have done as I promised," she said, then vomited. Bile spattered my sandal.

But the Angel's eyes remained fixed on me. "Do you have faith?" Its voice was neither a man's nor a woman's, but something in between. So, too, its face, which, had it not been marred by the lesions and that growth, would have been astonishingly beautiful—or handsome, if you prefer. Both words seemed equally inadequate.

Unable to speak, I nodded.

"Good," said the Archangel Zeracheil, then swung around awkwardly in that space too small for it, and hobbled toward the light of Lower Heaven.

As Ignatius had warned me, Lower Heaven was both more and less than I'd imagined.

We stepped from the Assumption—Ali's arm over my shoulder for her support as much as mine—and found ourselves atop a hill. I was struck by the sheer scale of things. We'd been taught that this was the largest of all Spheres. What the Priests hadn't told us (or perhaps didn't know) was that the distance to the firmament, which by my reckoning had increased slightly as we'd risen from the Apostle John's Sphere to that of Saint Peter, more than doubled here, and the suns were at least a kilometre above. The openness thus produced unnerved and disoriented me. I felt exposed, as if a protective mantle had been stripped away, and I wondered if this was akin to how Adam and Eve felt at the moment they lost their innocence and learned shame.

The second thing that struck me was that ordinary things, like trees and grass, grew taller here, perhaps twice the height they did in the Apostle Peter's Sphere below.

Other than that, the rest of the scene was unremarkable, even mundane.

There was no road outside the gate, or sign that there ever had been one; just a field of unusually tall, sere grass running down to a creek. Beyond that, an endless, overgrown wood, looking no different (save for the unusual height of its trees) than the forest through which we'd travelled in the Sphere below. I'm not sure what I'd expected, but I felt disappointed by the ordinariness of it all.

Next to me, Ali clutched her stomach and doubled over, retching again. Perhaps it was a sympathetic response, but I, too, was battered by a wave of nausea, and felt my gorge rise; I tightened my throat to keep my last meal down.

"You feel a natural disorientation," said Zeracheil. "It may last anywhere from a few hours to a few days. If you cannot walk, you may use the litter." The Angel pointed. Near the wall of the Assumption was a large palanquin with two poles; the platform itself was bare and carved from a single piece of oak. Despite the lack of bearers, the whole thing floated a metre above the ground. I would have been astounded to witness such a miracle—if we'd not been in Heaven.

I helped Ali onto the platform. It didn't move, not even a centimetre, as if it sat upon legs firmly anchored in the ground.

"Would you ride, too, David?" The Archangel Zeracheil towered over me.

"I . . . I would like to walk. I think it will help."

"As you wish." The Angel's manner of speaking was slow and oddly distracted, as if its attention was divided between this and another plane of existence. "You may find it easier by holding the poles. If you feel faint, they will bear your weight."

I did so, and was grateful for the support.

"You may push, and the litter will move. If you tire, let us know and we will do what we can to help you."

I leaned forward a bit, and the palanquin moved.

"This way," Zeracheil said, and began walking around the periphery of the Assumption, moving like an injured bird, the tips of its frayed wings dragging along the ground.

I followed, and would have fallen at least twice, had I not had the poles to cling to. Each step carried me farther than I wanted, and this disrupted the rhythm of walking my body had come to expect. I tried to adjust the length of my stride to account for this strange buoyancy, but still found myself slipping and sliding—worse, I started to fall backwards on extended steps. So I stopped striding altogether, and hopped, feet apart, pushing off on my back foot and landing on my front. It seemed to work reasonably well and was far less dangerous than trying to walk.

I caught up to Zeracheil as he turned the corner on the opposite side of the Assumption. "May I ask a question?"

The Archangel stopped and nodded, a somber dip of a head twice the size of my own.

"When are we to be judged?"

The Angel, its head still cocked, stared at me—or, rather, through me to some other place. "When you die."

I was not dead; leastways I didn't think I was, for my heart still beat, and my head throbbed with the ache of the living. "Then we are not to be judged?"

"All men are judged," Zeracheil said, "when they die."

I glanced at Ali to see what she made of this; although she seemed better, she stared off into the middle distance, rubbing her temples and showing no interest in the exchange. "But must we not be judged to enter Heaven?"

"You are here, are you not?"

"Yes."

"Then the answer to your question is no."

The relief I felt was tempered by unease at the strangeness of Zeracheil's answers—it was my first inkling that the minds of Angels ran differently from ours. I had more questions, but worried that in asking I might discover I'd misunderstood what the Angel had already said. I preferred to believe that I still had a chance of redemption. So I left my questions unasked.

Zeracheil turned and hobbled on, stopping on the margin of a narrow dirt track, the sort that wild game make. The path snaked down through the grass and disappeared into the forest. "Follow this to the house of Zeracheil," the Angel said, in the same affectless tone it said everything.

"Are you not coming with us?" I asked.

"We cannot travel farther." It indicated the wood that lay between, and I took this to mean the path was too narrow to accommodate its height or the span of its folded wings. "Stay on the path and beware the animals. They are unaccustomed to man." It unfurled majestic wings, throwing us in shadow.

"Wait!" I shouted. The Angel stood over me, its wings slowly collapsing onto its back. "What about those who were following us?"

"The door is closed," the Angel said. "They are barred from Lower Heaven."

"They would not have built the tower unless they believed they could breach the Assumption."

"God made them, and they cannot unmake themselves. They do what they must."

I didn't understand the Angel's cryptic answer. Nor its fatalistic nonchalance on the cusp of an invasion. "You must know they mean to take Lower Heaven."

The Angel's wings lifted in a perfunctory shrug. "If it is God's will."

"Don't you care?"

Zeracheil showed no expression. "God made us. We do what we must."

I'd come here at the urging of people who wanted to aid the Angels. But the Angels—or this one, at least—seemed indifferent to their own plight. I essayed no response, and Zeracheil must have taken this as a sign the conversation was at an end. It spread its great wings again; they beat heavily, throwing mad swirls of dust into the air. I closed my eyes against the miniature storm. By the time I opened them, the Angel was already over the wood. As awkward as it was on the ground, in the air it was the embodiment of grace. I watched it recede.

"Zeracheil called you David."

I turned to Ali. "He did." I could think of no reason to lie. "It's my real name," I said, then added, "I'd nearly forgotten."

"David," she said, trying it out on her tongue. "Zeracheil knew your real name. I'd have expected you to be surprised."

"It's an Angel," I said. "A messenger of God. And God has perfect knowledge."

"Then why didn't it know you lied about having faith?"

I felt my face flush. "I didn't lie."

By her expression, I knew Ali saw through me. And she was right; I was no longer certain of my faith. All that happened to me, everything I'd seen and heard, had planted the seeds of doubt. It's true I had not wanted to enter Heaven for fear of being judged; but, even more so, for fear of *not* being judged. I worried that here I would see the promise of judgement and reward for what they were: lies used to console and control the faithful. If you'd asked me right then, I'd have said this seemed to be the way of things, for here I was. Perhaps it was the lingering strands of my own faith asserting themselves—or, more likely, a desire to hear my own arguments from another's lips—but I leapt to the defence of my tattered beliefs. "The Angels have greater knowledge than men, but are not omniscient. Matthew says so."

"They cannot read the minds of men. And we would fight for them, though they wouldn't fight for themselves." Ali spat. "You and Matthew credit them too much."

I ignored her sacrilege. My sacrilege. "We should be going." I scanned the horizon for Zeracheil, and in the far distance saw half a dozen winged creatures, which might have been Angels—but they banked sharply, and I knew them for mere birds. "Zeracheil did not say how long it would take, and I would not wish to be in the wood after sun-off." I thought about the wolves in the Sphere below and wondered aloud how much bigger the ones here might be.

"The house of Zeracheil's is over the next rise," Ali said, "and there are no wolves in these woods, though there are bears and other such animals that might do us harm." With a grunt, she rolled herself off the platform onto unsteady feet, and drew her sword from it scabbard. "The animals are bigger than those in the lower Spheres, but their muscles and frames are weak by comparison. Like the Angels, they are fragile. Our swords should be sufficient protection." She took a first tentative hop, moving in the same manner I had decided worked best. "You are right, David. I believe a walk in Heaven would do us both good."

With that, she set off down the path, and I stared after her, open-mouthed, wondering if the Angels had told her these things—or if perhaps this wasn't her first time in Lower Heaven.

A Choir of Angels

Loping—which is what I'd come to think of our strange way of moving—through the wood, I was taken by the size of the flora and fauna. Flowers, plants, and trees were half again the size I would have called normal. So, too, with the few animals we saw. A mouse as big as a squirrel, a squirrel as big as a rabbit, and a hare the size of a dog, each disproportionately large compared to its diminutive relatives in the lesser Spheres. Without man to thin their ranks, I expected the woods to be teeming. Yet, there were far fewer creatures than we'd seen in the Sphere below. And, for all their size, the animals also seemed less hale. The hare's fur had looked patchy in places, and in the instant the mouse darted across the trail, I am quite sure I saw red lesions similar to Zeracheil's. I thought then of the four paltry birds I'd seen earlier, and wondered what might have happened to the multitudinous flocks that ofttimes darkened the sky in the Spheres below.

We topped the rise and descended into the valley beyond. As the ground levelled, the tangle of woods ended unexpectedly, and we found ourselves stepping onto a path of gravel leading into a garden. All manner of plants were on display—shade trees and fruit trees with leaves both broad and thin; shrubs, creepers, vines, and ferns of all description; and flowers, bed after bed of flowers, with blooms in all shapes and hues. I recognized only a few, which I knew by the stunted cousins on our estate. Most, however, were novel to me; I'd never dreamt there could be such variety and abundance in all the Spheres.

As we moved through the garden, I wondered who maintained it. The paths were too narrow and, in many places, the plants too close set for an Angel of Zeracheil's size not to snag its wings. Nor could I imagine the messengers of God devoting the time it would take, kneeling in front of the flower beds, instead of at prayer. Yet the gardens were meticulously cultivated—twice, ripe fruit fell when I brushed against a low-hanging branch, but there was not one stray apple to be seen. I had my answer sooner than I thought: I caught sight of a spider-like thing, a black bowl for a body, turning over soil in a flower bed, using its unnaturally straight legs like a set of small spades. I don't believe it was an insect or animal, at least not the kind of thing we think of when we use those words, for its carapace had the sheen of polished metal. Once I knew what to look for, I realized the garden was fairly overrun with the creatures, all busily digging, climbing, tilling, planting, and pruning.

About a kilometre from the wood, we came upon Zeracheil's house.

Each Angel, the Church had told us, lived in its own palace, and I suppose this was true after a fashion. But this structure was not palatial—it was perhaps twenty-five metres square, smaller, but cubic like an Assumption, and appeared to be made of the same white stone. There were five floors, each about five metres in height. Curiously, a wall on each of the stories seemed to be missing, exposing the interior, and I realized this was done so that the Angels could fly directly to that floor. There were no architectural flourishes or exterior decorations of any kind. The building itself, from the outside at least, looked not like a palace, but more like a warehouse, a perfection of function over form.

We circled until we found a side where there was no wall.

I had been concerned that, given the shelter the house provided, wild beasts might have taken up residence. But there were none—at least on the ground floor (nor were there staircases that would have permitted us to explore the upper floors). I guessed that the same thing that kept the wolves at bay was at work here, too. The rooms through which we walked were bare, save one in which we found a few furnishings: stools rising high as my chin, arranged around a square table under which I could walk with only a slight bend. There was no carpeting, but between rooms there were curtains that could be drawn for privacy. I saw nothing that resembled a kitchen, a bathroom, or a bedroom, and assumed these might be found in the upper stories—though, for all I knew, it might be that Angels had no need of sustenance or of rest. Curiously, there were no Crosses or any other religious adornments on the walls. This put me in mind of the description of Heaven in Revelations: *I could not see any temple in the city since the Lord God Almighty and the Lamb were themselves the temple, and the city did not need the sun or the moon for light, since it was lit by the radiant glory of God, and the Lamb was a lighted torch for it.* I suppose this close to God such tokens were unnecessary.

In the centre of the house was an atrium open to the sky, and here three Angels waited for us beside a pool that must have been fed by a subterranean stream.

All were remarkably similar in appearance—almost exactly the same height, weight, and girth. The same held with age, none young and none old. If they'd been men, I'd have guessed they were just shy of mid-age. Even so, there was something ageless about them, and if you told me they were as old as the world, I'd not have been surprised. As for their faces, they looked the same, much as brothers or sisters do, distinguishable not so much by the slight variations in their sculpted features as by the unique constellation of diseased pigmentation and ulcerations that seemed to infest them all. Like Zeracheil, the other two had visible tumours—one on its shoulder, like a hump; the other beneath its right eye, swelling it shut. Had they not had these deformities, they would have been uniformly striking. The two new Angels leaned back upon their wings, and I realized this, and the backless stools, were perhaps the only way Angels could rest. All three regarded us impassively through milky eyes.

I should have been anxious or relieved, but I was too exhausted to feel much of anything. However, beside me, I sensed the tension rise in Ali and coil like a snake. I had thought that anger reserved for me; but it seemed directed as much at the Angels now. Zeracheil stepped forward, and the other two Angels rolled forward off their wings.

"That one is the Archangel Uriel." Zeracheil indicated the Angel with the hump. Then, nodding at the one with the closed eye, said, "That one is the Archangel Raphael."

All three had watched me through those empty eyes since we'd stepped into the atrium; none had given Ali so much as a glance.

"You wish to know why we brought you here."

I conceded I did.

The Angel named Uriel said, "We have an indulgence to ask of you, David. Two, perhaps, depending on the outcome of the first." Its voice had the same lilting quality as Zeracheil's, but was of a slightly different timbre. Both, though, could have sung contralto or countertenor with ease. "You may accept or decline. And you will be given time to think before you do so."

I nodded. What else was I to do?

The Angel Raphael stepped towards me; Ali went rigid. "We wish you to perform a task that is impossible for us and likely dangerous for you." Raising a long, palsied finger, the Angel pointed straight up, to the firmament, squinting at me with its one good eye. "Between New Jerusalem and Lower Heaven are God's gift of the Waters Above. When the suns go off, we wish you to swim them."

God made the vault, and it divided the waters under the vault from the waters above the vault. I'd once asked Father Finn, who took great pleasure in reading us Genesis, how this could be, an ocean above Heaven, and he'd given me a reproachful look and his stock response, that faith made anything possible. I wondered how exultant he'd feel if he could have heard this confirmation from an Angel's lips. Yet hearing it brought me no joy. I tried to imagine an ocean of water above us, and felt its immense weight pressing down on my soul. "And what am I to do there?"

"Look, so that you might tell us what you find."

"You said it would be dangerous."

"We cannot be certain, David," Zeracheil said.

"You must breach the top surface of the Waters Above," Raphael said. "We are God's messengers, and must dwell in Lower Heaven, nearer men. *We* have not seen the Glory that is the City of God." Though I came to learn that Angels rarely evince emotion—leastwise emotion of the sort we'd recognize—there was something in its inflection that suggested longing. "You were sickened coming here. Above the Waters the transition may be greater. If you faint, you will drown. Nor are things in the Waters Above like those in the material world, for souls have no need of air. God might have provided none, or in its place made something completely different, something unfit for man or beast or Angel."

"If you speak to God, can you not ask Him what lies there?"

"We do not speak to God, he speaks to us," Raphael said, in a manner that made it clear it would not brook further discussion.

"If I decline?"

Though I was looking at Raphael, Zeracheil answered. "You may return to a lower Sphere as soon as it is feasible."

There is little point in relating the balance of the conversation. I asked a few more questions, which the Angels answered—or did their best to, though I am not sure they fully comprehended all that I was asking, just as I didn't fully comprehend some of their answers. By and by, I said, "I'm tired, and would like time to think on it more, as you said I might." This was only partly true; though I was, indeed, fatigued, I had more questions I wanted to ask. But not in Ali's presence.

The three Angels regarded one another with their cloudy, unfathomable eyes, something passing between them, though they never uttered a word. Zeracheil turned to me. "Rest, then," it said. "You may draw water from this pool. Take as much fruit as you wish. You will be safe as long as you stay in the garden. Behind is a room where you may sleep. We have made bedding such as we could. When your mind and body are more accustomed to Lower Heaven, we will hear your answer."

Thus saying, Zeracheil unfurled its wings and beat down, breaking the stillness of the morning sky. Raphael and Uriel followed, and in only a few seconds all three had flown from the atrium, and so were lost to sight.

Ali had already made her way over to the pool; there was a bucket there, and she picked it up and dipped it into the water.

I was certain this wasn't the first time she'd met Raphael. I considered asking her about this, and if she knew of the first boon they'd ask me, and what the second might be. But I decided against it. We'd managed little sleep in the last two days, and I was dead tired and still feeling more than a little sick. If anything, Heaven had been harder on her. I took my lead from Zeracheil and decided that I, too, would wait patiently until Ali's state improved enough that I might have a better chance of a reasonable answer.

I watched her tilt the bucket up; she drank deeply, then, closing her eyes, leaned back and emptied the rest over her head. Saturated, her usually shapeless clothes clung to every curve and hollow, and my imprudent heart thumped furiously in my chest; in that moment, Ali possessed me, infected me, burning brightly in my blood like a fever.

Dropping the bucket, she walked into the house, in the direction of the room where Zeracheil had said we might sleep, leaving dark, wet footsteps in her wake.

God Weeps

From a sleep haunted by visions of damnation, I woke on a bed of moss the Angels had arranged, feeling bleary and unsteady, as if I hadn't rested at all. Rising, I discovered that the corner Ali had staked out for herself was empty, though the outline of her shape was still pressed into the weave of plants. I looked out a small window, into the garden, thinking I might see her there, only to discover the suns were already beginning to dim. I had slept the night through and then much of the next day.

In the atrium, I found Zeracheil waiting for me, sitting on the end of the palanquin, a wing draped over either side. In one hand it held a slender stick, as long as I was tall. Fruit lined the rim of the pool, and a full bucket of water had been drawn. In silence, I ate and drank the small amount I could stomach, the Angel regarding me patiently the whole time.

When I finished, I said, "Where is Ali?"

"In the wood. She wishes meat."

I felt relief; I had worried that the Angels had returned her to the Sphere below—or worse. "I am rested," I said, though there wasn't much truth in it, "and ready to answer your question. If first you would answer some of mine."

"Free will requires you understand the consequences of your choices, and so you may ask whatever you deem important to this understanding."

"Why me? Are there not other men who would do this for you?"

"Men do not abide in Lower Heaven."

"Yet Ali and I are here."

"You are the first to have been beyond the gates of Lower Heaven's Assumption."

"You said I might leave. Is this true whether or not I agree to do your bidding?"

"Yes."

"Ali, too?"

"If you do our bidding, perhaps. If not, then no."

I had been afraid of something like this—it was why I had wanted a clearer head before I made any decisions. "You say *perhaps*. What do you mean?"

"What you find in the Waters Above will determine where Ali is sent."

"I will do as you ask," I said, "on one condition. That after I perform the first indulgence, and regardless of whether or not I choose to perform the second, Ali and I will be returned together to the Sphere below."

Zeracheil shut its eyes, and I held my breath. Whether it was communing with other Angels, or merely reflecting within the corridors of its own mind, I couldn't guess. After a moment, the Angel nodded, as if to someone not present, then opened its unsettling eyes. "Would you make an oath to God that you will consider the second indulgence after completing the first?"

"I would," I said, truthfully, though I couldn't imagine any circumstance that might make me accept the second—and I had good reason to want to leave Heaven as quickly as possible.

"We will not compel Ali to accompany you. But if she is willing, we agree to your condition."

"Thank you," I said.

The Angel Zeracheil pushed itself off the palanquin and essayed a slight bow.

"I have more questions."

"You may ask."

"When Ali told me an Angel speaks to her, she said *an* Angel. One."

"This is the way," said Zeracheil. "Each Angel may speak to one soul."

"When an Angel speaks to a person, is it the same way it speaks to other Angels?"

"The same, and different, as our minds are."

"Could you speak to me in the same way?"

"No."

"Is it because you already speak to someone else?"

"An Angel does not Possess you, and so your mind cannot hear."

"Yet an Angel may Possess a man? Any man?"

"Yes, if the man assents."

"If a man is Possessed, he hears his Angel, no matter where in the world he might be?"

"Yes," Zeracheil said, then added, "but not all listen."

"Then why not Possess me?"

"Some minds, strong minds, resist Possession. Such a struggle may end in madness. We would not chance that with you."

"Ali is Possessed, isn't she?"

"Yes."

"That's how you knew to open the door." And why I knew, with Ali unconscious, I'd have to shut it myself.

"She spoke with her Possessor."

"Is her Possessor the Angel Raphael?"

"Yes."

"Why did you ask me to swim the Waters Above? If Raphael speaks to her, why not Ali? She could describe what she sees to him."

"It was not part of her covenant. We asked. She refused."

"Why not compel her?"

"God has gifted man with free will. It is not for the Angels to take away."

I thought on this a moment. "When I asked you to send Ali back with me, you said *We will not compel her.* You didn't say *We cannot compel her.* Does this mean her Possessor can compel her, if it wishes?"

"She has a soul and so free will."

"And what of the vessel of the soul? May the Possessor compel that?"

Zeracheil stared at me for a moment, likely trying to understand my intent. "If its soul assents," Zeracheil said slowly, "its vessel may be compelled."

I wasn't comfortable that I fully understood Zeracheil's response, so I tried to think of another way to ask my question. "If I took an oath to do something, and changed my mind, might I still be compelled to fulfill my promise?"

"An oath in God's name," said the Angel, "is inviolable."

Ali's Angel had spoken to her, and, through her, guided us to Lower Heaven. Yet that, in itself, wouldn't have been enough. If not for my egregious sin, and the guilt and remorse it engendered, I would not have allowed Ali to bring me here. Had the Angels known this, too? And knowing this, had they *compelled* Ali the day I'd raped her? I'd never bested her in any of our practise sessions with Kite—save when she'd wanted me to. And yet, in my fragmented memories of that day, she'd struggled furiously. Yet I still managed to pin her to the ground.

I wondered, then, if the Angels had contrived everything that led me here. . . .

Staring at Zeracheil, his face a blank page, my suspicion hardened into a sickening certainty, one that shook my belief, not only in the Angels, but in a just and caring Creator—for how could I believe in a God who would let his Messengers use a girl in such a way, or coax a boy into mortal sin?

Worse, I believed Ali was about to commit another mortal sin, one for which there could be no forgiveness. *I don't blame you*, she'd said to me on the bridge. *If I had, you'd have been dead long ago.* Who, then, did she blame, if not the Angels? Her Angel. And so I knew she meant to kill Raphael.

I did my best to hide my alarm. "I would talk with the Archangel Raphael."

"That one has departed, to do God's will."

"Departed?"

"Raphael makes for the other side of Lower Heaven."

I had hoped to meet the Angel face-to-face and kill it—so that Ali might not. I owed her this much, at least. But with the news that Raphael had departed, I felt a surge of relief. Though I hated the Angel for what it had done, I had no taste for murder, and was grateful for the reprieve. Flying to the opposite side of Lower Heaven and back would, I imagined, require several days. With a bit of luck, we'd be back in the Apostle Peter's Sphere before then.

But there were still things I needed to understand. "When we return to the lower Spheres, will Raphael continue to speak to Ali?"

"Yes."

"If this is the case," I said, "I fear for her sanity."

"As do I." It was the first time I'd heard Zeracheil not use the ubiquitous *we* with which all Angels referred to themselves. "Yet she made a covenant."

"I know I have already promised to perform your first indulgence, and I will be as good as my word. But I have a second boon to ask of you." I drew a breath. "If I do this thing, will you release Ali from her pledge?"

"We cannot give back what has been promised to God—and to Raphael."

There was nothing to be done for the moment, then, save to complete the first task as fast as possible, so that I might hasten our departure. Raphael had said that before I could swim the waters, we must wait for the suns to go off. I looked to the firmament; the last light of day was leaking away, and the suns would be off within the hour. I told Zeracheil I was anxious to get on with it.

The Angel handed me the stick it had been holding, and explained what he wished me to do with it. A short time later it directed me to climb onto the palanquin. Zeracheil beat its great wings, lifting towards the firmament, and the platform rose, drifting obediently in the Angel's wake. There was nothing to cling to, so I lay flat, as far away from the dizzying height as possible, even though Zeracheil had assured me the hand of God would not falter. The platform rose smoothly and steadily, the gentle waft of air from the Angel's wings tousling my hair.

Presently, I caught sight of a strange shower of water, only a few metres wide. I looked up and saw that, far above, a narrow stream ran off the back of a dwindling sun, fanning out into the gentle rain before us. I knew what its source must be. As I watched it fall, I considered the intrigues of the Church and of the diseased Angels, and of my plotting the murder of one of God's Messengers, and couldn't help but think, *For us God weeps....*

The Vault of Heaven

I stood on the broad, convex back of the extinguished sun, its latent warmth creeping into the soles of my feet, the sharp contrast of icy water washing around them. With the suns out it was too dark to see anything above, so I had followed the diminutive stream, shuffling, tapping along with my stick as a blind man would, to its source: a fall of water, no thicker than a finger. Looking a metre or so above my head, I saw a twist of silver, reflecting the tiny bit of ambient light, then darkness above as if the water materialized from nothing. A perpetual miracle that ran down the back of the sun and leapt off its edge, scattering God's tears on the gardens far below.

Do not fear, the Archangel Zeracheil had told me. *An arm's length away on the stream side. Hold your breath—and jump. Jump with all the strength God gave you.*

Here, in the highest reaches of Lower Heaven, where gravity was a fading memory, jumping wouldn't be the problem. No, the problem would be directing my jump without being able to see what I was jumping toward.

I reached out until the tips of my fingers touched the tiny waterfall, then stepped back a full arm's length.

The opening, Zeracheil had told me, was roughly two metres square, too small by far for an Angel, but more than enough for a large man. For a skinny boy, plenty. Still, a small error and I'd smash into the surface of the firmament, hard enough, perhaps, to break bones. The most danger, though, was in the rebound. There was no telling where I'd end up. And there was nothing to grab onto on the back of this sun. I might bounce past the edge, tumbling to the ground a kilometre below.

When Zeracheil had perceived the fear in my eyes, the Archangel had curled a long hand over my shoulder, squeezed it lightly, and said simply, *Have faith*.

Faith. Wasn't that what I had always professed to have?

I crouched. *I want to have faith*, I thought. Raising my hands above my head, I clasped them around the long stick as if in prayer. If I hit the firmament, the stick would likely snap first, and I might just have enough time to do something. What I might do, though, I wasn't quite sure.

I believe, I said to myself, certain the doubt I harboured, the doubt the Angels didn't seem to suspect, doomed me.

Shutting my eyes, I sucked in a deep breath and sprang.

For a heartbeat, the rush of air. Then cold waters sluiced over me, slowing me.

Astonished, I realized I was in the Waters Above. For what seemed like a minute (later, when I related this to Zeracheil, I acknowledged it was probably only a handful of seconds) I drifted up through sluggish liquid. I breached the surface of the Waters Above, felt the chill of air, but dared not breathe.

I opened my eyes.

And gasped—unwittingly drawing a deep breath.

Against utter darkness, millions upon millions of points of pure light, a wash of unearthly brilliance, some so bright I could barely look upon them. I gaped open-mouthed at the splendour—and felt smaller than I had ever before.

Souls.

Zeracheil had told me to expect this. I nodded piously at the time, as if I'd believed, the same way I'd nodded at the stories told by the Priests. Back then, though, I *had* believed their tales about forgiveness, love and, of course, the immortality of the soul. Life after death. I had always liked those stories, wished them to be true with all my heart. Only experience had brought doubt, and I had come to the conclusion that they were wish fulfilment more than anything else.

Or so I'd thought.

Now, I felt all traces of disbelief wash away. Heaven was real, and the dwelling place of immortal souls. How could I not believe what was in front of my eyes? The epiphany was heartfelt, even if all else was too overwhelming to be comprehended in the moment.

I stared in wonder.

From my lessons I knew the most brilliant souls would be the Angels of the first sphere: Seraphim, Cherubim, and Thrones. The next brightest would be those of the second sphere: the Dominions, Virtues, and Powers. And the others—all the millions, perhaps billions, of others—the souls of men saved. One might even be my father's, no matter the Church said different.

I lifted my arm, fearful of what would happen if I made contact, knowing the souls were near and yet infinitely distant. Why shouldn't they be? The laws of time and space held no sway over God.

Water crept over my lower lip. In the diminished gravity, I sank very slowly, but sink I did; I kicked and bobbed back up, treading water now, the physicality of movement shaking me from my reverie, suddenly aware of the gelid waters, of the stick in my hand—remembering abruptly what I was to do. The task God had given me, through the agency of his Archangel Zeracheil.

I extended my arm completely, raising the stick directly over my head as Zeracheil had instructed me. There was a barrier, Zeracheil had said, invisible to the eye of man, and I was to touch it with the stick if I could. I waved the stick in small circles but it met no resistance. I kicked myself higher, as high as I could surge from the waters, waving the stick, and still nothing. I flung it, and counted to three before I heard it strike something invisible, perhaps five metres above my head.

That was it. That was all I was to do.

I opened my mouth to pull in a lungful of air, then stopped mid-breath. *The air. Raphael warned me.* If it was noxious, it was too late, for I'd already drawn several breaths. So I pulled in another tentative lungful, this time tasting it on my tongue and in my gullet—stale, with a metallic tang. But breathable. If it was poison, it was slow-acting, and there would be time enough to worry about that later. The important thing, the only thing, was to return to Lower Heaven that I might complete my first indulgence.

I looked a last time at the multitude of souls, and felt my own stir as if it longed to join. A soul I had not quite been able to believe in moments before.

Not yet, I told myself. *Too soon.*

I picked a glimmer out of the vast array, a small unprepossessing one and, focusing on it, mouthed a short, silent prayer for my father. Then, sucking in a deep breath, I dove, and swam back to the world of the living.

Map of the World

Occupying a top corner of Zeracheil's house, closed off on all sides, was a room with a large, panelled door, the only door I'd seen in the house. It swung open silently as Zeracheil approached, and the Angel stepped into the gloom thus revealed. I followed, and as soon as I'd crossed the threshold, the door sighed shut behind me. A momentary panic seized me in the perfect darkness; then a ball of light blossomed in the centre of the room. Zeracheil stepped up to it, put its hands together inside the ball, as if in prayer, then flung them wide. The ball expanded to fill the room, creating a floor-to-ceiling Sphere with Zeracheil at its heart.

"Do you know what this is?" asked the Archangel.

The sphere was lucid, blue-tinged on its surface, and contained within it the ghosts of other concentric spheres. Fourteen, all told. I reached out to touch it, my fingers passing through the outermost layer with only a slight resistance, the sort you might feel in putting your hand into a bowl of water. "A map of the world," I said, staring in awe.

"It is God's Eye," said Zeracheil. The Angel raised its hands again, this time holding them about a metre apart, then brought them together and the Sphere shrank to half the size. Zeracheil stepped out to stand at my side. It placed its hands on the ghostly blue surface, as if the sphere was a solid thing, and then rotated it beneath its touch. The Angel's hands stilled, and so did the globe's movement. "This is where you were," Zeracheil said, touching a spot on the outermost surface. "In the Waters Above." It turned to face me. "Do you know why we brought you here, David?"

"To ask your second indulgence."

"Would you hear it?"

"I promised I would." When I'd struck my deal, I promised easily, believing there was nothing that might move me to consider the second indulgence. Only, that was before, when my belief had faltered. In swimming the Waters Above, I'd felt a resurgence of the faith I'd thought lost. Did I still have doubt? Certainly. And I knew it would always be so. That was the lesson the Waters had taught me. That faith, without doubt, is not faith at all, just as courage, without fear, is not courage at all. I'd witnessed the choirs of Angels and the countless souls of men, and felt the grace of God upon my face. How could I now refuse to contemplate Zeracheil's second request? "Ask," I said.

"God wishes you to heal His Wound."

I do not believe Angels are much good at reading the expressions of men, but no one, not even an Angel, could have missed the astonishment and confusion writ on my face. "I don't understand."

"The world is God's Body, the Waters his Blood," Zeracheil said. "God bleeds, and the Waters Above diminish."

In waving that stick, I knew I'd confirmed the Angels' fear: the Waters were no longer as plentiful as they'd once been. Yet it seemed to me there was no small amount remaining; more below, I'd have guessed, than stale air above, and if in all the world's time it had only diminished this much, then it seemed to me that ages would have to pass before it would be perilously low. I said so to Zeracheil.

"The rain that falls to fill the rivers, that runs to lakes and seas, that slakes the thirst of plant and man and beast—all comes from Heaven. And returns to Heaven. Yet now, less rises than descends, and so the Waters Above diminish. When weighed against the extent of the Waters, the difference is small. But this is how the Devil works. Small differences are like small sins, and over a lifetime they will blacken your soul, until there is no hope of salvation. So it is with the world. The rains fail below, and with them the harvests, for there is not enough in the Waters Above to sustain all."

I pictured the sere fields and the dwindling shorelines in the lower Spheres. Droughts that worsened each year—or so Kite had told me. And in my travels, I'd seen nothing to persuade me this was not the case. Rather, what I'd witnessed convinced me that on the heels of drought, like yammering dogs, came famine, plague, and war. "Can God not replenish the water?"

"He gave us the Waters that all the Spheres of the Apostles might thrive. It is the River of Life, and His Blood. How much more would you ask of him?"

If Zeracheil's words were an attempt to make me feel shame, they succeeded. Still, the Angel hadn't answered my question. "If God will not replenish the Waters, what can be done?"

"No one can retrieve what Satan has already stolen. But you can stop the Fallen One from taking more." Zeracheil repeated the first gesture he'd made several times, and the Sphere grew again and again, and with each successive magnification I saw more detail on the surfaces as they flew past. They were not smooth, as I had supposed, but textured, showing the outlines of recognizable things: hills and valleys and rivers, the spectral regularity of geometric shapes that I took to be cities, towns, and villages. The image dove down into the world, until the surface of the last Sphere, that of the Apostle Paul, passed beyond the walls of the room, and only a diffuse glow was left. Zeracheil continued to gesture in the same way and I suppose the image was magnifying over and over, but little seemed to change. Then, after a few moments, a tiny, seething ember appeared in the centre and Zeracheil stopped.

"Hell."

The Angel must have noted my look of incredulity, for it said, "Do not be fooled. Hell is vast beyond imagination, weighing more than all the Spheres combined. Even here, in Lower Heaven, its pull is felt." The Angel rotated the image, then gestured, and a thin silver thread lanced the room, running from the ceiling to where it sparked against the surface of the ember. "Hell is an absence that devours, and from which nothing escapes." Zeracheil reversed the process, and the ember receded, but the silver line remained; we raced back along its length. When the lowest Sphere dove through the room, Zeracheil froze the image. The thread was cut off at the undersurface of the lowest Sphere, that of the Apostle Paul, directly beneath a structure. I had no idea how tall or wide that building might have been, and there was nothing in the image that would have provided a clue to its actual dimensions, but its proportions were the same as an Assumption. "God wishes you here, David," Zeracheil said, pointing to the ghostly image in the lowest of all Spheres, "to staunch the flow of His Blood."

"How? How could someone like me do such a thing?"

"God has not revealed this to us."

I shook my head in disbelief.

"You must have faith, David."

I didn't. Leastways, not in the Angels of Lower Heaven. Although the turn of their minds might be different, I believed they schemed as much as those holy men of the Church. Perhaps they were not to blame for that; perhaps their proximity to men had infected them. I looked into Zeracheil's blank eyes. "My faith is not as strong as you might suppose."

"God chose you for two reasons, David. Because of the *strength* of your faith, and because of the gift of memory He granted you."

I thought it odd that God would share this with the Angels, yet be silent on what I was to do to staunch His Wound. "I have a good memory. Why is this important?"

Zeracheil motioned with his hands for a time, and the world collapsed until Lower Heaven once again appeared just inside the walls of the room. "There are no maps of the lower Spheres, where men live short, violent, and Godless lives. And in those Spheres above, where the Church holds sway, you would be jailed or crucified if you carried such maps. Even if it were possible, sufficient detail of all the Spheres would require volumes, and be impossible to conceal. However, you might safely carry a map of all the world in your memory."

"To get there I will have to pass through the Assumptions."

"Not everyone in the Church opposes the Angels."

The Jesuits. They controlled the Assumptions—at least those in the Catholic Spheres. Unlike the rest of the Clergy, who made it a virtue not to question the nature of the world, the Jesuits believed in an explicable order, which God did not jealously guard. For them, a virtuous life was one in which they were *obliged* to study the laws of Nature. After all, had God not ordained the laws of Nature? And had he also not given us the faculties to unravel their mysteries? At times, this approach had set the Jesuits against the main body of the Church. "The Society of Jesus aids you?"

"They would not act against the Holy See, but have misgivings about the war on Lower Heaven. They will help us in what small ways they can, and hinder the Church in the same fashion."

"And in Spheres below where there are no Jesuits?"

"Discontent grows there, as it does in the Catholic Spheres. Everywhere men look up with envy, though some not so far as Heaven."

"The Fallists?" They had been wiped out—or so the *Addenda* told us. But I'd learned that not everything in the *Holy Books* could be trusted.

"Yes. And others in the Lower Spheres."

"You've struck bargains with your enemy's enemy."

"We are above, they are below. The Church is conveniently between."

I considered this for a moment, then said, "That's all the more reason for Rome to move quickly to take Lower Heaven. Don't you fear an attack?"

"We expect an attack, but do not fear it. Its success or failure is of no consequence."

Ali had said as much, though I hadn't credited it at the time: the Angels seemed indifferent to the Church's ambitions, or to their fate. "How can you not care about the Kingdom of Heaven? How can you allow men to enter, and so commit a sin that would consign them to Hell?"

"God has given men free will. They make choices, just as you."

"The Church *will* come."

Zeracheil shrugged. "The Angels have little time left in this Sphere. Men will have less."

Little time? "I see no drought here."

"No more or less than below," Zeracheil said. "The Waters Above do more than slake the thirst of God's creatures, David. They wrap all the Spheres, protecting them from God's radiance. As Glorious as it is, such radiance is too much for men—and even Angels—to bear." Zeracheil then did a strange thing: it placed a hand on the diseased side of its face, and dragged a finger down; necrotic skin sloughed away under its fingertip and dangled from its cheek. In its place glistened a new lesion. "In your lifetime, it is likely Angels will no longer abide in Lower Heaven. Nor any of God's other creatures." The Angel held out its fingertip; on it was a pinkish smear. "In Lower Heaven, God's presence is muted by the firmament. But you were in the Waters Above, David. Did you not feel His radiance?"

I *had*—in my heart and my soul. But I hadn't thought about my body. Raising my hand I touched my cheek, an echo of what the Angel had done to itself; I felt a faint tingle, the sort you might after sitting too close to a fire.

"You've felt God's touch," Zeracheil said, triumphantly. Until now I'd seen no semblance of emotion on the face of an Angel. But Zeracheil's expression was rapturous. "The flesh knows it. And knowing its imperfection, longs to wither away, leaving nothing that might thwart communion with God."

I believe the Angel wanted me to feel the same joy at having experienced God's touch, and I suppose I did to some degree; but I was uneasy, too, for it seemed Zeracheil's joy was occasioned as much by the touch of God as by the mortification of its flesh. The Angels would die— or at least the poor vessels that contained them—in an ecstasy of pain. I hid my revulsion as best as I could. "If this is your wish, why would you staunch the flow of God's Blood?"

"To save man, as God has adjured us."

To save man? An unsettling notion occurred to me then. "Will God's radiance spread past Lower Heaven?"

"If you do not staunch the flow of God's Blood, all Spheres will, in time, be as Lower Heaven, and the flesh of men will wither, too."

My throat went dry. "When?"

The Angel quoted Matthew speaking of the end of the world: "*But as for that day and hour, nobody knows it, neither the angels of heaven, nor the Son, no one but the Father alone.*"

I suppose I should have been more concerned with the fate of the Spheres, and the millions of souls that would suffer. Instead, I asked, "What of Ali?"

"If you choose to do God's bidding, she will accompany you."

Upon hearing this, my spirits rose. I was grateful, even, for if we did not have this to bind us, we had nothing; I'd no doubt she'd abandon me the moment we departed Lower Heaven. "If I choose not to go, what will happen to her?"

"She will make her way to God's Wound as best she can, to do what she might. This is her covenant with God, through her father's oath, and hers."

So there it was. If my faith was not enough to compel me, nor the world's demise, Ali's presence would. *The Angels*, I thought, *know my heart better than I know it myself.*

I gazed upon the ghostly outlines of all the Spheres of the world, and worried anew, for it would take days, at the least, to commit what I must to memory. "I would begin now," I said, filled with a sense of urgency, and wondering again how far and fast the Archangel Raphael might fly.

Avenged

Each day for the next four days, I came to the map room (as I'd come to think of it) to look through God's Eye at the world. It responded to my touch in the same way it had to Zeracheil's, and I turned it this way and that, examining Sphere after Sphere. I quickly discovered that the map was not accurate in some respects: it showed forests in places where I knew there to be only fields, and vice versa; the streets and outlines of buildings matched, more or less, what I'd seen in the heart of larger cities, like *Los Angeles Nuevo* and *Rome*, but the ramshackle sprawl of houses on their outskirts was missing. Indeed, entire towns through which we'd passed did not even appear on the map. When I asked, Zeracheil told me this was the world as it had been when God created it, and though I could trust the hills and valleys to be largely unchanged, I could not be certain when it came to the works of men.

Here and there were coloured symbols on the map, more often than not in or nearby cities, and these, Zeracheil said, marked the homes of believers—by which I took him to mean partisans of the Angels—and if I magnified these points sufficiently I might see their names. I also noted that the Assumptions through which Ali and I had passed were white, but many others, including the one now buried within the Babel tower, appeared grey. I asked the Angel about these, too, and Zeracheil told me that only the white Assumptions still functioned.

So I committed to memory the general topography of each Sphere in its entirety, including all its white Assumptions, mapping countless routes between Heaven and God's Wound. Then I studied the roads along which we might travel between Assumptions, choosing those that spanned the shortest distances, and marking alternatives in case we had need of them. As I did all this, I weighed our possible routes against what I knew of the Spheres we'd been in (and what I'd learned of other places from Ignatius, Kite, and Meussin), considering those things that might disrupt or hasten our progress, and then modified the routes in my head accordingly. My best guess was that the journey would take about a year—if all went well.

During this time I slept no more than five hours a night, and worked each day until exhaustion blurred my thoughts, making it impossible to focus. Only then would I climb onto the palanquin and descend. When I woke, no matter how early, there was always fruit and a freshly drawn bucket of water waiting. I saw little of Ali, and spoke not at all to her, for she was always asleep when I returned to the room Zeracheil had given us, and gone before I woke. Sometimes I caught glimpses of her in the garden, practising her sword work on large dummies she'd contrived from fruit and leaves and vines, and was distressed to note they were either the same size and shape as a wingless Angel—or as me.

In the few minutes I was not closeted in the map room or asleep, I observed the workings of Zeracheil's house. Angels came and went, and I did my best to sort them out, but at a distance they all looked alike. Often they would arrive in twos and threes, landing on the middle floors. For the most part they treated me as if I were invisible. With dread, I watched for an Angel with a growth under its eye. Once, when the palanquin was lifting me to the map room, I passed a floor on which a group of Angels had just landed, and I thought one might be Raphael, for it had a growth beneath its eye, but when it turned, fully exposing its face, I saw its tumour had progressed much further, and had already taken its eye and crossed the bridge of its nose.

Toward the end of the fifth day, when I could think of no more I might learn with God's Eye, I used the palanquin to return to the ground floor and sought out Zeracheil. I found it in the room with the table and stools, where it often sat with other Angels when they communed in silence. On this occasion the Archangel sat alone, its head bowed and hands folded in its lap, perhaps lost in prayer.

Zeracheil raised its head as I entered, and I was taken aback; the skin on the side of the Angel's face sagged, where the neoplasm had been. Its tumour had been neatly excised, yet I could not see any traces of the incisions such an operation would have required.

"You would leave," Zeracheil said.

"Ali and I, yes."

"As we have promised," Zeracheil said, "two days hence at sun-on."

"Two days?" I'd observed an increase in comings and goings of Angels the previous day, which had only fuelled my impatience. "We would leave now."

"Ali will not be ready."

The previous night, when I'd returned to the room to sleep for a few fitful hours, she hadn't been there. "Has she been sent elsewhere?"

"She is where you sleep."

"Then why must we wait two days?"

"She is with her Possessor, Raphael, who—"

I spun, and loped from the room. In two great strides I crossed the Atrium, and on the third caught at the curtain covering the door to our room to arrest my progress—only my momentum ripped the fabric off the rings that held it, and I careened into the door frame, my right forearm taking the impact. I fell to the ground in searing agony, the curtain twisting around me. But, for an instant, I had a clear view of a horrific scene: Ali, face down, legs and arms bound, pinioned to the ground. Atop her, the Archangel Raphael grunted with an unholy pleasure.

I staggered to my feet; jarring pain knifed through my right arm, and my vision bleared. Yet the madness that possessed me must have impelled me, for the next thing I clearly remember was my one useful hand gripping the delicate edge of a wing where it met the Angel's back, and yanking Raphael off Ali and flinging it with such force that when the Angel smashed, face first, into the wall behind, I heard two loud *cracks*, like the sound of dry kindling snapping. Then I found myself standing over it. One wing was at an impossible angle, and a terrible wound had opened on its head from which spilled anaemic blood, pinkish and thin, with the consistency of water. Where genitals would have been, I expected to see a disfigured, tumescent penis, or even something like Meussin's wooden phallus, but there was nothing but that ambiguous flap of skin. However, on its lips and dribbling down its chin was blood, not of an Angel, but thick and crimson like a man's. "You asked it of us," Raphael said, between wheezing breaths.

I turned, and saw that Ali lay insensible on the floor; on the side of her head, a circular wound the size of a silver bishop oozed blood. Her sword leaned against the wall beside the door, and I walked over and picked it up, shaking it free from its scabbard. Turning to the wounded

Angel, I felt nothing but a preternatural calm. "That day at the river, she could have stopped me," I said. "If you'd let her."

With that I plunged the sword into the chest of the Archangel Raphael where its heart would have been—had it been a man—driving it down until its tip bit into the floor with the ring of metal on stone. The Angel spasmed, and let out a keening wail that shivered through my bones. It tired to rise, one great wing thrashing, the other, blood-flecked and useless, flopping piteously. I held the sword firm, pinning the Angel for perhaps half a dozen heartbeats, until it stilled.

Whatever reserve of energy animated me, it fled, and my legs gave out.

I stared up at a blank ceiling, the room reeling around me. Waves of pain, more intense than any I'd ever experienced, spiked my forearm. Through gritted teeth, I managed to gasp out, "I think my arm is broken," though I wasn't quite sure to whom I was speaking.

And that's all I remember.

Purgatorium

When consciousness returned, I found myself lying on a cool, smooth surface. It was dark, and a damp, slow-churning mist enveloped me, obscuring anything more than a few centimetres from my nose. My arms were crossed over my chest, and it felt like a shroud had been wrapped around me. In that moment, I believed myself dead and awaiting judgement. I took comfort in this notion and, for the first time in a long time, I relaxed, content to lose myself in the nothingness.

"*David?*"

The whisper cut through my torpor, shattering the illusion. An invisible weight settled on my chest and limbs. I tried to unfold my arms and move away the shroud so that I might push myself into a sitting position—and gasped as jagged pain surged from my right arm through my body in excruciating waves.

"Lie still." Ali's words cut through my agony.

I drew ragged breaths as the pain ebbed, each wave diminishing until my arm was merely the nexus of a dull, persistent throb.

"Open your eyes."

The ubiquitous mist seemed to have worked itself into my brain, gumming its works; my body was infinitely heavy and movement an impossibility. I didn't want to open my eyes. All I wanted to do was lie there, veiled. I felt the world slipping away. . . .

A sharp rap on my shoulder jolted me awake again. "You must stay conscious!"

I groaned, and screwed my eyes shut even tighter.

"Your arm is wrapped to your chest—don't try to move it."

My left arm lay below my right and, lifting it, I gently probed my broken limb. What she said was true. My right arm had been immobilized, secured by strips of broad cloth wound around my torso; beneath this I felt a makeshift splint on my forearm, formed of two pieces of rough wood, and packed with moss.

"Here."

Something dribbled into my mouth and seemed to scorch the back of my throat, shocking my eyes open—and precipitating a fit of coughing.

"More?"

I shook my pounding head—and felt that I might retch, or faint, or both. Swallowing back the bile, I blinked. The fog no longer seemed so impenetrable, or perhaps my eyes had adjusted, but I saw Ali's shadowy outline sitting next to me, knees drawn up, arms wrapped around her shins, one hand clutching an unstoppered wineskin. I tried to ask her a question, but my voice was an incomprehensible croak. I swallowed once, twice, to lubricate my vocal cords, then managed to rasp out, "Where?"

"On the back of a sun in the Sphere below Lower Heaven."

My muddled brain took a moment to grasp this; when it did, I realized the fog that rolled around us was, in fact, a cloud. I'd seen wispy ones as a child, but none for years.

"Can you sit up?"

The binding had been wound under my left arm, leaving it free. So I used my good arm to slowly, carefully, push myself up. My other arm ached profoundly with each pulse of blood, and I felt woozy, but managed.

"Here." Ali extended the wineskin. "A gift from the Angels. It will dull the pain."

Taking the skin from her, I tried an experimental sip. It tasted good. I drank again, and the wine burned down my throat and coursed through my chest and into my limbs. After taking another swig, I tried to hand it back to her. She waved it away.

"Keep it."

The cloud was on the wane, and I could see her more clearly now. A white bandage, with a dark stain at the temple, had been wrapped around her head. She looked at me, but her face held none of the anger or resentment to which I'd become accustomed; instead, it was strangely blank, as if I didn't matter in the least to her. And perhaps I didn't, now that we were out of Heaven. "How long?"

"You've been out for three days."

As if in answer, my stomach grumbled loudly.

"We've no food."

"I'm not hungry," I lied. "What . . . what happened?"

"The Church breached Lower Heaven. This is a way out that's not watched." Ali frowned. "The Angels told me you killed Raphael. Is this true?"

I took a good swig this time, wanting to dull the memory. "Yes."

Ali stared off into the fog, saying nothing.

I hadn't expected gratitude; neither had I expected to experience a twinge of guilt for what I'd done. Yet I did. "It attacked you."

She shook her head slowly.

"Raphael wounded you—"

"You petitioned the Angels to stop speaking to me. That is what Raphael was doing when you killed it." She touched her bandage lightly, then looked at me. "They did this to me to please you, David."

"To please me?"

"They believe you are the only one who might complete the task God has given them. They would gladly die to protect you." She shook her head, as if at their folly. "Taking the Angel's voice from my head was a minor behest for them. I tried to argue Raphael out of it, for the Angels could have aided us on our journey. On the task *they* gave us. But in its eagerness to please you, it wouldn't listen." She made no attempt to hide her bewilderment—and antipathy—as she spat out these last words. "When I regained consciousness, they said they took you to a healing place, where they knit your arm—and *prayed* for you."

"But I killed Raphael!"

"It is no matter to the Angels that you killed Raphael," Ali said. "They don't believe God has given them free will. They are here to do his bidding, as best they can. What happens to them is neither good nor bad. It's just what happens—because it must."

"No." I had killed an Angel, and had expected to be punished. Wanted to be punished. "They are God's messengers."

"And animals are God's creatures," Ali said. "Yet they, too, are as soulless as Angels, and so without free will. If you kill a goose, is that murder?"

Despite my anger at what they had done to us, I couldn't believe the Angels were no more in God's eye than meat for our table. "So Angels have no free will?"

"Who knows? Christ's Blood, I'm not sure *we* have free will. Perhaps we practise a necessary self-deception, to convince ourselves our lives have meaning."

A week ago, I would have tried to argue her out of such a nihilistic perspective, but now I didn't have the energy—nor was I so sure she was wrong. We sat in silence for a few moments, each lost in our own thoughts. I took another drink from the skin. Only tendrils of cloud now washed around us, drifting listlessly around our ankles; the edge of the sun had emerged, a few metres from the toes of our sandals. "You still haven't explained how we got here."

"There was no other way to leave Lower Heaven."

"But how did we get *here*?"

"Passages above give access to the suns below."

"How could you possibly know—" I stopped, recalling the coloured lines running between the surface of each Sphere and the firmament below. Not knowing what they were, I hadn't paid them much heed. But she'd understood. "You've looked through God's Eye."

"My memory is not perfect like yours, but I told Zeracheil it wouldn't hurt for me to know the way, too, in case," she paused to give me a look here, "you were killed."

I tried not to hide my uneasiness at her practicality. "You thought to use the tunnels to escape."

"The Angels are not the most practical of creatures," she said. "Someone has to be."

"When the Church breached Lower Heaven, you had the Angels bring me on the palanquin to the entrance above this sun."

The slightest dip of her head was an acknowledgement.

"Like the corridors of the Assumptions, the tunnels would be too small for the Angels. And the palanquin won't work if it's too far from them. So you would have carried me." I craned my neck; it was dark, but I could see an even darker square directly above me, through which two things that looked like thick ropes hung, one reaching the back of the sun next to me, while the other dangled a few metres below the opening. Vines she'd twisted together.

"So you have no rope?"

"The Angels have little use for such things."

We were half a kilometre above the surface of the Sphere, and I thought it unlikely Ali would have found vines to reach that distance. Nor was I sure how I'd undertake such a lengthy descent with a only one good arm. The wine must have been dizzying my wits, for the next thing I said was uncharacteristically sarcastic. "A wonderful plan. We are stranded on the back of a sun. And if we don't die of thirst," I lifted the wineskin, "then it will be of hunger." I thought my barb clever, in the way a drunk is always amused by his own impoverished wit.

"We are not stranded," she said, "and hunger will be the last of your worries when the sun goes on."

She was right, of course. The suns lit the world, but they heated it, too; in a few hours we'd be parboiled in our own skins. "Then how are we to get down?"

She pointed behind us. "We fly."

Turning my head, I stared open-mouthed at what looked like a pair of Angel's wings. Two metres high and more than twice that across, they were darker than the night, as deep a shade of black as the Angel's wings were of white.

"When an Angel injures its wing, it uses this like we use a cast, to hold the bones firm until they mend. It allows it to continue flying so its muscles don't atrophy. "

Propping the whole thing up was a frame in the middle, comprised of spindly looking rods to which was attached a harness of some sort. I looked at the opening, as large as the one through which I reached the Waters Above, but too small for these wings. "How did it get here?"

"It breaks down into a bundle that would fit in a rucksack, and that weighs next to nothing," she said. "We haven't the reach or strength to beat the wings, but they will hold us aloft, and we can bend them enough to have some control, so that we might glide to the ground."

There was a slight gust of wind, and slow waves undulated across the dark fabric. "We are not Angels," I said.

"Perhaps not. But for three days I practised, first from hilltops, and then from the suns of Lower Heaven. On the fourth, I added extra weight to equal yours. We will fall faster and harder here, but the Angels told me it should work nonetheless."

We? I stared at the unbuckled straps dangling from the front of the harness.

"Sun-on is only a few hours away. Can you stand?"

I nodded numbly and handed Ali the skin. I suppose I should have been more alarmed, but the wine seemed to have done its job. Rolling onto my knees, I levered myself to my feet. My broken limb throbbed mercilessly, and my legs shook, but it was nowhere near as bad as I feared.

Ali handed back the wineskin. "Drink."

I thought about it for a moment, wondering if it would be wise to dull my senses further. Then I tipped the skin back, mouthing a silent toast to Ignatius, drinking deeply until wine trickled from the corners of my mouth and the skin sagged from emptiness. I flung it over the edge of the sun, and watched the cloud swallow it.

Ali walked to that preposterous contraption.

The thing had been made to fit an Angel, and would have been lifted onto its back. But Ali merely walked into the midst of the frame and turned around. Resting, as it was on the ground, the upper straps just touched her shoulders. She picked it up with ease, and the wings lifted slightly on their own, as if eager to take flight.

Ali directed me to stand in front of her, facing away. When I did so, she wrapped a thick belt around my waist, drawing me back into her. As she reached around me to buckle it, I felt her breasts press against my back—and the quick beat of both our hearts. She pulled a single shoulder strap around my good arm and cinched it down. I'd braced myself for a stab of pain, but I was conscious of nothing other than the point of her chin on my shoulder and her breath tickling the nape of my neck.

"We can't both run or we'll trip over each other. So you must carry me piggyback. Can you do that?"

"I think so."

"Ready?"

I didn't answer her question; there was one I needed to ask first. "If I'd still been unconscious at sun-on, what then?"

"The Angels said you would wake."

"But if I hadn't?"

"You want to know if I'd have left you behind." She paused. "No."

"Why not?"

"I need you."

She'd said the same thing to me before, about getting her to Rome. At that time I'd thought the anger in her words directed at me, but later realized it was self-loathing. If Ali hated anything, it was needing someone else. "To lead you to Hell."

"No. I can find my own way, if I must."

"Then what?"

"I am with child."

I can't explain what happened next—only tell it: my legs churned of their own volition.

"David!"

As I ran my heels hit Ali's shins, and we staggered and almost fell; Ali swung her legs up, wrapping them around my waist. The weight was almost too much for me, and my arm was on fire, but I lumbered forward.

"*Wait!*"

To the sides I saw the great wings cant forward as the wind ran under them, and felt an insistent upward tug. I closed my eyes, not wanting to know when the edge would come, listening only to the slap of my sandals and the snap of the fabric.

On my sixth stride, my right foot found no purchase and we pitched forward. Moisture from the cloud streamed across my face as we fell, like two stones, into the pall of night.

Then the breath of God caught our wings—and, miraculously, we flew.

End

ABOUT THE AUTHOR

Robert Boyczuk has published short stories in various magazines and anthologies. He also has two books out: a collection of his short work, *Horror Story and Other Horror Stories*, and a novel, *Nexus: Ascension* (both by ChiZine Publications). More fascinating details on Bob are available at *boyczuk.com*.

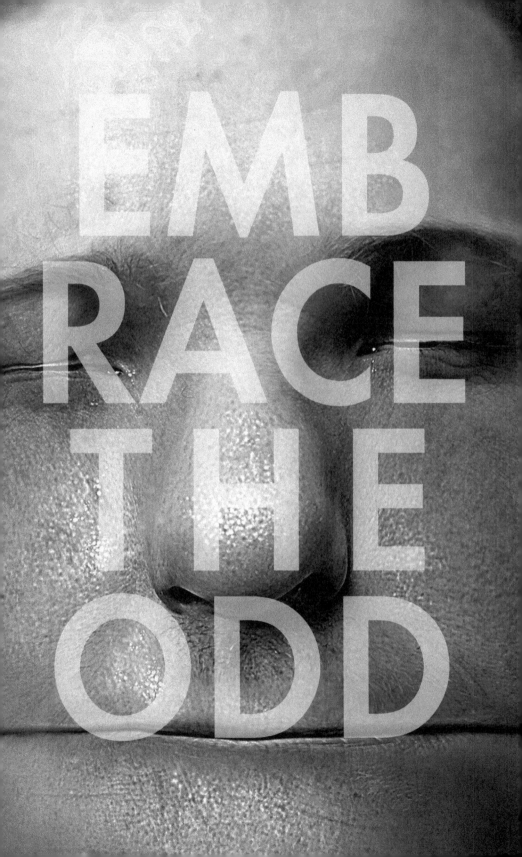

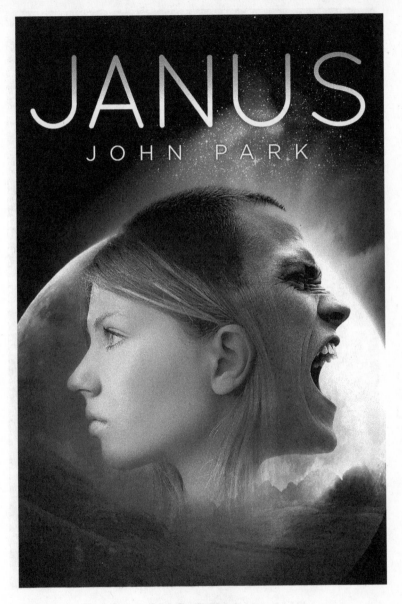

JANUS

JOHN PARK

AVAILABLE SEPTEMBER 2012
FROM CHIZINE PUBLICATIONS

978-1-927469-10-1

REMEMBER WHY YOU FEAR ME
THE BEST DARK FICTION OF ROBERT SHEARMAN

AVAILABLE OCTOBER 2012
FROM CHIZINE PUBLICATIONS

978-0-927469-21-7